The Wedding

MARY HELEN PONCE

Arte Publico Press

Houston, Texas

This volume is made possible by a grant from the National Endowment for the Arts, a federal agency.

Arte Publico Press
University of Houston
Houston, Texas 77204-2090

Ponce, Mary Helen.
    The Wedding.

    I. Title.
PS3566.0586W44   1989   813'.54   89-6933
ISBN 0-934770-97-2

The paper used in this publication meets the minimum requirements of the American National Standard for Permanence of Paper for Printed Library Materials Z39.48-1984.

To Ana, my lovely daughter . . . who decorates my life.

For the chicks and guys from the barrios who remember the big, fun weddings . . . and fights.

Part I

Chapter One

Blanca and Cricket

Blanca Munoz had known Sammy-the Cricket most of her life. He was just another guy, a nondescript dude that hung around Main Street smoking Lucky Strikes, looking tough while waiting for something too happen. Cricket could not be called handsome but he wasn't ugly either. His wide face had deep pock marks, his dark eyes were slanted and his straight black hair was worn in a ducktail, and much too long. Nor was Cricket popular, except among Los Tacones. Cricket was too mean to be popular, as he almost always picked on other guys. Worse, he did not drive a fancy car (which made even the homeliest guy passable), nor did he dance especially well. Blanca was not impressed by Cricket's build, as he was much too thin, with arms that dangled to his knees and legs that bent in the middle. What most impressed Blanca was Cricket's meanness.

The first time Blanca began to think of Cricket as a potential suitor was at a dance the summer she turned eighteen. Although she had heard glowing reports from Lucy, her best friend, about the guy called Cricket and how he sure could fight, she had not paid attention to him until this night.

Cricket, who lived across town near the lumberyard, was not a part of her circle of friends. He was much older. All of 22! Worse, he was a pachuco who hung around with the Tacones gang. Blanca knew where most of the pachucos ended up, and she had vowed to herself not to get mixed up with a zoot-suiter. She had promised her Uncle Ernie (an ex-pachuco and ex-con) to stay clear of guys wearing drapes. But then, Blanca reasoned, most of the cute guys belonged to gangs. Ain't nobody left! Worse, the other guys were too square! They not only dressed like squares, but they drove cars that had no class. Still, Blanca had to admit, she was a bit curious about the guy with the funny nickname, Cricket.

Sammy Lopez had earned his nickname in the numerous fights that errupted most Saturday nights between the two Valley gangs: the Tacones and the Planchados. Once when he had knocked the shit out of a guy, Cricket stomped on top of him with his long legs. Just like a cricket! While other guys swapped right hooks or smacked each other with brass knuckles, Cricket, his thick-soled shoes as weapons, long legs flaying, kicked his victim senseless until the others pulled him away.

That starlit night of the dance, Blanca took her time getting ready. She plastered her face with Max Factor pancake makeup, lots of Maybelline and Tangee Real Hot Red lipstick, then rolled her pompadour higher than usual. Maybe tonight I'll meet a nice guy, she thought, blotting her wide lips with a piece of toilet paper. Just maybe. . . . After all, Lucy knows which guys are hep to the jive!

Blanca's best friend, Lucy, liked to follow the pack and thought of herself as a real cool chick. She enjoyed nothing more than a good fight. She even liked to throw a few punches, a thing she had learned at her Aunt Tottie's Bar, a beer joint known as "el sobaco," the armpit. Lucy had invited Blanca to the dance.

"You gotta go, man!"

"Yeah?"

"All the guys are gonna be there!"

"Gosh!"

"Put on your new high heels. And lots of Maybelline!"

"Okie dokie."

The dance was at el Salon Parra, a rundown, wooden building in a remote part of Taconos, where most wedding dances and some private parties took place. The owner, Señor Parra, was a mild-mannered, church-going man of medium height, with a slight paunch and thinning grey hair. A good businessman, he went out of his way not to anger the local zoot-suiters, most of whom he hated and, given the option, would have run out of town. During a fight he never called the cops, but instead looked the other way. He knew Los Tacones got even with stool-pigeons who called the coppers. He once saw Cricket slash the tires on a police car when the cop was inside the hall. During a fight Parra remained calm, thankful he had gotten the rental fee before the dance. Aside from that, he hated having to replace shattered windows and broken chairs. What Señor Parra did best was mind his own buisness, which is why the dance hall was booked solid throughout the year.

The night of the dance, Blanca and Lucy met their friends Sally and Rosie on the corner of Main, then they waltzed across the street to the dance hall. They sipped cold drinks and looked around. Within minutes El Gato Cortez's band began to play and the dance floor filled. Throughout the night Blanca danced with various dudes. Now and then she and Lucy danced together, but only if Lucy could lead. They passed the night dancing the boogie-woogie, sipping whiskey sours, sizing up guys decked out in the latest drapes and waited for something to happen. Close to midnight, just after the band had taken its final break, all hell broke loose when the Planchados gang started a fight.

The fight began when the Planchados, undetected in the dark street, cruised by the dance hall and threw a beer bottle at some guys outside the hall. The bottle crashed into the crowd and hit el Sapo, one of the Tacones who was standing alongside Tudi and smoking a Lucky Strike. Tudi immediately picked up a rock and hurled it at the retreating car, a low-slung navy blue Ford with gleaming white walls. The rock made a direct hit; the sound of splintered glass filled the air. The Ford came to a screeching halt, the driver slumped forward in the front seat. The Planchados, stuck inside the stalled car, began to cuss at each other. Their screams and those of the crowd outside were heard by the crowd inside the dance hall. Within minutes the dance hall doors opened. Out poured Cricket, Topo, Frankie and Paulie. They ran to the stalled car, yanked out the Planchados, dragged them to the parking lot and began to punch away.

When Blanca and Lucy saw the guys run out the door, they immediately knew something was going on. They put their drinks down, crushed their cigarettes with their shoe heels and dashed outside to where a circle had formed. They elbowed their way to the front and began to egg the guys on.

"Knock 'im out."

"Watch it! He's gonna . . . "

"Here come the coppers!"

Blanca, her husky arm looped around Lucy's thin waist, watched Los Tacones fight. "Gosh, whatta really good fight," Blanca shouted to Lucy. "Man alive!" She noticed there existed a code-of-honor among the pachucos. They fought one-on-one, rarely ganging up on just one guy. When Blanca spotted Cricket sparring with Skippy, the leader of the Planchados, she could not take her eyes off him. She was fascinated by how Cricket dodged in and out, waiting to connect with his victim. Just like Joe Louis! In the dim light Cricket appeared graceful, his lithe body swaying to and fro with the punches. "The guys sure gots lotta guts," groaned Blanca, squeezing tight against Lucy. "They just gots ta win." When next she looked, a prone Planchado lay at Cricket's feet. She decided then and there that Sammy-the-Cricket was for her.

The fight ended right before the cops came roaring down the street. The Planchados, their tailor-made jackets stained with sweat and blood, took off in the splintered Ford. The Tacones dusted themselves off, evaded the cops, broke out a bottle of Hill & Hill and strutted back to the dancehall, with Cricket in the lead. The dance continued as though nothing had happened. Only the Tacones's rumpled drapes gave them away. And although Cricket did not ask Blanca to dance, she could hardly take her eyes off him the entire night.

Next day, Sunday, Blanca took a different path to church, one that took her past Cricket's house. Before leaving, she gave herself a sponge bath, scrubbed her armpits and spread on Mum deodrant. She inspected her clothes and decided on a soft pink jersey dress with big shoulder pads and a draped skirt. The material clung to her generous hips and full bust. "I wanna look so fine," Blanca wailed as she squeezed into the dress while humming along with the Ink Spots, "I wanna look like a hep chick!" She stood in front of the dresser and stared at her reflection. She turned this way and that, re-rolled her pompadour up high and re-checked her makeup. "Shit, I look too tired," Blanca frowned, "but the dance chure was fun." She smeared on more Max Factor pancake #2 to hide the bags that rimmed her brown yes, traced eyebrow pencil over her shaved eyebrows, hitched up her seamed stockings and then sauntered off for late mass. As she approached Cricket's house, she quickly took out her Maybelline and a plastic compact. With the tip of her finger, she extracted Tangee Red lipstick from the tube, slashed a red line across her full mouth and then continued to walk toward church.

As luck would have it, Blanca later thought, Cricket was just then getting up. He slept late most mornings and weekends. His job in the garbage plant and his partying with the guys kept him out most nights until the wee hours. But that warm summer morning, when he looked out the sticky bedroom window and spotted Blanca coming up the street, he quickly grabbed a comb, gave his greasy ducktail a flip, splashed water on his pock-marked face and grabbed his boppers. He casually sauntered outside.

"Oh, hi, Sammy. How d'ya feel?" murmured Blanca, her eyelids fluttering. "How ya feeling after last night?"

"All reet," grinned Cricket, as he fell into step with Blanca. His bloodshot eyes behind the dark glasses could barely focus. "Did ya watch the fight?"

"Yeah! Man alive, it chure was good. Did ya gets hurt?"

"No way! Nel."

"You chure can fight," gushed Blanca, her thick lips glistening with red lipstick. "You fight just like the champ," she added, smoothing her pompadour.

Cricket glanced down at the husky girl that walked beside him. She ain't so hot, he thought, just a dumb broad. But she's got some nice tits and a big ass. Well, nuthin's perfect. As they approached the church, Cricket spotted Tudi across the street. With a diffident smile, he shrugged his bony shoulders and told Blanca, "See ya later." He secured his dark glasses and walked away from the husky girl in the pink outfit who stared after him. He was determined not to let the guys see him and later accuse him of being hung up on a chick. After all, I gots my pride, he reasoned.

After that Blanca and Cricket were seen cruising the streets of Taconos Sunday afternoons, along with other couples who were all dressed but with nowhere to go.

Chapter Two

Blanca

Like most of her friends, Blanca had attended school only to the eighth grade. She had been put back in the third grade because she was a slow reader. Years later, when her family returned in November from picking fruit in Fresno, she was called to the office and told she would have to repeat the seventh grade.

"Blanche Muñoz?"

"Yes."

"Ummmm. You're starting school very late. I doubt very much if you can catch up with the rest. I, uhhh, we think it best you remain in seventh grade and . . . "

"But . . . "

"Of course, you can always take a few tests. Just English and Math. If you pass them, then . . . "

"Oh! Well, I guess I can stay in the seventh, but I'm too big and . . . "

"But you'll be with all your friends!"

"Yeah? Well, okay."

By the time she reached eighth grade, Blanca was almost fourteen, a big cheerful girl with fully developed breasts, round hips, thick ankles and a slight case of acne. She was a friendly girl and got along well. But, she would tell herself, I'm too dumb. All I know is 2 and 2 are 4, Columbus discovered America, and how ta pick fruit. I ain't ever gonna graduate. I hate school.

It never occured to Blanca to plan on going to high school. "What for?" she told Lucy, "no one in my family did. Why should I be any different?" She cared neither for books nor for the Anglo teachers, many of whom she felt treated her like a dummy. She was therefore relieved when in her last semester her close friends were saying, "I'm not gonna go to high school, I wanna work."

"Me too."

"I hate books."

" . . . and the teashers. They're so mean! They only pass their favorites, like Celia and Rosemary. I'd rather work."

"I wanna buy me some high heels and . . . "

"I gotta help my folks."

"My little sister needs some clothes and . . . "

"Yeah."

When Blanca finished eighth grade, she found work in a flower nursery said to have belonged to Japanese farmers who had been sent to Manzanar, a camp near the mountains. At the nursery she cut and bundled carnations and stuck them in large vats full of water. She worked all summer, dragging herself home to Taconos in muddied clothes, her hands swollen, fingers calloused. The work was seasonal and soon ended.

Lucy was the only girl Blanca knew who worked steadily in the fields, picking lettuce, tomatoes and cucumbers in the ranches that dotted Footridge Boulevard. And although most afternoons Blanca saw Lucy jump off a truck, dressed in dirty denim pants and a long-sleeved shirt, each Saturday night Lucy emerged from her small house dressed to the nines in clothes bought in San Cristobal. So Blanca went off to work in the muddy tomato fields with Lucy, but told her mother, "It's just a part-time job. I ain't gonna do this forever." She soon tired of stooping over and of the the wet, cold dirt, so she began to think of another job. None was to be found.

"I don't know how to do nuthin," wailed Blanca to Lucy. "And I gots ta get me a job when the tomatoes end. And not in them fields either, cuz the mud makes me itch and I'm getting fatter 'cause I eat too many tomatoes."

A year later, one cool October day, Blanca determined not to return to either the carnations or tomatoes. She took the bus to the employment office in San Cristobal. She felt nervous, apprehensive. She wore her best white blouse, a dark skirt and very little make-up. Blanca knew that Anglos looked down at Mexican girls who wore pompadours, draped dresses and heavy makeup. That morning she had taken a sponge bath, dusted her cheeks with Pure Peach rouge, outlined her thin eyebrows, then combed out her pompadour into a thick wave. If I wanna get a job, she grumbled as she got on the smelly, crowded bus, I gotta looks like a square. She then walked the five long blocks to the employment office, took her place in line and began to look around.

The people standing ahead in line, concerned only with their own problems, ignored the busty, round-faced girl. Now and then Blanca looked up and stared at the people going in and out of the double-glass doors. Near the unemployment line several arguments broke out, some of which could be heard at the back of the room. "Getting some unemployment is the shits," Lucy had told Blanca earlier. "Them people acts like it's their goddammed money. They look at Mexicans like they was shit. Man, I'd rather work in the tomatoes than kiss up ta them."

That day, when it was her turn, Blanca approached the front booth where a tall, skinny woman with a sallow face creased like an accordion instructed her on how to fill out some color-coded cards. The woman ordered her to take a seat and wait for her name to be called. When she scanned Blanca's attempt at writing, she snickered aloud to a co-worker and, in a tight-lipped monotone, told Blanca, "You were supposed to fill out this line too."

"Oh!"

"And list all your work experience."

"Experience?"

"Yes. Right on these lines. From here to here you list . . . uhh, put down the names, places where you've worked, your supervisor's name, wages earned, and . . . "

"But I ain't hads no job!"

"Well, then we can't really help you, can we?"

"But I gots to . . . "

"The problem is . . . you Mexicans have no skills."

"And you gringas have too many wrinkles," hissed Blanca, her eyes beginning to tear. "You all gots turkey skin." She stalked out of the office, her face red with embarrassment, stopping only to check her stocking seams.

Lucy's right, admitted Blanca to herself as she slowly walked to the bus depot, her dark eyes blazing. Them people are sure nasty. They don't wanna pay out no disability nor nuthin. Or give us jobs. But man alive, I don't wanna pick no tomatoes for the rest of my life. I'm just gonna have to find me my own job, that's all.

Blanca knew it was useless to try to find a job in Taconos. Although Taconos had a post office, it lacked department stores and larger employers. Only a smattering of small markets, a butcher shop, a dry cleaners and a Mexican bakery were to be found. I'll never find me a job in Taconos, sighed Blanca, 'cause everybody already gots the jobs I can do. If I could gets hired in San Cristobal, I wouldn't have ta go so far.

In San Cristobal, few Mexican-Americans were hired as clerks or cashiers in stores, such as Thrifty or J.C. Pennys. Chito Ornelas, who after World War II returned to the barrio in his Marine uniform loaded down with medals, was one of the few guys to work at a clean job. Chito worked as a janitor at Pennys where he swept floors and cleaned toilets. In his spare time he helped unload huge crates of merchandize. Mary Lopez, who worked at the Easy Credit, was first hired during Christmas to gift-wrap. Later she was promoted to sales clerk because she was hard working, good with figures and did not mind having to sweep the store each evening. During her lunch hour Mary cleaned the glass shelves that held sparkling rings and bracelets. But Mary's lucky, Blanca moaned, as she boarded the smelly bus that went back and forth between San Cristobal and Taconos. Do I gots to do like Cruzita and find me a job in L.A.? Do I havta work in the garment district like them old ladies? Shit!

For weeks Blanca trudged to and from San Cristobal, ashamed of having to borrow money once more from her mother and fearful of having to look for work in L.A. Blanca feared having to leave the barrio. "I don't know how ta sew, type or add," she grumbled to Lucy. "And I don't wanna be no damn waitress. Man Alive! What am I gonna do?" She tried cleaning house for two Anglo women in San Cristobal, but when she put Purex bleach into the white clothes without seeing the red socks stuck inside the washer—everything turned pink—she was handed bus fare and all of two dollars and told not to come back. Day after day she walked the streets of San Cristobal in search of work. Twice she ventured as far as Burbank, where small pottery factories had taken over the greyish buildings where years earlier airplanes were built.

When she heard of an opening in "los turkeys," a poultry farm in Razgo, Blanca quickly washed out her one good blouse, counted her loose change, then walked down Main Street to the bus stop and went to apply. Much to her surprise, she was immediately hired to work by Mr. Rodnick, the owner who supervised a full crew of Mexican women. Rodnick thought that Blanca, with her husky arms and stout built, would make a good worker. She was given a huge canvas apron that came to her ankles and set to work alongside the other women.

The small town of Razgo, located south of Taconos, was known for two things: its Italian winery that sold Dago Red by the gallon and its poultry farm. Small motels dotted Razgo's main street. At one time the motels had been occupied by aircraft workers who had rented rooms by the month, then by servicemen who upon being discharged, chose to remain in California. Today there was little to see or do in Razgo, other than visit the winery to sip wine and nibble on black olives and salami sandwiches. The only other building worth noticing was the poultry farm.

The Brown Egg Poultry farm sat away from Razgo's main road, in the middle of a weed-covered lot behind the railroad tracks. The building, built in the 1900s when the town was first founded, was old and delapidated. The once white paint, now yellowed, had begun to peel off the walls. The windows were dirty, with torn screens and cracked windowpanes. The weed-covered lot was full of empty bottles and dented cans.

The main room in the Brown Egg Poultry Farm resembled a barn. It was a large, wide open room painted a sickly grey. Most of the workers were Mexican, but here and there an Okie could be found. The women's main job was to pluck feathers from dead turkeys and chickens after they were first immersed in hot water. The fowl circled above them on pulleys, dripping warm, pinkish blood. Once the poultry was plucked clean, it was moved to another room where husky workmen stored the dead birds in huge, cold storage rooms. From there the poultry was sold to restaurants, hospitals and markets.

The first day of work Blanca bumped against a hanging turkey. She cringed and felt sick, but quickly got over it and took her place in line. The foreman, a fat, red-necked Okie named Brother, quickly told her what to do: "See here, Miss. First pull them feathers off the neck, then them on the uhhh, the other parts. Last of all, do them legs, then go over the bird until the critter ain't got a single feather. See?"

To Blanca, the dead birds, with their sharp beaks and dull eyes, still appeared to be alive. She hated to touch the cold, clammy flesh. She constantly wiped her hands on the long apron that hung to her ankles, aware she would have to get over this if she wanted to keep this job. Man Alive, Blanca mumbled to herself, as she stood on her feet pulling at dead birds, "I never knew turkeys had so many feathers . . . or such a big shit hole!"

From the first, Blanca hated the job at los turkeys. The dark, wet feathers stuck to her apron, hands and legs. She hated working in a room that looked like a barn. The bloody smell of flesh, and the blood that stained her canvas shoes made her want to throw up. Blanca knew, though, that in Taconos los turkeys was considered a good job. If nothing else, it sure beat the heat of the tomato fields. At work she rarely complained about the job, but once safe at home or with Lucy, she let loose with a barrage of curses.

From the start, Blanca enjoyed the camaradarie found among the women workers, most of whom were older. The women made Blanca feel at home.

"Welcome to the turkeys, Blanche. Ya married?"

"No. Not yet anyway, but . . . "

"She's not stuped!"

"So, who's asking you, Sadie? You already put three husbands in the grave."

"Listen to you. My husband died in the war. The rest were just . . . "

"Just what?"

". . . Friends."

"You mean, sugar-daddies."

"Well, what about you, Lupe? You ain't no saint. You gots three kids and none gots the same last name!"

"So what? I support them, don't I?"

"Cut it out! Blanche is gonna think we're all bad."

"I was only kiddin! Can't ya take a joke?"

"Watch et. Here comes the boss."

During lunch the women would sit outside on old benches to share tacos and coffee kept warm in small glass jars. Most of them had children. All worked to help pay the rent, buy food and clothes and to now and then pay a bail bondsman or lawyer to free a husband or son from jail. But they were a happy bunch who passed the time telling off-color jokes to make the tedious job of plucking dead birds go faster.

"I saw you last night with your honey!"

"Oh really?"

"He says he loves me!"

"Ha, ha. He only wants one thing!"

"He wants your paycheck, stuped!"

"He sure dances good!"

"He ain't gots a job!"

"I does."

"No way I'm gonna support some wino."

"So, whose asking ya to?"

"Good tacos."

"Pass the chile."

The women would remind Blanca of how lucky she was to be single, have a steady job, live at home and not have a drunk hanging around each Friday to take her pay. Blanca listened to the women talk, smiled shyly and rejoiced in her good luck.

From the first, Blanca's priority was to buy new clothes. She needed dresses, slips, bras and panties to replace the faded cotton underthings she had worn for years. With her third paycheck, unable to resist a sale, she bought a satin bedspread with yellow and blue flowers. Later, when she spotted a set of plastic dishes at Thrifty's, she put them on lay-away for her mother. She splurged on a silver-chromed vanity set: mirror, brush and comb for $2.99 at Kress. But Blanca tried to stay away from the clothing stores that each week displayed stylish dresses on tall, skinny mannequins, where eager-faced clerks urged her to open a charge account.

Most of Blanca's friends, especially those who were single working-girls, lived for shopping! Each Saturday around five o'clock they could be found in front of a favorite store—Pennys, Sally's or San Cristobal's Fashions—spending their hard-earned cash.

"Gosh Rosie! Lookit that coat. I gotta try it on!"

"You look too dark in purple."

"Oh yeah? Says who?"

"Let's go to the Mode O Day."

"Neh, their stuff's too square, man."

Being single sure is the life, Blanca often thought. I can do what I wants, go where I wanna go and ain't nobody gots nuthin to say about it. Her mother rarely asked where she was going nor what time she would return. Since her father had died years before, Blanca was under no obligation to explain her whereabouts to a male relative. Now and then her Uncle Ernie, an ex-con who had served time in San Quintin, tried to give her fatherly advice.

"It's up ta ya to help yer mama."

"Sure, Tio Ernie."

"Don't let no sonavabich take advantage of ya, get it?"

"Yeah, I get it."

Once out of his sight, Blanca giggled at the unwelcome advise of Tio Ernie, a short, husky man who had learned how to butcher at Folsom and who slapped his wife around every chance he got.

Each payday Blanca cashed her check at the corner store, then gave her mother money for room and board. The rest she kept for herself to spend as she pleased. Now and then she tucked a ten-dollar bill inside a shoebox kept under her bed. As did most Mexicans, Blanca mistrusted banks and liked her money where she could get her hands on it.

"I gotta buy me a bedroom set," Blanca confided to her cousin Dora. "One just like Lucy's: maple, with lots of drawers. She gots hers for nuthin down . . . and the payments, they're only fifteen dollars a month. She said she can pay it off in three years. But first I gotta buy me some new tenies for work. Last week my check was too little 'cause I didn't work on Monday. I was too tired from the dance."

I ain't saving nuthin, she now and then groaned. Maybe next time I won't have ta pay fer them shitty aprons and gloves . . . and have money for other stuff. For the moment, though, it sure is good to be single and not have ta tell anybody where I'm going, no how.

After she met Cricket and things became serious, Blanca attacked the turkeys with renewed energy. She plucked away, humming softly to herself, assured this job would enable her to have a nice wedding. I'll be the first in my family to get married in the church, she gloated. I'm gonna make my mama so happy! And Lucy so jealous! Gosh! I never did gets to high school, but I'm gonna have me a big wedding. I'll show 'em. I'll make Cricket buy me a white dress with a long, long veil, and some white high heels so I can look tall. I'll have lots of bridesmaids and ushers, a good hall and a groovy band. And a nice reception with lots of chicken mole. And a cake from that bakery in L.A.

My dance will be the best one in Taconos. With the Gato Cortez Band. And when everything's over, Cricket and I can maybe (just maybe) drive to Fresno or somewhere on a honeymoon. Blanca's round face paled at the thought of so much happiness! She plucked away at the turkeys, smiling to herself, as around her the older ladies sighed and shook their heads.

Chapter Three

The First Date

The first time Blanca Muñoz and Sammy-the-Cricket went on a date was on a mild November night. Cricket had just gotten paid and was feeling flush. The accountant at the garbage plant, a near-sighted guy called Smarts, made a mistake in calculating Cricket's overtime and overpaid him by fifty dollars. When he got his check, Cricket could hardly believe his luck, so he asked another dude standing around to read out the figures to him. His eyes behind the dark glasses lit up and his thin mouth stretched into a wide smile. He shook his ducktail back and forth, all the time wanting to get out of the garbage plant, just in case Smarts had made a mistake. His first thought was to take off to Bunny's in L.A. to put a down payment on a pin-stripe suit, like the one he had seen on Skippy, the leader of the Planchados. But he changed his mind when he realized he still owed Bunny's for shirts bought that summer. Once he cashed his check, he stopped off at Tudi's to shoot the breeze and guzzle some Hill & Hill. He was lounging comfortably inside Tudi's car, humming along with Frankie Laine singing "That's My Desire," when he happened to see Blanca going by on her way home from the turkeys. He sat up, smoothed back his ducktail and remembered how Blanca had admired his fighting the Planchados some weeks back. Cricket poked his head out the window and said, "Hey man, whereya goin ta?"

"Oh hi, Cricket. I'm goin' home from the . . . from work."

"Yeah? And whatcha gonna do tonight?"

"Nuttin."

"Ya wanna go to the chow?"

"Huh? I guess. Who else is goin?"

"Tudi and his chick. We'll pick ya up at eight. I'll just honk and . . . "

Eyes wide in surprise, Blanca dashed home, her full breasts bouncing as she skipped across the cracks in the sidewalk. At home, she flung open the bedroom closet door, pulled out a new pink blouse and a gabardine skirt, and ran to take a sponge bath. She rubbed her armpits briskly, thinking, "I chure hope I don't stink too much. I ain't gots time for a chower. Gosh, I hope Cricket don't think I dress too square 'cause I ain't wearing my black dress with sequins, but I gotta save it for the dance. She rubbed Mum under her armpits, dabbed Evening in Paris cologne behind her ears and on her thick wrists, then sat in the cramped living room with a bed at one end to wait for Cricket. Now and then she peeked out the window, looking for Tudi's car, wondering where Cricket was. She had just straightened her stocking seams for the tenth time when she heard the back door open and Lucy barge in.

"God, esa! Ya didn't tell me Cricket and you was . . . "

"We're just going to the chow, to the drive in, I think."

"Yeah? Well, make him take ya to a nice place after. Shit, a movie ain't nuttin."

"It is ta me," answered Blanca, turning away from the window. "We're gonna see *Gone With The Wind.*"

"Ya seen that ten times! Ever since it came out, at least five years ago, ya seen it!"

"It's my favorite! I can't help it if I likes that Clark Gable. God! When he picks up Scarlett O'Hara and . . . "

"Going ta the drive-in fer a date ain't nuttin. Shit, ya gotta get a guy to take you to fine places. To the Palomar or Zenda."

"Maybe Cricket ain't gots money," Blanca answered, her voice low. "I don't care . . . "

"That guy ain't got no class, esa! How come he ain't askin ya to the Zenda?"

Just then they heard a car pull up in front of the house. Honk, honk, honk. "I gots ta go, Lucy," Blanca called as she bolted out the front door. "See ya later."

Once inside Tudi's car, Blanca adjusted her black skirt, happy to see that Cricket had changed his shirt and now looked better, what with his ducktail all slicked back and without his dark glasses. She smiled at him and at Tudi, then looked out the car window, hoping the chicks walking by would see her in the car with Cricket. They rode around Taconos for a while. In the back seat Cricket lit a cigarette and inhaled deeply. He smiled at the heavy-set girl next to him and leaned back into the plastic car seat.

Tudi took little notice of Cricket and Blanca. He knew Sally would soon be home from her job at her dad's butcher shop, so he drove around in circles, killing time. At the corner pool hall lounged Paulie, Sapo and Frankie, all dressed to beat the band. It was Saturday night and the Tacones wanted to show how cool they were in their tailor-mades.

Each of the Tacones, except Tudi, took pains to dress in the latest draped pants and white shirts with French cuffs and a jacket that spelled class. Paulie, El Pan Tostado, had no choice but to have his pants fitted to his full body, otherwise he told the guys, "I look like chet." Tudi rarely looked at what he wore. He was wearing the same pants worn last weekend, but with a clean shirt.

"I likes nice tings," he often explained to Sally, "but I don't wanna spend all my cash, like Cricket. I gotta pay off my car, ya know, make payments . . . and give my mom some too. No way I'm gonna buy more drapes at Bunny's."

Tudi liked Sally, a chubby girl with light brown eyes and a friendly disposition. Her favorite color was yellow, a color she told Tudi made her feel good. Most of the time she wore a yellow dress or sweater, which reminded Tudi of warm sunshine. Sally was nice to everyone and was often asked to be a bridesmaid. Her girlfriends also knew that she always gave a nice wedding present. She was generous with money and, when at the movies with Tudi and their friends, bought popcorn and candy for everyone. When not working at the sewing factory in San Cristobal, Sally worked with her father, Don Archuleta, in their butcher shop outside Taconos. She often gave Tudi tender pink pork chops to take home to his mama, which is also why Tudi liked her so well.

Of all the chicks that lived on Honeysuckle Street, Sally had the nicest house. And the nicest furniture. And the best clothes. Tudi sometimes wondered why Sally hung around Lucy and Blanca. "You sure ain't like Lucy," he often told Sally. "How come you and her . . . "

"Ain't nobody else dresses charp," Sally told him, frowning slightly. "Ain't nobody else goes ta the Zenda either." Now and then Sally invited Tudi over to listen to records. Each time he felt awkward and embarrassed. The living room where Sally served him baloney sandwiches with Fritos was furnished with a wide plaid sofa, matching chair and braided throw rugs in soft shades of brown. Now as he, Cricket and Blanca drove past Sally's house for the third time, he decided to park his car and save gas while waiting for Sally to come outside.

Tudi parked the car and got out, stomped out the Camel cigarette dangling from his hand, stuck a piece of Juicy Fruit in his mouth, ran a comb through his thick hair and then knocked on the door. Within minutes Sally, wearing a yellow blouse and grey skirt, came out the door and got into the car and made herself comfortable. She said "Hi!," then squeezed Tudi's arm. He started the car, put it in first gear, rolled up the window and drove off to the drive-in."

"What are we gonna see?" asked Sally, adjusting her skirt. "What movie are ya . . . "

"The one at the Towne is gonna be good."

"Nel. I ain't gonna take a chance. Them Planchados hang out there. Ain't that right, Cricket?"

"Speak fer yourself, man," grunted Cricket from the back seat. "I ain't chicken."

"Let's go see a gangster movie," urged Sally, aware Cricket wanted to start an argument. "The one wiz that fat guy, uhhh, Peter Lorre is real good!" "I wanna see somethin with cowboys," offered Tudi, "with John Wayne and . . . "

"Man, them movie's are too square!"

"Yeah. But I like it when the cowboys . . . "

"Well, okay. Whatcha say we take the chicks to see, uhhh, Humphrey Bogart?"

"Simon! That guy don't take no chet from no chicks. Or nobody."

"But I wanted ta see 'Gone With The Wind,' " wailed Blanca, looking at Sally for support. "They're chowing it at the drive-in."

"Man, that one's too old. I knows the story by heart."

"Go ahead to the drive-in, Tudi. The chicks wanna see 'Went Wiz the Wind' . . . "

They drove to the drive-in about six miles from Taconos, getting there just as it got dark. While driving, Tudi kept looking around, on the alert for cars resembling those driven by the Planchados. Man, I sure hate driving on strange streets, thought Tudi. Lately he hated driving anywhere far from Taconos. He felt safe only in the Valley, on familiar streets and alleys. "I knows them Planchados ain't after me," he often told Sally, "but if I keep hanging around Cricket, they'ze gonna gets me too."

He parked the car, adjusted the speaker, then leaned back to enjoy the cartoons that preceded the movie, happy to be with Sally. They returned from the snack bar just as the movie was about to begin. Just then Cricket happened to turn around.

"Shit," hissed Cricket, yanking off his boppers, "the Planchados are behind us! And lookit over there," he pointed. "Them cars too. Man, Tudi! Whatcha have ta bring us to this . . . "

"Act like you ain't seen em," advised Sally, trying not to gag on her popcorn. "Don't look at em."

"I gotta go to the pisser," announced Tudi. "Man, what if they gets me in there?"

"I'll go with ya," offered Sally, "I gotta gets some popcorn and . . . "

No sooner were Tudi and Sally out of earshot, than Cricket let out with a litany of curses.

"Son-ava-beesh. Them guys was probably followin us, but that jerk didn't sees them."

"Who?"

"Tudi! Thass his job, to look out for . . . "

"Maybe they just came ta see the chow."

"Yeah? I don't trust them mudders."

Blanca, her face white and lips trembling, said nothing. I shoulda listened to Lucy, she sighed, running her hands through her limp curls. I shoulda told Cricket to take me to a nice place. That way them Planchados wouldn't start nuttin. She could almost smell her damp armpits; her pink blouse was straining at the sleeves. She lit a cigarette, took a puff and tried to watch the "Coming Attractions" now on the huge screen. Just then Sally and Tudi returned from the snack bar, their arms laden with popcorn, cokes and Milk Duds. While Sally passed the food around, Tudi lit a cigarette and turned to Cricket.

"Them guys are okay, Cricket. I gots in the line next to Skippy, and he ain't said nuttin."

"Yeah? They knows you'ze chicken, that's why."

"More popcorn, Cricket?"

"If it hadda been me, they woulda runs the udder way."

"Wanna soda, Blanca?"

On the screen, a dark-haired Scarlett O'Hara, in a red dress that showed her full breasts, danced with a tall, handsome Clark Gable, her green-eyes gazing up at him. In the back seat, Blanca moved away from Cricket, who kept shifting in his seat, and staring out the windows.

"Man, this sure is a good chow," sighed Sally. "Lookit all them guys flirting with Scarlett O'Hara. Gosh, she sure gots a little waist."

"Yeah, I know," answered Blanca, pulling in her stomach. "She chure is pretty."

Just then someone tapped on the car window. Tudi rolled open the window, while in the back seat Cricket braced himself. "Ese, gotta light?" asked Mudo. "I ain't got no matches."

"Whatcha doin here, Mudo?" hissed Cricket. "Dont'cha know them Planchados are . . . "

"I ain't botherin em," Mudo grumbled as he lit a cigarette. "I just wanna see 'Gone Wiz the Wind.' I ain't here ta pick a fight with them guys," he concluded, taking a puff of his Lucky Strike. "I just wanna . . . "

"Okay, Mudo," said Tudi as he closed the window. "See ya en Taconos."

In the rear of the car Cricket took a deep breath, then slowly let it out. Shit! Somethin was happening to the Tacones! Jezus! Even Mudo was acting chicken, and Tudi had talked to that mudder, Skippy. What the hell! Ain't nobody give a shit about nuttin.

Before they knew it, the movie was over. Around them cars began to warm up, then circle around the asphalt and move towards the exit. Tudi turned on the ignition and idled the car. I better be prepared, he sighed, his sweaty hands gripping the steering wheel. He looked toward the exit. Sally ripped open the box of Milk Duds and popped one into Tudi's wide mouth.

"Whatcha waitin fer," asked an irritable Cricket from the back seat. "Ya gonna stay here all night?"

"Neh. I was waitin for the traffic ta . . . "

"Get going! Ain't nobody left in the joint . . . "

Tudi turned onto the exit lane, his eyes searching all around. He stepped on the gas, got behind the car ahead, a grey Merc that in the dim light looked vaguely familiar. He put on the lights and his heart skipped a beat. In front of them was a car full of Planchados!

"Man, it's Skippy!" cried Tudi. "Whatcha want me ta do?"

"Ram 'em. Chow em whose boss."

"Just drive," suggested Sally, adjusting her bra strap, "an when we hit the main drag, give it some gas."

"Nel," screeched Cricket. "They'ze gonna say weez chicken . . . "

"Just drive," repeated Sally, making sure Cricket heard her. "Just take us home, then you can chase them guys to San Cristobal." Once they hit the main road, the grey Merc took off down the middle lane, leaving Tudi's blue Chevie behind. Right before the Planchados turned left, the driver of the Merc stuck his hand out, pointed his middle finger and shouted, "Here, Cricket," then tore off towards the safety of San Cristobal.

Blanca never forgot that first date, nor how brave Cricket acted. "Imagine," she later told Sally, "Cricket wanted to ram them guys off the street!"

"Yeah, well it wasn't his car."

"Whadda ya mean?"

"Nuddin."

After that night, Cricket began to think of Blanca as a cool chick. After all, hadn't she been on his side when them Planchados almost jumped them at the drive-in? Sally began to have second thoughts about Cricket and Los Tacones, but she continued to send Tudi pork chops.

Cricket proposed one night in May while he and Blanca were in Tudi's car parked near Topaz Canyon, the local lovers-lane. In the front seat Tudi and Sally were snuggled tight. Parked next to them in a flashy midnight-blue convertible, Josie and Wimpy sipped whiskey and puffed camels. They had just been to a swell dance at the Salon Parra and were now beat from so much boogie-woogie. Inside Tudi's car Blanca snuggled close to Cricket.

"Man, whatta good dance!"

"Yeah!"

"But I gotta git home, or my Ma will . . . "

"Yeah? Well I ain't ready yet."

"But what if . . . "

"Tell her you're my old lady . . . and we're gonna gets hitched."

"Really? Gosh! Wait till I tell Lucy!"

Chapter Four

Blanca

Coached by Lucy, Blanca hinted to Cricket that it was up to the groom-to-be to pay for the bride's dress, but Cricket played dumb and ignored her. At home she stood in front of the cracked bathroom mirror to practice how, once she cornered Cricket, she would look him in the eye and tell him a thing or two. But when faced to face with her fiancé, Blanca could not say anything. Blanca knew that the Tacones hated chicks who tried to give orders, dames who acted like they wore the pants. She decided to wait until they were alone.

One night while parked in Topaz Canyon, Blanca, dressed to the nines and reaking of Tabu, snuggled up to Cricket.

"Honey, I saw the prettiest dress in . . . "

"Well, buy it, man!"

"I mean a wedding dress! You know, for our wed . . . "

"Well, whatcha waitin fer?"

"Do you really think I should . . . "

"Simón! It's your money."

"Cricket sure pissed me off," Blanca later moaned to Lucy, "He thinks he's so good 'cause he beat the Planchados, but he acts so damn stuped and keeps making excuses fer not talking about my wedding dress. Every time I start to ask him about whose gonna pay . . . he takes off and leaves me with my mouth hanging open. He pisses me off . . . "

After they took the chicks home, Tudi and Cricket rode around the empty Taconos streets, sipping whiskey and smoking stale cigarettes. "That Blanca sure pisses me off," hissed Cricket to Tudi. "Man, ain't nuthing a guy can do 'cept throw em ta the dogs. No way that dame's gonna shut up. I tell you man, she's beginning to get my goat. All she wants to talk about is the wedding . . . and her damn dress. Ya gotta show them chicks who'se da boss . . . ain't no other way."

Blanca then decided to do one of two things, hound Cricket for the money or stay on his good side and pay for everything herself.

Some couples in Taconos were married for three years or more and were still making payments on wedding rings and wedding pictures, even after the first kid was born. Weddings were expensive, everybody new that. But so much fun! A neighbor girl, Suki, had borrowed money from her folks to pay for her wedding reception. But my Ma ain't gots no money, Blanca sighed, and my Tio Ernie ain't gots a steady job. The bridesmaids gotta pay for their stuff, so I can't borrow from them. What am I gonna do?

Most married girls in Taconos helped out at home. Blanca paid room and board, as did Rosie and Josie. Only Sally kept all her money, which is why she liked to spend it on her friends. Single girls from poor families often bought furniture for the front room so as to show off. Others bought hope chests which they crammed with sheets, towels and blankets bought on lay-away at Pennys. But after hinting to Cricket about the money needed to pay for the invitations and food, and getting no better answer than a grunt, Blanca decided to take care of the wedding details herself . . . and the heck with Cricket.

I'll buy the flowers from the nursery where I worked, and my Ma can make the mole. And if I gotta, I'll make payments on my dress. Maybe Lucy can loan me money for the cake, cause they cost too much in L.A., or maybe I'll buy it in San Cristobal. But dammit, once Cricket and I are hitched, he better let me have his check, so I can get the stuff I wants. That cheapskate ain't gonna take my check! And the first thing I'm gonna do is tell him he ain't gonna buy no more suits at Bunny's . . . or else!

Cricket and Los Tacones were always competing with the Planchados to see who dressed the best. To the guys from Taconos, it was a matter of pride to show that guys from a hick town weren't all that square. "Dammit, Cricket goes to L.A. all the time," Blanca complained to Lucy. "He gots ta get the latest stuff. He's always charging more stuff. Last month he bought three shirts. And he's so damn cheap with me! He don't even wanna buy me my . . . "

"Sometimes he just goes with the other guys, then comes

back with another jacket or pants. Man alive, Lucy! He ain't gonna have money for nuthing," sighed Blanca, her face flushed and sweaty. "And I wanna go on a honeymoon!" She finally cornerd Cricket.

"Gosh, honey, you look so fine! Are them new pants?"

"Yeah."

"They gots some new styles at Pennys. Wanna go see . . . "

Cricket, his homely face contorted with laughter, stared at Blanca, then snarled, "Nel, esa, my pants gotta be from Bunny's. I ain't gonna buy no threads from no Pennys. Shit, I ain't square. I gotta look sharp, man. Like them Planchados. I'm hep."

"But what about the wedding?" walled Blanca, her face gaunt in the dim streetlight. "Whatta about my dr . . . "

"What about it?" Cricket's eyes like black coals, stared down at the husky girl clinging to the sleeve of his new jacket. He flipped at imaginary dust on his lapel and pushed his bride-to-be from him. "What about it?" he demanded once more.

"I was just askin," answered Blanca, her clammy hand against her thudding heart. "Nuthing."

"Goddammit," Cricket hissed, "ya sure like ta get my goat. Ya better get it straight right now. Nobody tells me how ta dress, nor where ta buy my drapes. Get it?"

Blanca was getting more apprehensive as her wedding day grew near and as she continued to see Cricket sporting new clothes.

It's too late to back out, Blanca thought, her face blanched and taut, ain't no way I'm gonna let my Ma down. I'm the first one in my family to leave by the front door, and there's no way anyone in Taconos is gonna make fun of me. I just won't say nuthin, and hope for the best. With that in mind, she began to work overtime and put all the money she could save in the hiding place under her bed.

Chapter Five

Sammy-the-Cricket

Samuel Lopez, known in Taconos as Sammy-the-Cricket, lived with his widowed mother, Doña Petra, in a wooden house on a weed-covered lot. Their house was identical to the others on their block, which were said to have been built as tool sheds by the railroad company during the early 1900s. The house was in need of repair; the small windows were broken in several places, and the back steps were falling apart. But to the widow Petra and to her son Cricket, this was home.

Before being crushed to death by a freight train, Cricket's father had worked as a day laborer in the ranches near Taconos. Rumor claimed that Cricket's father was drunk and did not see the train approaching. His close friends, other drunks who hung around the rail yard, swore the train was going too fast to stop. No one paid any attention to those who witnessed the accident. The rail line, nevertheless, paid the widow Petra a small sum without acknowledging responsibility for the accident. The company also presented her with a free train pass to boot. The grieving widow was advised by friends and neighbors alike to take the money, which she did. But before she could cash the check, her older son, El Sully, was caught breaking and entering. El Sully was taken to county jail and sentenced to five years in the can. The insurance money was used to pay a bail bondsman and, later, a lawyer from Los Angeles who got the charges reduced. Her husband's funeral also came out of the check and so did the money to buy the tool shed converted to a house.

Cricket's earliest memory was of a small dark house crowded with bodies, matresses and warmth. The warmth came from the wood stove that sat in the corner of the kitchen where every morning his mother made tortillas. A large box with odd pieces of wood sat next to the stove. Doña Petra took pride in her wheat flour tortillas. She had learned to make these in Sonora, and liked to cook them for her sons, especially for Cricket, the homeliest, but her favorite.

As a kid Cricket hated school. By the third grade he could barely write his name and address correctly. His classmates sometimes made fun of his attempts to read. He liked recess best, during which time his long legs carried him across the playground in record time. By eighth grade he had grown close to six feet, taller than most of the teachers, all of whom he hated.

"I'm gonna gets Mr. Thatcher."

"Yeah? How come?"

"No reason, I just hate his guts."

"Whatcha gonna do ta him?"

"Pour gasoline inside his car, then light et."

"Man, you chure gots guts."

When he turned thirteen Cricket quit school, as had his brothers before him. He had already repeated seventh grade and was not about to hang around for a third try. He never regretted leaving school. He hated books and teachers alike. In fifth grade, after being reprimanded by the principal for smoking in the playground, Cricket poured sand into the gas tank of the principal's shiny car. He was caught by the janitor, a kind old man whom Cricket kicked all the way to the office. Once in the principals' office, Cricket denied having committed the crime. Because only the janitor had seen him and he was under-age, Cricket was hauled to juvenile hall, where his head was shaved and his picture taken. Cricket vowed to get back at the janitor who, scared out of his wits, retired to the desert. Cricket returned to school the next year, full of new tricks picked up from the other punks who clogged juvenile hall.

As the youngest son in a family of tough dudes, Cricket was determined to be tougher and meaner than his brothers. He vowed to take no shit from nobody, just like the guys in juvenile hall had taught him. He often thought that if his brother Sully, then serving time for shooting a cop, had been really tough and had kicked the shit out of the copper rather than shoot him, he wouln't have been sent to Folsom.

"Man, Sully, ya shoulda kicked his ass."

"I dids, but he still gots up."

"Ya shoulda used brass knuckles!"

"He gots some too!"

"Yeah? Well, ain't nuttin ta do but shoot the bastard."

"Thass what I done."

From a young age Cricket could outrun everyone: his older brothers who, if they caught him, would knock the shit out of him, his teachers, the cops and guys out to get him. His favorite pastime was kicking dogs. He liked to hang around the alley that bordered the liquor store on Main Street to watch for dogs. Nearby he stashed a supply of rocks. When dogs came by, he kicked out at them, then armed with the rocks tore off after them. Most of the dogs knew him by sight and smell and took off whenever they saw him.

Cricket never regretted leaving Taconos Elementary School. Most of his friends and neighbors, guys who hung around the corner smoking and shooting the breeze, had dropped out of school too. All they talked about was getting girls and low-slung Chevies, and of how to get jobs other than those in the fields or as unskilled laborers.

"Man, I been to the machine chops tree times!"

"Yeah? And whatcha find?"

"Nada. Ain't nuthing if ya ain't gots experience."

"Ya gots experience, Cricket. Tell 'em ya can steal and slash tires."

"Ha, ha, ha. Yeah, and beat the shit outta coppers."

"Ya want yer jaw busted?"

"Neh! I was just kiddin."

As had his father and brothers before him, Cricket first got a job in the fields swamping potatoes. When that job ended, he hired on to work at a nearby packing shed, loading crates of tomatoes and lettuce. When the packing house moved to Los Angeles, Cricket stayed behind to try his luck in the shops in San Cristobal and Razgo.

Cricket felt awkward having to use mechanic's tools. All he had learned from Sully was how to slash tires, steal batteries and lie through his teeth. The only thing he knew to do with a tire wrench was sling it at someone who pissed him off. He got a job pumping gas in a service station, but when told he had to change flat tires too, he quit, but not before emptying the cash box. He then applied at the machine shops in San Cristobal where he had heard they hired anybody, but the smell of gasoline and oil made him sick. Worse, when asked to turn on a soldering iron for a demonstration, Cricket was ashamed to admit he could not read the directions on the machine.

"First ya turn on this switch, then . . . "

"Which switch?"

"This one, the one that says ON."

"Oh! I thoughts that was ONE."

"Huh? On second thought . . . "

Cricket felt uneasy around loud machines too. Loud motors gave him an earache, and loud machines drove him nuts. None of his brothers had ever owned a car, except for the time Sully stole one. And although Sully was an accomplished thief who littered their back yard with radios and record players, Cricket never cared to tinker with them. He hated getting oil on his big, wiry hands. "All I gets is work in the fields," Cricket hissed, "but all that mud is the chets."

What Cricket hated most was working in the muddy fields. The hours were long and the pay low. What he hated most was the mud that stuck to his face and neck. The older men who worked alongside him were not easy to intimidate. Worse yet, all worked faster than he did. "This mud's the chets," Cricket often grumbled. "I gots too much class ta be workin like a nigger." He looked forward to the end of the tomato season, when he could sleep all day while waiting to see what else came up.

As the leader of Los Tacones, Cricket hated for the chicks to see him caked in mud, or worse, riding home from the potato fields on a flatbed truck. Once, as he was getting off of a truck, he spotted some chicks nearby and told the driver to let him off in the alley. But the driver forgot and stopped in front of them. Cricket jumped off in the middle of Main Street and tried to steal away, but one of the girls with peroxide-yellow hair called out to him.

"Hey Cricket, where ya been? Dancin in the mud?"

"Uhhhh."

"Hey, Cricket, is that a new suit?"

He ran home, kicking out at dogs, cussing a blue streak and vowing to get even with the stupid truck driver who was ruining his reputation.

One summer Cricket got a job with a trucking company. He lied about his age, forged a social security card, cut his hair, and stole a pair of work shoes from a store in San Cristobal. The job took him to Bakersfield, where along with a fat guy named Toby, he took produce to and from the wholesaler to market. Cricket was assigned to help Toby load sacks of potatoes to be taken to Central Market in Los Angeles. At first Cricket liked the long ride on top of the huge truck, but when the truck broke down and he had to help Toby check under the hood, he began to cuss and screech at Toby. Cricket was replaced the next day.

By the time he was seventeen, Cricket had a reputation for being in trouble with the cops. He was picked up for petty theft and taken to jail, lined up and identified by witnesses who later saw him face-to-face in court and changed their story. They hated to tangle with a character whom even the cops feared.

By eighteen Cricket was a tough, wiry guy with slick black hair, thin lips, dark slanted eyes and arms that hung to his knees. He got in with Los Tacones, a gang of Pachucos that hung around Kiki's Pool Hall on Saturday nights. He began hanging around with Tudi, a neighbor whom Cricket considered too square, because Tudi gave his mother half of his pay. Worse, Tudi sometimes ironed his own pants! That Tudi's too stuped, Cricket thought. The moola he earns ain't his mudder's. Ain't nobody gonna make me give em my pay. Not even my Ma. Mostly, he hated to pay for the food and cigarettes his brother Sully took with him when running from the cops.

Cricket was his mother's favorite son. Of all the brothers, he alone resembled his father. The others were short, like her side of the family. All had been in trouble with the law. Cuchi had served time in Folsom. Sordo, who was deaf in one ear, was convicted of stealing a car from a police garage. Sully had shot a policeman who had caught him stealing a frozen turkey for Thanksgiving. Of all her sons, Cuchi scared the widow Petra most. He talked to himself all the time, walked in his sleep and liked to play with matches. The only time the poor widow was at peace was when Cuchi was in jail, Sully was out-of-town, hiding from the cops, and Cricket was out with Tudi.

Like most guys in Taconos, Cricket longed for nothing more than a steady job, an indoor job away from the muddy fields and the cold, damp air. He yearned to wear custom-made suits made at Bunny's in Los Angeles, to drive a shiny car with white walls and to have a steady chick.

The summer he was sixteen Cricket went steady with Lola, the pretty girl who lived next door. They would meet by the tall pepper trees that lined the rail yard, where they sipped sodas. Or they went to the show on Saturday nights with Lola's brother Rana. They broke up when Cricket found out Lola had denied knowing him to Toots, a guy from San Cristobal thought to be a square. When he found this out, Cricket got so angry that he went out to kick dogs and plan how he was gonna get Lola's new boyfriend.

Cricket had sworn to punch Toots in the kisser. One night when he spotted Toots near Lola's house, Cricket took out his knife and under the cover of darkness slit Toot's two front tires. He then went home and from the kitchen window watched Toots deal with the flats. When he saw Lola point towards his house, Cricket realized that Lola knew him a lot better than he had thought. He quickly pulled the curtain closed and then took off to find Tudi, whom he knew would swear he and Cricket had been together all night.

When told by a friend that they were hiring in the garbage, Cricket got a ride with Tudi to go apply at the sanitation plant on San Cristobal Road. He wore a clean shirt, kakhi pants and shoes with regular heels. Right before he went into the building, he took off his dark glasses. He feared being spotted as a pachuco, so did his best to look square. Much to his surprise, he and a member of the Planchados were hired. While waiting to be processed, Cricket gave the Planchado a cool stare, then nodded, aware of how important this job was to them both. He knew there was a time to fight . . . and a time to do nothing. He did nothing.

Cricket found hauling garbage to be hard work. Although the sanitation plant was located in the San Cristobal Valley, the garbage trucks went everywhere, even to Beverly Hills, where the drivers were told not to make noise while the rich slept. And in some areas of Los Angeles, the garbage trucks were not allowed in residential areas until nine in the morning. The garbage cans all weighed a ton, even those from expensive homes. Cricket hated to work with smaller guys. Because he was bigger, he was in charge of hauling the cans to the garbage truck. As the day wore on, the cans felt heavier and heavier.

"Them drivers gots it made," Cricket sniveled to Tudi, "all they do is sit on their ass. I gotta do the shitty work . . . while they sits inside the truck ta drink coffee." Still, he was grateful not to be back in the fields.

One time Cricket was assigned to work with Richie, a tough guy from San Cristobal. Richie was not a pachuco, but at dances he hung around with the Planchados. That night Cricket bandaged his hand, then told the foreman he could barely lift his arm. He was told to drive instead. Richie cussed up a storm, but had to haul the cans while Cricket sat up front in the truck, at ease and smoking his Lucy Strikes.

On Saturday nights Cricket and the guys got higher than a kite on marijuana. Burt, a member of Los Tacones heard that the Planchados smoked pot 'cause it helped them work faster, so he introduced Cricket to "yesca," as he called the thin, brown cigarettes he bought in L.A.

"If ya smoke Mary Jane before work, ya won't get tired."

"All the guys in the garbage do it, man. That's how come they don't gets tired."

"Try it!"

Cricket did.

Sometimes Cricket smoked so much marijuana his eyes changed color, or so it seemed. The whites of his eyes criss-crossed with red capillaries looked pink from far away. He took to wearing his dark glasses at all times so that the foreman would not see his blood-shot eyes and fire him. When high on dope, Cricket worked harder than ever. Often his boss would pound him on the back and say, "You Mexicans sure work hard." Cricket would grin, then continue working, confident his boss liked him and wouldn't fire him when now and then he reported to work late.

After three months on the job and being assigned to work with Fats, a husky weight-lifter who liked nothing more than to grunt, Cricket decided this job was what he and the guys had always dreamed of: a clean job a steady job. After six months he took his money out from under a crack in floor and drove with Tudi to Bunny's to put money down on a custom-made suit, three shirts with French cuffs and shoes with three-inch heels. Next he bought an old used car and began to think of Blanche Muñoz as his old lady.

The car, an apple green 44 Ford immediately caught Cricket's eye. It's shiny green paint and white-wall tires gave it a snappy look. Even Tudi agreed that the car was mighty fine, so Cricket bought it. He gave nothing down, signed his name on the dotted line pointed out to him by the salesman and grinned at Tudi from behind the black boppers. He had barely left the parking lot, feeling nervous 'cause he didn't have a driver's license yet, when the car groaned and then stalled. Cricket and Tudi managed to push it to the side of the road. Cricket returned to the car lot, yanked the salesman outside, punched him in the eye and demanded another car. As they scuffled between the latest models, the cops were called by a secretary. When Cricket heard the familiar wail of sirens, he pushed away the bloodied salesman, called him a sonavabeesh and tore off down the alley to the stalled car which, after he and Tudi pushed it downhill, fired up and took him back to Taconos in record time. Later that night Tudi looked under the hood and discovered Cricket's new car was held together with bailing wire.

A few days later, Cricket and Sully, drove by the car lot where he had bought the Ford. He threw rocks at the office windows and at the cars in the lot, leaving behind a glass-strewn mess. He never went back, but instead sent Tudi to make the car payments on the apple-green car that he hardly drove.

In Taconos it was commonly thought that only girls wanted big, church weddings. But Cricket had always liked being in weddings. He also enjoyed the fuss of being with the guys and driving to L.A. for wedding pictures in souped-up cars with gleaming white walls. More than this, Cricket felt it his sacred duty to have his best friends, in tuxedos, riding in low-slung cars with loud pipes that kept the cops writing out tickets. Secretly, Cricket wanted it said that his wedding had been the best in Taconos. As soon as he began to get a steady paycheck, and once he and Blanca had started going steady, he began to think of raising his status among the pachucos of the San Cristobal Valley by getting hitched to his chick in a wedding that would outclass all others.

Chapter Six

The Batos

When the batos noticed Cricket making goo-goo eyes at Blanca Muñoz, they began to tease him about being hung up on a chick. At first he denied he even liked Blanca, let alone thought of her as his steady chick. But when he kept taking her out and later walked her home from Sally's, Los Tacones knew it was serious. When high, the batos liked to compare chicks, especially those who refused to go out with them, chicks who hated pachucos and even hated "squares" who wore drapes. The guys had their favorites too, chicks not worth the price of a movie and others too ugly to be seen with.

One night, right before a party at Sally's, the guys picked up Cricket, then went cruising the streets of Taconos to kill time before checking out the chicks. As they rode around the dusty streets they talked about what they liked in chicks and teased Cricket.

"Hey Cricket, ya hung up on Blanche Muñoz?"

"Neh, she's just a chick I wuz dancin wiz . . . "

"She wants ta boss ya," added Paulie, el Pan Tostado, adjusting his tie.

"Ain't no dame gonna tell me what ta do!"

"You said it!"

"Right."

"She walks like a cherry . . . "

"Oh yeah? How can ya tell, Topo?"

"Ya can't," inturrupted Sapo, smoothing his moustache. "A guy can't tell nuttin. Taday chicks do what they wants . . . they comes and goes till midnight. In da old days a guy could call da chots. Ain't no way ta tell if they cherry, except ta bang em up a liddle . . . ha, ha, ha."

"Yeah!"

"You bet."

"My chick better be a cherry when I gets hitched," snarled Frankie, sipping from a flask, "or else."

"Or else what," asked Tudi, chewing on gum. "Or else what?"

". . . I'll knock the chet outta her," explained Frankie, smoothing his flying ducktail. "Chow her she ain't gonna fool wiz me . . . den dump her in front of her pad so che can fool some udder jerk."

"Man, a chick hasta knows how ta act right wiz a guy," chimed in Topo patting his curly hair. Remember Sophie? That chick I took to da chow?"

"The one wiz them big tits?"

"No, stupid. That dame was Jovita . . . "

"Da one with peroxide hair?" asked Tudi, fiddling with the radio. "The chick wiz orange eyebrows?"

"Neh, that was Mabel . . . "

"Man, Topo, ya chure had lotsa chicks," sighed Paulie, tucking in his shirttails. "How come ya ain't gots hitched?"

"Why buy a cow when milk is so cheep?" answered Topo. He stretched his legs, lit a cigarette, then inhaled deeply.

"Aha, ha, ha," chortled Sapo, his eyes crinkling with laughter. "Ya said et, man!"

"So what about Sophie," persisted Tudi, "she found out ya wasn't a cherry?"

"Don't mess wiz me, ese," growled Frankie, giving Tudi a dirty look.

"A guy ain't suppose ta be cherry," added Paulie with authority. "Da guys suppose ta had lotsa experience . . . "

"Right."

". . . But a chick better keeps her legs crossed . . . "

"Oooooow," grunted Topo, scratching his crotch. "Oooooow, baby, baby." " . . . And not let nobody in . . . else che ain't nuttin but a whore," continued Frankie. "Ain't dat right, Cricket?"

"Right."

"Yeah, but what happened ta Sophie?" asked Paulie, his big chest heaving, "da one wiz da big tits."

"Man, ya got sumtin wiz tits?" asked Topo, smoothing his suit lapel. "Ya still gots ta have a nipple ta sleep?"

"Nel!" screeched Paulie, laughing aloud. "I just wanna know

what about Sophie, dats all."

"Sheeet . . . " groaned Sapo, "I chure would lak ta gets me some . . . "

"And Sophie?" hissed Topo to Frankie. "Ya gonna tell us what's wiz her, or what?"

"Ain't much ta tell, ese. She wanted ta gets hitched wiz me so bad!"

"Oooooow," laughed Topo, lighting up cigarettes for himself and for Cricket, "how bad she want ta get hitched? Come on, Frankie, ya gonna tell us, or what?"

"Whatcha want me ta do? Draw ya a pichure?" grinned Frankie.

"Yeah, ese. How many times ya . . . "

"Ain't how many times dat counts, ese. First I toll her she gotta prove ta me she's cherry . . . den I wuz gonna buy her a ring."

"Yeah?"

"And what happened, man?" asked Tudi, his brown eyes flashing. "Did she let ya in?"

"Of course! Me and everybody else . . . "

"Aha, ha, ha," screeched Paulie, el Pan Tostado, rocking back and forth against the car seat. "Aha, ha."

Among the batos it was commonly said that any chick who did "it" with a guy, even if they were going steady, was sure to put out for other dudes.

That night, Los Tacones got tired of bullshitting and waiting for Sally's party to start. They returned to Tudi's car and went off to kill time. Paulie sat in back with Topo, his ample behind taking up half the seat.

"So what of Sophie?" asked Paulie, chewing on a fingernail. "Ya didn't finich tellin 'bout the chick wiz dem knockers . . . "

"Sheet," hissed Topo, yanking at Paulie's lapel, "ya gots somethin wiz spotlights?"

"I just like em," growled Paulie, "ain't nuthin wrong wiz dat, eees et?"

"Yeah, well, some batos like em," snapped Topo, "ain't nuthin wrong wiz dat. But me, man, I like a good ass. Ya know, somethin I can grab onta."

"No," added Sapo, squeezed against Cricket and Tudi. "Ya gots et all wrong. Ain't much ya can do wiz big titties and a big ass. Gimme a chick wiz long, long legs and . . ."

"Yeah?" snickered Topo, "legs ain't nuttin if a dame ain't got no tits."

"Tits ain't nuttin," argued Tudi, "what counts is . . ."

"Oh yeah? Ya an expert on chicks?" growled Frankie. Shit, Tudi, I bet ya ain't had more than one chick yer whole life . . ."

"Aha, ha, ha," laughed Sapo, smacking his hand on the car dashboard. "Ya a cherry, Tudi?"

"Man, I ain't sayin dat," snapped Tudi, his hands gripping the steering wheel, "but big tits and a big ass ain't all that . . ."

"Ain't nuthin a chick needs more," affirmed Frankie, "cept ta be a cherry. No guy wants leftovers."

"Ya said et," groaned Topo, looking out the car window. "Any bato settles fer anudder guy's leftovers is gonna regret et."

"How come?" asked Tudi, as he turned the corner. "How come sumthin that happened before's gonna change how ya feel bout somebody."

"Ain't no guy gonna fergit, stuped. Whatcha tink . . . deys gonna know somebody else gots ta his chick first, that's what!"

"Yeah, but what if . . ."

"What if what?" snarled Frankie. "Man, Tudi, ya talk like you don't know nuttin. Ya better learn ta be a man, ese, udderwise ya gonna be sorry. A chick ain't cherry ain't worth a tu . . ."

"What if she's nice?" wailed Tudi, chewing furiously on a piece of Juicy Fruit. "What if . . ."

"Don't cut no ice," snarled Cricket, "once ya chow em whose boss, they gotta be nice, or else . . ."

"Man, when I gets hitched my gal better be nice ta my Ma," Frankie said. "She better not give my mudder no lip. Not like dat bitch my brudder married."

"Suki?"

"Yeah, she's my seester-in-law an all dat, but if I was my brudder . . ."

"Ya ain't."

"I ain't saying I am, Tudi! Man, sometimes ya give me a pain in da ass . . ."

41

"Turn to da left," ordered Cricket, flexing his knuckles. "Give a U-turn, Tudi, den park over there. I wanna see what chicks are at da party."

"There goes Rosie," snickered Sapo. "Man, che gets more skinny every time I see her. She looks lak spaghetti!"

"Ha, ha, ha," laughed Tudi, his mouth open wide, "her legs look like two sticks. Ha, ha, ha."

"Looked Lupe," said Frankie, "looket her. I used ta take her outs, ya know, just ta do her a favor . . . "

"She gots some big knockers," grunted Paulie, "I seen em up close and . . . "

"Ya ain't seen chet, ese," said Topo, "ya just like ta brag."

"Dat Lucy gettin in the red convertible?" asked Sapo, straining to see across Tudi's shoulders.

"Chure looks lak her," answered Tudi, lowering the car radio, then looking to where Sapo pointed. "Chure looks lak . . . "

"Hedy Lamarr?"

"Neh, the udder one wiz dem big eyes."

"Joan Crawford? Aint che da one wiz dem big choulders?"

"Yeah! She acts too tough fer a dame . . . always wants ta give orders . . . "

"Lucy likes ta give orders," offered Tudi, turning the radio knob back and forth. "I heard her tellin off dat guy called Güero, ya know, he hangs out at Tottie's Place.

"Yeah? Well, that bato's a sucker fer . . . "

"Shhhh, here comes my chick," snapped Sapo, opening the car door. "I don't cuss round her. Ya gotta chow respect, ya know."

"Respect? Fer a chick? Ya outta yer mind?" gasped Topo, smoothing his hair back with his fingers. "Sheeet, I don't cuss in fronta my Ma, but a chick . . . "

"Come on, Tudi," Paulie said, pushing the car seat forward, "it's time fer da party. Man, I can smell the food already!"

Chapter Seven

Lucy

Lucy Matacochis was Blanca's best friend. She was two years older and much wiser in the ways of men. She was of medium height, almost skinny, with thin brown arms, small pointy breasts and a tiny waist and shapely legs. Lucy's dark olive complexion went well with her dark, glittery eyes and thin lips that could snarl or pout at will. On weekends Lucy's hennaed hair, worn in the latest styles, was decorated with an array of rhinestone clips bought at the Five and Dime. She changed her nail polish at least twice a week to match favorite outfits. Lucy thought of herself as a real tough cookie, and used her quick temper to intimidate everyone, including her mother. She won most arguments by default, or by snarling and shaking her fists. Being that Blanca never argued back, she and Lucy got on very well.

Lucy came from a family of tough women. Her older sister Chita was once in juvenile hall for stealing record albums from a Los Angeles store. When due to be sentenced, Chita appeared in court wearing pig tails, a plaid skirt like the ones worn by Catholic schoolgirls, and white bobby socks. Aunt Tottie, who owned a beer joint, hired a slick lawyer that throughout the hearing referred to Chita as an innocent child. Chita was put on probation by a judge who drank like a fish and had been given a case of Jim Beam by Aunt Tottie. Moved by the sight of Chita in pigtails, the judge placed her on six months probation.

Although born in Taconos, Lucy had lived in Fresno for a time when her father, a stooped, fierce-looking man, who tired of working at low paying jobs and moved the family there to find a steady job in a packing house. From the start, Lucy could not adjust to Fresno. She hated living in "the sticks," as she put it, and pleaded with her father to let her visit her sister Chita who was now pregnant by a pachuco called Sapo. She stayed behind in Taconos with Aunt Tottie. "This place is too dead," Lucy lamented to Chita, "and the guys are all stupid. They wear work boots all the time and smell of sulphur. I hate it here! It's too dead!"

Every chance she got, Lucy took the Greyhound bus to visit Chita and Aunt Tottie or to see what was happening in Los Angeles.

When she turned sixteen, Lucy informed her father that she was returning to Taconos. He slapped Lucy in the face, called her names and shoved her out the door, along with a battered suitcase stuffed with clothes and makeup. His screams were heard all the way to the Fresno peach groves. But Lucy, not the least intimidated, snarled right back and shook her tiny fists in his sallow face. She said goodbye to her mother and stomped to the bus depot, where she boarded a Greyhound back to Taconos.

Lucy moved in with Chita, Chita's boyfriend Fish and Chita's kid from Sapo. She was given the dark screened-in porch for a bedroom. She hated it, although it faced the street and she could check out the guys cruising by. I gotta put up with this dump, Lucy told herself as she filed her long nails, at least till I gets me a job. Then I'll move somewhere else, or something. Every other day she painted her nails a bright purple or hot magenta, determined not to look like a hick. Ain't nobody gonna take this from me, Lucy vowed. My nails gotta look cool, or my life ain't worth a shit.

In seventh grade Lucy had been caught giving the finger to a teacher and was asked to either shape up or get out. She decided right then and there that if she stayed, she would eventully kick the shit out of the stoolie who had told on her. She left Taconos Elementary for good, making sure to take with her the comic books stashed in her desk and the bottles of nail polish hid in the schoolroom closet. She could barely read and write and had problems with long division, but school was not for her. After sitting around for a time and baby-sitting for Chita, she found work in the tomatoe fields, a job she enjoyed at first because she got to flirt with the husky truck drivers who hauled the tomatoes to the city markets. But when she caught three colds in a row and her tight blouses began to hang on her skinny frame, Lucy decided to find a "clean" job. She lied about her age, piled her hair high on her head and even lowered her hemlines and then took off for San Cristobal to put in work applications at the Five and Dime, sweat shops, pottery shops and at Thrifty Drugstore where a bleached blonde in a Peter Pan collar looked her over and said, "We'll call you when there is an opening."

"I don't gots no telephone."

"Oh! Well then, I'll send a card. Okay?"

"Yeah."

Just when she was getting desperate, tired of Chita's screeching kids and Fish's leering eyes, Lucy's folks moved back to Taconos to the same old house three doors from Blanca Muñoz. Chita, now back with Sapo, who had been in Folsom, moved to another place near the railroad tracks. A heartbroken Fish left town.

Lucy and Blanca quickly became friends. Lucy taught Blanca how to pluck her eyebrows, peroxide her hair and jitterbug to Tommy Dorsey. Most evenings they sat in Lucy's room listening to the radio while the dust from passing cars swirled around them. Mostly they talked about how to get a job. Lucy took the husky, pimply Blanca under her wing, gave her advice on how to make up to a guy, but couldn't help her find a steady job no how.

Lucy's Aunt Tottie, at 34 a loud, jolly "grass widow" who lived with her boyfriend Chucho, decided to open a beer joint in Taconos. She hired Lucy, her favorite niece, to help on weekends, but when she saw how well Lucy got on with the men, Tottie talked her into working full time. It was clear Lucy could take care of herself.

From the start Lucy set the ground rules. "I don't take no shit from nobody, see," she hissed at more than one startled customer. "I don't take no shit. Get it?"

The men that hung around Tottie's Place found Lucy's attitude tantalizing, even challenging. Imagine! A chick who talked back to men! They stared at her small breasts, shapley legs and small, mean mouth. Buisness quickly picked up, but from the start the men kept their distance.

The very first week, Lucy dashed a mug of cold beer into a customer's leering face. The second week she punched a guy called Güero, a hulking, beefy ex-Marine, with her clenched fist. Güero fell in love on the spot! Rather than smack Lucy back, Güero bought Lucy a beer, then took her home. He later sported a huge black eye and bragged about how he had gotten it.

"My honey, she hits me."

"She must really love you, ese."

"What else she give you, Güero?"

"Nuttin."

"Tell er ta hit you again, man."

"Neh. My wife might get suspicious."

When it was clear to Güero and the guys that hung around Tottie's Place that Lucy could fend for herself, they treated her with respect and bought her drinks while Aunt Tottie beamed her approval. She had taught Lucy how to play the game and was impressed at how fast Lucy had learned. "Ya gotta drink and cuss like a man, so's ya can call the shots," Tottie advised Lucy. "Show em ya ain't scared and they'll come running after ya."

"Yeah?"

"Yeah. I oughta knows."

As petite as she was, Lucy could work ten hours on her feet and then dance all night long without feeling tired. Most weekends she took off to the Zenda Ballroom in L.A. straight from work, stopping only to change into a tight, slinky dress with a deep slit and shoes with ankle straps and three-inch heels. She went outside to wait for a ride. Sometimes she went dancing both on Saturday and Sunday nights, then dragged to work with bleary eyes and a droopy smile. But one thing was lacking in Lucy's life. She didn't have a steady guy! Like other dames, Lucy longed for a steady guy who was hep, a sharp dresser with a shiny car. But more than this, a dude with a steady job who would buy her an engagement ring, even a hope chest.

In Fresno Lucy had gone steady with Tuchi, a tall wiry fellow. They would go riding through the peach groves, drinking whiskey and smoking packs of Lucy Strikes while waiting for something to happen. And then one night Tuchi got knifed in a fight. He died in Lucy's arms.

The very next day, Lucy dressed to the nines and walked to the funeral home. Everyone in town was there. The girls quickly formed a circle around Lucy and hugged her tight. After all, hadn't Tuchi died in her arms? Even Tuchi's brother, drunk on whiskey and sorrow, hugged Lucy and told her how much it meant to know she had held Tuchi during his final moments.

It was a great funeral. Everyone from the Fresno barrio was there, even the cops! The church bulged with guys with dark circles around their bloodshot eyes and with hands at the ready. The dudes wore draped pants with long tapered jackets. Long chains hung from their waists; thick-heeled shoes scraped the green cemetery lawn.

Among the chicks at the funeral, none could hold a candle to fifteen-year old Lucy, decked out in a new dress, a black veil, black high heels and Ripe Cherry lipstick. From afar she looked like a young girl dressed in her mother's clothes, but up close, the tiny breasts fairly burst from inside the dark dress. Her small waist was accentuated with a rhinestone clip that throughout the somber event glittered brightly. The tight, jersey dress skimmed over her small hips and down to her curvy legs encased in black ankle-straps.

Lucy was the star of the funeral. She eclipsed even Tuchi who, laid out in a padded coffin, was also dressed to kill. When it was time to put Tuchi in the grave, Lucy rose to the occasion. While the priest mumbled his prayers, Lucy made as if to jump into the grave, but was restrained by Lencho, a really cute guy who scooped her up in his muscular arms and carried her to his car. Lencho gave Lucy a shot of whiskey and took off with her to the peach groves. By the time they returned to Tuchi's house for the food, Lucy was almost in love. I gotta play et cool, Lucy knew, 'cause Tuchi's brothers are tough dudes and lookin at me kinda funny. But I don't give a shit! Ain't nuthin they can do ta me. She did, however, give Tuchi's mother a locket given to her by Tuchi at Christmas. That generous gesture saved her from further gossip.

"Living in Fresno is the shits," Lucy told Blanca. "It's worser than Taconos, so ya can just imagine. Ain't nuthin going on. All people here do is work, then go to town on Saturday night to spend their money. They spend all day Sunday cleaning out the buckets and stuff for the job. Man alive! I tell ya, Fresno is the chets. One thing I notice though, all the guys gots steady jobs. Even kids work in the packing houses or in the fields. That's more than we gots in Taconos!"

By the time she had settled down back in Taconos, Lucy, at sixteen, decided to forget men and just have a good time. But now and then she yearned to meet her ideal and settle down with a guy who wasn't a real pachuco nor a real square, but something in-between. A hep guy who could cut a rug . . . and had a steady job.

One thing Lucy was certain of, she was not going to have a bunch of kids. "No way I'm gonna end up like Chita," she hissed at her timid mother. "I ain't gonna get pregnant at fifteen, nor mar-ried at sixteen. I ain't gonna be like that stupid Chita, stuck with a bunch of kids from different guys."

"They're so stuped," snarled Lucy. "They're so stupid, that's why they gots so many goddammed kids. Shit, I'm not gonna have me no five kids. I'm gonna have fun!" Lucy's mother, as afraid of the daughter as of the father, merely nodded her greying head and kept out of her daughter's way.

Once settled in in Taconos and making good money at Tottie's Place, Lucy realized nothing much had changed. "There's nuttin ta do," she wailed to her shocked mother. "I hate working nights. I don't gets ta go nowhere, except to the beer joint. I'm gonna miss another party. I want some new clothes. I wanna live in L.A. I wanna go dancing!" Day after day she sat on the swaying porch to paint her nails and pluck her thin eyebrows while next to her the radio blasted out the latest in sounds. She sat until early evening, filing away at her nails, staring towards Main Street on the lookout for new guys in town.

When things got too boring, Lucy thought back on her life and of the boyfriends she once had. This she usually shared with Blanca.

"Gosh, Lucy! I didn't know ya had so many boyfriends!"

"Yeah. The one I really fell for was El Junie. He was from Parlier, near Fresno. One time he took me out to the peach groves, then gots fresh with me."

"God!"

"I told him ta take me home or I'd knock the shit outta him. He thought I was kiddin, so I scratched his fat face wid my nails. I chipped 'em good, but scared the piss outta him. When he wasn't lookin I jumped outta the car and hitched a ride home. Man, you shoulda seen his face. But I taught him a lesson. The next day he brought me a lug of peaches, but I told him to give them to some other fool. Ha, ha, ha . . . "

"What happened to El Weasel?"

"Whatcha want to know?"

"Did ya go all the . . . "

"Neh, he was only good for a cuppa coffee and a cigarette."

Earlier Lucy had fallen head over heels in love with Weasel, a guy from Maravilla who hustled in a tire factory on Firestone Boulevard. Weasel's name was really Arthur, but he became Weasel because of his long, narrow face and small squinty eyes. One night at the Zenda Ballroom, Weasel spotted Lucy in the crowd. He let out a yelp, smoothed his moustache and moved in. He and Lucy danced together the whole night. During the intermission they went outside to sit in Weasel's magenta convertible.

An ecstatic Lucy told everyone that Weasel was "The One!" "He's so fine!" she squealed. But when the Tacones found out a guy from L.A. was invading their turf and making it with a Taconos chick, they went after him. The magenta convertible was never seen again. Lucy was both pleased and angry that the Tacones had scared off El Weasel. But it pissed her off that Weasel had not put up a fight and had not acted like a man. Still, Lucy was curious to find out what had really happened to Weasel, so she asked Aunt Tottie to drive her to the Maravilla Housing Projects to look for Weasel. Later Lucy found out that Weasel had been married the whole time and was the father of two kids. Lucy vowed to hate men. "Men ain't nuttin but liars and cheats," she wailed. But once she found out about Blanca's wedding, Lucy got over her hate. After all, weddings always attracted guys from outa town!

Chapter Eight

Father Ranger

When told by his superiors that he was being transferred from Thorpe, Texas to Taconos, Father Francis Ignatius Ranger, O.M.I., was estatic. He thought he'd died and gone to heaven. The dry Texas weather had so aged him that at times he forgot that at thirty-two he was still a young man, albeit a wrinkled, disenchanted priest. He immediately began to prepare for the move. Into the battered suitcase bought when he had first left home for the seminary, he packed a pair of swim trunks and his favorite Duke Ellington albums. He thought of the blue Pacific, the miles of orange groves and the sunny weather that awaited him once he left behind him the barren town of Thorpe. He packed in a frenzy, planning how on his days off he would take off to the concert halls and small jazz clubs in Hollywood. Once I'm settled, he thought as he rolled up his chasuble and rammed it into the bottom of the canvas suitcase, I'll get to hear some real music.

For the past five years Father Ranger had suffered (or so he liked to think), from lack of culture. Thorpe was a small ranching town near the Texas-Mexico border. The town was inhabited mostly by Mexicanos who earlier had came north to work on the cattle ranches. They were simple, hard-working people who each Sunday trekked to the small church for mass, then home to prepare for the coming work week. Thorpe had a general store, three gas stations, a drugstore and one "good" restaurant, The Buckin Bronco. At The Buckin Bronco everything was eaten with puddles of ketchup.

Father Francis looked forward to being in Taconos. He had not been to a concert since his last vacation in Los Angeles, when he went to see his idol Duke Ellington at the Hollywood Bowl. Now and then he listened to his collection of old seventy-eights on the dilapidated record player left behind by his predecessor, the Dominican Father Ambrose. Father Francis's fingers itched to be at the piano, to imitate the Duke. Once he gave the incoming pastor a tour of the Thorpe parish and verified travel arrangements, he said his last mass for the congregation. He tried to keep a straight face as he told the townsfolk how much he would miss them, but would remember them in his prayers.

Father Francis left Thorpe on an extremely hot day, anticipating the temperate weather and the cool ocean breezes of the California coast. When he finally got off the stifling, crowded train, he was shocked to find that it was just as hot in California! Union Station in Los Angeles felt like an oven. His canvas suitcase seemed to melt to the ground. Pedro Solis, sent to pick him up in an old 1940 Ford, found Father Francis sitting at a counter, cold drink in hand.

To the irritable young priest, the idea of sitting in a small dusty car was almost unbearable. Not even the marble columns and cool tile floors of the station lobby helped cool him. As he waited for Pedro Solis to bring the car around, Father Francis Ignatuis Ranger took a lily-white handkerchief from his pants pocket and began to mop his brow. He felt betrayed; his red ears began to itch and burn from the heat, his priestly collar was about to choke him. He had so yearned to escape the debilitating heat and the simpleminded people of Thorpe. And here I am now, he grumbled, as he wiped the back of his neck with his handkerchief, smack in the middle of California, and it's hotter than hell! He put on his black jacket, aware that Pedro Solis needed to be impressed. He adjusted his wilted collar and helped load his belongings into the car trunk. Mr. Solis held open the car door. Father Francis wearily climbed inside, stretched out his long legs and sighed, Sunny California, indeed!

"Is it always this hot?"

"Hot? Wait until July, padre!"

"July?"

"Yup. And August too. It gets in the 90s . . . "

"Good God!"

Once settled in Taconos, and full of energy and goodwill towards his fellow men and women, Father Ranger began to reorganize the parish. He hated the dusty furniture left behind by his predecessor, Father Juanito, whom he had heard described as an old fart, and could hardly wait for the archdiocese to send him the annual budget, one he prayed would allow him to paint and to refurbish the old fart's former house. "The people of Taconos are kind-hearted and generous," he wrote to Father Murphy, "and I intend to win them over, or die trying. The first thing I want to do (after I get the rectory in order), is buy a new car. From past experience, I know nothing impresses the young men like seeing their pastor, el padrecito, driving a cool heap."

As he had previously done in Thorpe, Father Ranger put all his efforts into working with the women of Taconos, this time with better results. The Altar Society membership quickly grew. Even Doña Luz, a short, stumpy woman who liked to give orders, joined, but insisted on being in charge of the food booths during the summer fiestas. Being that her only competition was Doña Pepita, a woman who was quite generous and put too much meat in the tamales, she won out. The newly-formed Marian Club for girls between the ages of 13 and 18 grew from three to fifteen members immediately after the first ice-cream social was held in the parish hall. As in Thorpe, Father Ranger had little to do with the parish men. He gave lip service to the men of the Holy Name Society, all of whom he thoroughly disliked. "Hypocrites," he hissed, while giving them communion, "drunkards." He felt all of them were heavy drinkers and wife-beaters and only went to confession and communion between drinking bouts. Even the altar boys, none of whom knew proper Latin, aggravated him. He tried his best to befriend the gangly, brown-skinned youngsters, but they continued to take off with the sacred wine.

He was most troubled by the young punks of the barrio, those too old to be in school yet too young to get decent work. They hung out inside dusky pool halls which, to his jaundiced eye, seemed to sprout on every other corner. "They aren't bad kids," Father Ranger wrote to his superior in his monthly report, "mostly they need guidance, religion and a steady job." Father Francis often thought at times that he was back in Thorpe. Everything seemed alike, from the dark, unkempt rectory with a front screen door that let in huge, green flies, to the simple-minded people who gaped at his embroidered chasuble, with hard, suspicious eyes.

"Everything seems the same," he wrote Father Murphy, "except that unlike the guys in Thorpe who wore Levis and cowboy boots, these punks from Taconos wear either kakhis or pegged pants, and shoes with thick heels." To Father Francis Ignatuis Ranger and his superiors at the Los Angeles Archdiocese, anyone wearing draped pants was a pachuco, and should be dealt with accordingly.

When in Thorpe, Father Ranger had often told the mothers of street-gang members that their sons would not go to hell, but perhaps to jail. Of course, this did not help the mothers cope with their restless sons. In California, Father Francis knew, was to be found a new breed of gang member, who was tougher, more intelligent, better-dressed and, in a few cases, even religious!

"The California pachuco is unique," wrote Father Ranger in his yearly report. "He is better nourished, lives in poor to modest homes, often has an eighth grade education, smokes marijuana and drinks whiskey and goes to mass on Sundays! In addition, there is a kind of honor among them, a loyalty hard to penetrate. This camaraderie did not exist in Texas, but is quite evident among the gangs here. Try as I might, I cannot communicate with them."

To Father Murphy he explained, "I hate the Taconos pachucos, not for what they represent, but because of the pain they cause their saintly mothers. Just last week two women, whose sons were picked up on suspicion, came by to borrow money to pay a bail bondsman. And today I heard tell that two rival gangs: the Tacones, from here, and The Planchados, the names tell you a lot about their mentality, no?, are at war. They hate each other's guts, are constantly fighting and have set a date to meet to have it out! I pray to Saint Francis without ceasing!"

The Taconos pachucos hated Father Ranger with an intensity that even surprised them. On more than one occasion they had seen him talking to the cops and felt he was in cahoots with the coppers. They called him a rat, and a stool pigeon, especially when soon after he arrived, the fuzz patroled the Taconos streets twice a day. Much of the hate began one summer night at a church fair when Father Francis called the police after Bugsy beat the shit out of his arch-enemy, El Wimpy, a pale pimply guy who wore suspenders to keep his drapes up. When thoroughly bloodied, Wimpy and Bugsy were pulled apart, then arrested for causing a disturbance. Wimpy was carried to an ambulance and Bugsy was pushed into a familiar black and white sedan, then hauled off to the county jail. Once the police left, Father Ranger went outside to talk to Wimpy's distraught parents, and his frightened girlfriend. He overheard some kids refer to him as *el padre stoolie*. He recoiled at the insult, his face turning a bright pink and his neck beggining to itch. He was hurt by this sudden shift in the altar boys he had befriended. He tried to explain that he had only called the cops to keep the guys from killing each other, but it was pointless. He knew he would forever be called a stool pigeon, and he would be hated just as much as the coppers. Left to shift for himself among the more pliant female members of the congregation, Father Francis resigned himself to what he felt was his personal cross, the intense dislike of the people of Taconos. At night, on bended knee he recited his breviary, eyes closed, hands clasped together. He prayed to Saint Francis while in the living room Ella Fritzgerald softly sang the blues. Within a year Father Ranger had become a permanent fixture in the barrio of Taconos. He officiated at funerals, weddings and at what he most loved, baptisms. The brown, cuddly infants served to remind him of his vocation. When he poured the holy water on the newborn babies, their lusty cries warmed his heart.

In early summer, Father Ranger organized jamaicas, or parish bazaars, as he preferred to call them. It was then that he came alive! His ruddy cheeks practically glowed with health and vigor. His bright eyes matched the clear blue sky that hovered over Taconos. Everyone in the small community was put to work, from the very elderly to the young children, who were made to sweep the church hall. Father Francis enjoyed looking at the smiling faces of his parishoners, a change from the year before, when it appeared everything he did was wrong.

Father Ranger felt both anger and compassion for the pretty young girls who came to the rectory to see about the wedding banns that by Catholic law had to be announced a month before the wedding. "Weddings are not my favorite thing," he often told Father Murphy, who now and then visited. "Neither are funerals, but in a way, weddings are a sure death for some of the girls from here."

He officiated at funerals with resignation, as for many of the poor of Taconos, death was it's own reward. But he thought of big, church weddings as a waste of both time and money. To him, marriage was not always a new beginning for a couple, but certain death for the pliant brides-to-be. Marriage, he knew, would seal their destiny. For the groom, little if anything would change. Of that he was certain.

"The double standard is entrenched in the barrio," he wailed to Father Murphy. "Married men come and go at will. They are free to find other women, abandon wives and children at whim, then return to claim their rights as hombres. This is the custom, and there is nothing I can do but advise an engaged couple to think seriously of the step they are about to take. Amen!"

When the rumor that Blanche Muñoz and Sammy-the-Cricket Lopez planned to marry reached him, Father Francis's first instinct was to visit the Muñoz family to offer his condolences. He barely knew Blanca's mother, a small grey-haired lady who rarely came to church, but felt he should caution her. In his eyes Cricket was the most despicable of pachucos.

"He's ugly, mean, illiterate and arrogant," he hissed to Father Murphy on the phone. "Even Los Tacones, the local gangmembers, hate his guts. He thinks nothing of running over street dogs, then backing up to roll over them again."

One Sunday after mass, when he spotted Blanca in a back row, he tried to corner her to ask about the wedding rumor. But Blanca, wise to his priestly ways, evaded him as though he were the very devil! She knew of more than one chick whom Father Francis had counseled "get rid of him," while the potential groom was outside waiting in the car.

He thought of talking to Blanca's mother, but knew she would side with Blanca, claiming her daughter was in love. A self-supporting young woman like Blanca, he thought, is too good for that Cricket jerk. Well, he sighed, there's nothing I can do, only pray and prepare the necessary forms.

Father Francis Ignatius Ranger often reflected on the similarities between the women of Thorpe and those of Taconos. He recalled how, when newly-arrived in Thorpe, he had looked around the small, dusty town and thought: there is very little for young women to do here, other than work at the Five and Dime, clean house for bigoted Anglos, or get married. But, isn't that what I preach? he often asked himself. Don't I advise women to in all things emulate the Virgin Mary? Marry and have children? Blanche only wants to marry and have kids, he sighed. And there's nothing I can do about it. He then arranged to meet with Blanca and Cricket. "And if all goes well," he told the happy Blanca, "I'll announce your wedding banns."

As a priest, I cannot deny a Catholic the sacraments, he concluded. He prayed for guidance . . . and patience, then left for the Shrine Auditorium in Los Angeles to attend a Stan Kenton concert, where he quickly forgot Blanca, Cricket and his problems with Los Tacones.

Chapter Nine

The Bridesmaids

When the young women of Taconos who lived on Honey-suckle Street first heard Blanca Munoz was getting married in the fall, they became more and more friendly to her. "Blanca, you wanna go to the show on Sunday?"

"Hey man, let's go play some records. You too, Blanca. You dance so fine!"

"Are you losing weight, Blanche? You look so skinny! It must be love!"

They began to include Blanca in small gatherings and invited her to the Zenda Ballroon, the huge dance hall where on Saturday nights bands from all over the country, Mexico and Latin America played Latin jazz and other new sounds, and where the guys and chicks from L.A. and Valley barrios faithfully went. And although Blanca still liked to dance the boogie-woogie and older dance styles, she hated not to know the latest steps. So she went along with the chicks who hoped to be part of the wedding: Lucy, Sally, Rosie and Josie. Each wanted to be a bridesmaid and share in the excitement of the big day.

"Has she asked you yet?"

"No, but we're best friends. She better."

"I hear Sally's gonna be in the wedding. God, she's in more weddings than the priest!"

"So what? Just 'cause you ain't . . . "

"Ain't what? Ya mean I ain't gonna be asked?"

As was the custom, the more bridesmaids and ushers, the better the wedding. That way there would be more bridal showers, many more presents and more money could be collected from the ushers to pay for the dance and band. And so the girls hung around Blanca.

Blanca did not think it unusual to have ten bridesmaids in her wedding. Her cousin Suki had had twelve. Jessie, who lived across the street had been accompanied by nine couples, and recently, Lucy had told Blanca about her cousin Becky from Fresno who had all of thirteen couples in her wedding.

"Man Alive! That was no wedding," Lucy said to Blanca, "it was a circus! Nobody fit near the altar, the cars were lined up for a mile and the guys, even the ushers, got parking tickets. Worser, the bridesmaid's dresses were so ugly! They looked like shit. And like a big fat rainbow. They ran outta food too, and cake too. The band was lousy . . . all they played was old stuff. The only good part was when a fight broke out and . . . "

"But I want a big wedding."

"Hey, honey, I ain't saying ya can't have one. Just don't make it no circus, get it?"

"Yeah, I gets it."

When it came time to order the inviations, Blanca took the bus to San Cristobal and went to the San Cristobal Stationary Shop. The skinny man who took the order tried not to laugh as Blanca gave him the names of those in the wedding.

"Are you sure the name is T-U-D-I? Not Theodore or Thomas?"

"No, Tudi. Just like I said."

"Well, uhhhh. And the groom's name is Cricket?"

"Yeah, but ya can write it S-A-M-M-Y."

"That spells Sammy! Didn't you say his name was Cricket?"

"Well, come ta think of it, it's really Samuel, but . . . "

Getting everyone's name on the invitation was a problem. "Mexican names are too damn long," lamented Blanca to the clerk. "Everybody's got two or three names." But the bridesmaids had given her specific instructions.

"I want my name written as Celia Louise," chanted Sally. "And I wanna be Lucille Marie," chimed in Lucy." Even shy Rosie insisted she be listed as Rose Marie Rios. "God," hissed Blanca, pressing her hands to her forehead. "All them names is givin me a headache. What happened to plain ole Sally? And everyone knows Lucy's real name is Luz Maria. Ain't no way all these names are gonna fits. She walked around the shop, staring at an assortment of cards, files and pencils. She finally decided to order invitations that were just a little bit wider than the others, and asked the clerk to make the print smaller. Even though they look like valentines, she grumbled to herself, at least everybody's name gots on it . . . even Porky's. "Sure hope everybody will be satisfied," she told the clerk as she took two ten dollar bills from her purse and paid, "'cause ain't nuthin I can do about names. I don't want nobody ta be mad at me, especially Lucy. But them invitations sure look like valentines!" Even with all these things to do, Blanca sighed, weddings are so much fun. And now that the invitations are done and everyone gots their names on 'em, they ain't gots nuthin ta say. Blanca knew everyone would be happy now and that meant lots more showers . . . and presents.

The ushers, not wanting to appear cheap, had agreed to pay for the bridesmaids' bouquets, all except for Topo, who was still making payments to a bail bondsman and pleaded, "I still gottsa pay them guys that sprung me from the can. I ain't gots no lettuce for flowers. Whatsa matter wiz plastic flowers, man? They lasts longer?"

"Its the custom, man," replied Tudi, his brown eyes steady. "Ya owe it to the chicks."

"I don't owe nobody nuttin," snarled Topo, his big teeth gleaming pearly white. "But ta show ya I ain't no chip-skate, I'll pay . . . but you gotta catch me next time. This week I gots ta pay some tickets, or the cops are gonna haul me in and . . . "

"Again?"

"Yeah. But ain't no big deal. They makes some good chow at the County. Last time I gots six pork chops . . . the dudes in my cell was Jews . . . or somethin, so I gots theirs too."

The bridesmaids, relieved to know they would not have to pay for their bouquets, rushed out to splurge on makeup and henna packs for their hair. Sally swore to lose ten pounds while Rosie gorged on fried potatoes, hoping to put some meat on her skinny frame. Lucy took off for L.A. to try on padded bras and fancy garter belts. Only the bride-to-be, worried sick over lack of money, stayed away from the stores.

Blanca chose Lucy as Maid-of-Honor. Lucy had experience and knew how to do things right and, unknown to Blanca, had quickly (and quietly) eliminated other contenders.

"Lucy, ya wanna be my Maid-of-Honor?"

"Gosh, ya sure ya want me? I mean, what about Sally?

"She sez you already told her you was . . . "

"I was just kiddin!"

"But I'm not. Come on, you can choose the colors for the dresses and the . . . "

"Well, okay. If ya say so."

Later, when it was time for the bridesmaids to select a partner, Blanca regretted her decision.

Just before the first meeting, which was supposedly held to introduce the guys and chicks to each other, Blanca whispered to Cricket that as Maid-of-Honor, Lucy wanted to choose her partner. Cricket immediately began to cuss up a storm. He screeched at Blanca who, pale faced and with trembling lips, could only stare at this different, angry Cricket.

"No way. I'm gonna picks the Best Man. Ain't no chick gonna tell me what ta do . . . "

"But . . . "

"No way. Ain't her wedding. Lucy tinks she's the boss, but I ain't gonna . . . "

"But she's my best friend!"

"Don't cut no ice wiz me."

"She ain't gonna like et."

"Tough shit. Lucy just wants ta gimme orders. Tell her to give 'em to some other jerk.

"Okay, honey. If you say so."

"I say so."

To most of the bridesmaids, the meetings were the best part of being in a wedding. They began about two months prior to the wedding and were usually held every other week, or when something important came up. The first meeting held for Blanca and Cricket's wedding took place on a mild July night at Blanca's. Everyone came! All the bridesmaids looked sharp. Lucy wore a tight black dress with a short peplum and a rhinestone pin at the waist. Her fingernails shone a bright magenta, as did her thin, sallow mouth. Sally was decked out in blue pedal-pushers, then the latest in pants for women, and a white blouse which she tied in front. Now and then her belly-button peeped from underneath the white blouse. Rosie wore a chartruese dress with black polka-dots and a wide, black belt that emphasized her tiny, tiny waist. Each time everyone commented on her waist, Rosie pouted to show her dimples. Even Blanca wore a new outfit, the one she had worn earlier for her cousin Becky's wedding in Fresno, but which had not been seen yet in Taconos.

The guys looked sharp too. Cricket wore pin-striped drapes with a light-blue shirt with French cuffs. Tudi wore his favorite beige pants with a spot on the cuff. Paulie wore navy-blue pants that were altered to fit his expanding waist; they had a shiny bottom. Once everyone sat down, had drinks and talked a bit, Blanca (with Lucy's coaching) called the meeting to order and told everyone what was going on.

"Them invitations are gonna be ready in about three weeks. Ya gotta pick them up from me. Gatsby's is gonna give the ushers, uuuh, you guys some kinda deal, so gets them there, okay?"

"We still ain't gots the band 'cause . . . but the dance is gonna be at the Elks in Burbank. Okay, you guys?"

"All right!"

"Yeah!"

"How suki! I like the Elks. The last time I was there there was three fights! Man, them Burbank cops are bad mudders. They arrested all the ushers and knocked the chet outta the groom. Whatta good dance!"

Later in the evening, records were stacked on the record player, drinks were passed around, the lights were dimmed and everyone danced. The meeting and the ones that followed soon turned into full-blown parties.

Paulie, El Pan Tostado, was usually the first of the guys to arrive. His dark face shiny with perspiration, black hair coated with brilliantine, he headed straight for the baloney sandwiches cut into small squares and stacked on a bright platter bought at the Five and Dime. When no one was looking, El Pan Tostado grabbed a handful of sandwiches and gobbled them down in record time. By the time the other ushers arrived, he was ready to begin on the chips and booze, as in the kitchen Lucy fumed.

"Man, El Pan Tostado's eating all the sangwiches . . . you shoulda hid them for later."

"How was I ta know he's such a pig?"

"God, Rosie! You're more stuped than I thoughts. Didn't ya see him at Sally's party last week? He ate all the tacos by himself. All we gots was rice and beans."

"Whatta pig!"

"Here, hide these cookies in the washing machine. I gotta go ta the store and buy more baloney. All on accounta that porker."

"Yeah."

Couples going steady smooched on the dark porch; others argued near the fence. Later everyone climbed into souped up cars and, radios blaring and tires screeching, took off to park near the cemetery.

By the second meeting, which had been called to discuss the important issue of who would ride with whom in the wedding cars, most of the bridesmaids and ushers had already picked a partner. Lucy immediately latched onto Frankie, whom Blanca disliked because he thought his shit didn't stink. But he was a good dancer and drove a sharp car. Sally kept waiting for Tudi to choose her, but Tudi said nothing. Rosie kept clear of Paulie, El Pan Tostado, afraid she might get stuck with the fat pig. Soon everyone was paired off, or so it seemed to Blanca. Just then Lucy stormed up to her and screeched, "Cricket ain't gonna tell me who ta ride wiz!"

"But Lucy, ya gotta ride with Tudi! He's the . . . "

"Not even if they pays me am I gonna be seen with that Jack O' Lantern."

"Ya gotta, Lucy. Cricket said . . . "

"I don't take orders from nobody."

"But Tudi's the Best Man!"

"Not ta me, he ain't. He's a clown . . . and ain't gots no teeth."

"But he's gonna buy some for the wedding!"

"So what?

"I think Tudi's nice."

"Well you go with him, then."

In the end Lucy agreed to be Tudi's partner, to march into church with him and pose next to him in the pictures. "But, she screeched, "ain't no way I'm gonna ride in the car to L.A. wiz him. I'll march with him, but that's all. Got it?"

"Okie dokie."

Lola, Blanca's older sister and the only family member to be in the wedding, chose Topo as her partner because Topo was a good friend of Chuy, her husband who was currently serving time. They had been in jail together and were still buddies. Tudi was befriended by Sally, a plump, cheerful girl with reddish-brown hair whom everyone liked. She agreed to be with him whenever Lucy started to sulk. Only Paulie, El Pan Tostado, was left to shift for himself. He chose Tencha, a heavy-set girl with round eyes who, like him, was as black as the Ace of Spades.

Chapter Ten

The Cushions

Once the most important wedding decisions had been made and once the squabbling bridesmaids agreed on who looked best in which color, it was up to the bride-to-be, Blanca, to take care of some of the more minor details of the wedding. She had to choose a bridal bouquet (gardenias were then in vogue), pick a ringbearer and junior bridesmaid, call on Father Ranger to fill out forms so that the wedding banns could be announced in plenty of time, and select wedding cushions to be used by the bride and groom at the altar.

With Lucy's approval, Blanca first hitched a ride to the Japanese nursery where, once assured her old boss remembered her and would give a good discount, she ordered the bouquets: white velvet-like gardenias with Lily-of-the-Valley and mossy ferns for herself, purple orchids without ferns only for Lucy (although Sally screamed to high heaven) and pink baby-roses with crespón, a dark green fern, for the bridesmaids. "All I gotta do now is see about the cuchens," Blanca told Lucy, and see how much Cricket will gives me towards other stuff."

"Yeah? Well good lucks."

In Taconos, the Mexican tradition was for the Maid-of-Honor to provide the satin cushions on which the bride and groom knelt during the wedding mass. Another responsibility of this madrina, or godmother, was to host the wedding breakfast and, on the wedding morning, to help dress the bride. To Blanca, it was important that the cushions match her dress and be pretty, with lots and lots of lace and ribbons. She waited, hoping Lucy had not forgotten.

Wedding cushions were not generally sold in stores, nor always in bridal shops. The small pillow-like cushions were made to order to match the material and style of the bride's dress. They were always white and usually made of the identical satin or chiffon worn by the bride. The cushions were trimmed with an abundance of lace, ribbons and soft-pink rosettes. Oftentimes, the bridal couple's initials were embroidered on the cushions with tiny seed pearls. After the wedding, the cushions were stored as a memento.

From the first, Lucy had assured Blanca that she would see to the cushions. A local seamstress would make them for a small fee. But Lucy, busy experimenting with henna packs on her dark hair and filing her sharp nails before painting them once more, forgot. Nevertheless, a persistant Blanca kept after her, reminding her each time they met.

"Lucy, whatcha gonna do about the cuchens?"

"I ain't hads no time. I gotta gets to the beauty shop first, then Josie's gonna do my nails in Purple Passion."

"Oh, boy! Are you gonna peroxide your eyebrows too? Like the last time?"

"Neh, they gots too orange after . . . and I wanna look so fine!"

"But what about the cuchens?"

"What about them?"

"Nuttin."

While Blanca was busy with other things, without asking her permission, her Aunt Consuelo from Fresno stepped in to take care of the cushions. Tia Chonita, an elderly woman who now and then visited, was Blanca's favorite relative. She was the only sister to Blanca's dead father. Tia Chonita was an independent woman who at sixty still worked in a packing house and faithfully dyed her hair blue once a month. When she heard of the wedding, Tía Chonita merely pulled rank,   saying that as Blanca was her only   living relative on her brother's side, that it was her given right, her sacred duty to make the cushions.

Tia Chonita got up early one Saturday and took the bus to the local Five and Dime in uptown Fresno. She headed straight to the yardage department, her favorite place in the store, and selected cotton backing, fluffy white cotton, heavy-duty thread, a swatch of creamy satin, several yards of lace and, last of all, an assortment of bright embroidery thread. The thread, she explained to the harried clerk, had to be pure silk. She then bought assorted colors of crochet thread, different sizes of needles and a tiny box of straight pins. She dashed home, her blue-grey hair blowing in the breeze, to begin to sew what she instinctively knew would be the most spectacular wedding cushions this side of Fresno, or Los Angeles, for that matter.

Before the cushions were cut and basted, Tía Chonita decided that rather than make a freehand design for the cushion cover, she would buy a ready made transfer-pattern, similar to that used on pillowcases. Off she went, back to the Five and Dime, her flowered apron clinging to her skinny frame. After some deliberation, she picked a pattern with birds, butter-flies, flowers and ribbons, one she felt was the prettiest in the whole store. She especially liked the birds that perched on the flowers and the tiny butterflies that looked down at them. Once at home, and after she had washed her hands in warm soapsuds, she began to cut the material for the cushions. She first cut the cotton backing, then the cushion lining and last of all the outside cover made of satin. She then transferred the pattern of birds and flowers to the satin material with a hot iron, being careful not to scorch the shiny cloth. Each cut piece was then laid on her bed in the order it would be sewn. She then oiled her Singer sewing machine, dusted off the pedal and set to work. Last of all she took down the wicker sewing basket with the embroidery thread and loop and began to sew.

What most bothered Aunt Chonita was deciding what color thread to use. Bright blue for the birds? Must butterflies always be yellow? Can I make the birds purple? The flowers, she decided, would have to be red. Bright red with green leaves. My cushions will be so pretty, she gushed. My dead brother would be so proud! I just hope Blanca likes them. Nowadays girls are so different. All they want are things bought from stores . . . and from Los Angeles. But I'm going to surprise my niece. I'll tell her they're to be very simple, and then . . .

The following weeks Tía Chonita worked from dawn to dusk to make the cushions she knew would be like no others. When finished with the embroidery, she prepared to crochet the edging in bright pink. Before touching the satin cushions, she washed her hands carefully, fearful she would stain the cushions. Alongside the crochet edging she attached strips of lace and tiny pink ribbons. When finished, she sat back, exhausted but happy at the sight of two fat satin cushions that glowed like beacons, covered entirely with birds, butterflies and flowers, entwined with lace and with bright pink crocheting at the edges. A masterpiece! Her masterpiece! She ironed flat the edges that refused to stay down, then wrapped the cushions in crisp tissue paper and placed them inside a cardboard box. Now and then she thought of adding Blanca's initials to the middle of each cushion, but decided it might detract from the perfection of the blue birds and red roses. As she sat on her rocking chair, she smiled at the world, happy that she had demanded, no, insisted on making the cushions. Finally Tía Chonita went to the Greyhound depot and bought her ticket to San Cristobal in anticipation of her niece's wedding. She sent Blanca a note written on flowered stationary and sent it in care of Tío Ernie who had been to visit. She was delighted when Blanca answered and said things for the wedding were coming along, all except for the Ring Bearer and the Junior Bridesmaid, whom she had not yet picked.

Three days before the wedding Aunt Chonita arrived at the Greyhound bus depot in San Cristobal lugging an old valise and a cardboard box in which nestled the bridal cushions. Blanca and Tío Ernie drove down in his jalopy to meet her. Blanca hardly recognized the old lady with blue-grey hair, an expectant look on her face. Not until Tío Ernie poked her in the ribs did she walk up to the old lady clutching a big cardboard box. He helped her to the car, threw the battered suitcase in the trunk and was about to do the same with the cardboard box when Tía Chonita grabbed his arm.

"Not that one."

"Why not? It fits with the . . . "

"No, I want it in front." "Okay."

Once at Blanca's, Tía Chonita greeted everyone, drank a cup of coffee and removed her stockings and wide elastic garters. She and Blanca's mother talked for a while, then Blanca showed her the wedding dress hanging in her closet. But Tía Chonita cut short all conversation and headed back into the kitchen and, without asking, took a large knife from the kitchen counter and prepared to open the cardboard box. She sat the box on her lap, pulled at the twine, yanked off layers of tissue paper, and slowly took out two white satin cushions ablaze with red flowers, blue birds, purple and yellow butterflies, edged with bright pink crochet thread and white lace.

"Looky," she cried, her wrinkled face beaming with pride, "looky."

Blanca's mother stared and stared at the cushions, trying to think of something to say. Just then Aunt Chonita pushed her aside and, her greying head bobbing, walked to the living room where Blanca sat talking with friends.

In the small entry way, Blanca smiled at her cousins from San Jose, all of whom she had passed on to Lola, and talked with friends, some of whom could not make it to the wedding, so had come by to wish her well. She served them coffee and Kool Aid, hoping they would soon go home, so that she could go to bed. Just then she looked up to see her Aunt Chonita coming toward her, arms laden with tissue paper.

"Look, how pretty," cried Aunt Chonita, holding aloft the vivid cushions.

The instant Blanca saw the cushions emerge from their bed of tissue paper, she put her hand to her head and softly moaned. Shit! Them cushions look just like dish towels. Just like the stuff sold in Tijuana. Wait till Lucy sees them, she's gonna die laughing. Damn, Blanca thought, all I needs is for Jorge Negrete to sing one of his songs . . . and I'm back in Mexico!

Like most chicks in Taconos, Blanca and her friends hated stuff that they thought was too low-class Mexican, such as embroidered pillowcases and dishtowels.

"Shoot," hissed Blanca, ogling the cushions that to her tired mind resembled dishtowels.

"Sí! Very pretty," added her mother, "muy bonitos."

"You likee?" asked Tía Chonita, her wrinkled brown face set in a smile. "You like?"

"Of course, she likes them. Blanca, tell your Tía Chonita how much . . . "

Blanca, husky arms crossed over her stomach, looked across the room at her aunt holding high the two cushions that in the harsh light shone like bright, sparkling beacons. She took a deep breath and walked across the room, then put her arms around her aunt. She could feel Aunt Chonita's thin shoulder blades beneath the cotton dress. "They're very purdy," she said to the old woman who was now re-wrapping the cushions. "So purdy. And so different! Ain't nobody ever seen anything like em."

Across the room, Blanca's mother took one look at her daughter's face, then bustled around the kitchen, avoiding Blanca's eyes.

Chapter Eleven

The Ring-bearer

Among those being considered for ring-bearer was Blanca's nephew, Petey, a kid Blanca could not stand. Her first choice had been Joey, a sweet, polite neighbor boy who wore glasses, was an altar boy and who, unlike Petey, never threw rocks at dogs or cats. Blanca had thought of asking Joey's folks to let him be in her wedding, but she was embarrassed to death to visit people she did not know. But once more Blanca was overruled by her mother, who insisted that she ask Petey.

"But, he's your sister's little . . . "

"That little snot."

"Blanquita! Your sister will be so hurt. Ay, m'ijita, what will I tell her when she asks . . . "

"Tell her I gots Joey."

"But Petey likes you and Cricket so much!"

"Yeah? Well I can't stand him."

"So what? What matters is you don't hurt Lola. Go ahead, go tell her that you . . . "

Fed up with the whole thing, Blanca threw up her hands, rubbed her angry eyes and said, "Well okay, Ma, but somebody better wipe his nose." She stalked out of the room, banged shut the door and headed towards Lucy's house. Within minutes her mother dashed out the back door and across the street to Lola's, determined not to give the angry bride-to-be a chance to change her mind. Apron flying, hair askew, she charged into Lola's small kitchen.

"Ay, Lola, you won't believe who Blanca wants for ringbearer!"

"Who did she choose?"

"Don't pretend you don't know."

"Petey? My Petey?"

"Sí. After all, your cousin Gloria's daughter is in the

wedding . . . "

Petey was a thin, wiry boy whom no one had ever seen without a runny nose. Although only seven, he cussed like a grown-up and was not at all upset when his mother shouted at him, "Shut up Petey, you're beginning to sound just like yer father." He loved to shock people. Among the things Petey most hated was to take orders from his mother. He often heard his father say, "A real man don't pay no attention to wimmin." Petey also hated to take a bath and to dress up. He preferred to run around in a torn tee-shirt and faded pants held up by suspenders. He was a champion at marbles, which he played each day and night. He was so obsessed with the game that school suffered and he had already repeated second grade. On top of his cowlick he wore a small beanie studded with soda caps. When he smiled, his crooked teeth shone brightly. When told he would be in Blanca's wedding, Petey began to whine, "I don't wanna be in no damn wedding!" To this his mother replied, "Why you damm little squirt. You think you boss yerself, do you?" Whamm! She smacked Petey across the forehead and the beanie fell to the floor. She followed the retreating Petey out the door, screaming loudly until he was out of sight. Later that evening Petey was sent to tell Blanca how happy he was to be in her wedding. Right before he went out the door, his mother wiped his nose clean.

"Ya gotta carry a cushen with the rings," Blanca told Petey.

"Okay, but do I gota to wear a . . . "

"A tuxedo?"

"My friends are gonna laugh at me."

"Yeah? Too bad! Make sure ya wipe yer . . . "

Once Petey had visited Blanca and was out the door, Blanca's mother smiled at her as if to say, there, that wasn't so bad, was it? But Blanca looked the other way, pissed-off at everybody. Dammit, she thought, all my relatives wanna be in my wedding. Shit! All I need now is for my cousins from Fresno ta wanna stay with us. This is supposed ta be my wedding, but everybody is stickin in their spoon. Darn, if only I wasn't so tired . . . Working overtime is the chets.

Some days, especially in mid-afternoon, the July heat was unbearable to Blanca. The daily walk to and from the bus stop took all of her energy. Ain't so bad in the mornin, she often thought, but walking home after pluckin them dead birds is the chets. She often woke feeling tired, naseous. Lately the turkeys appeared to have more feathers and lots more shit in their butts.

"Shit, a wedding is sure a lot of work," Blanca lamented to Sally. "I shoulda eloped ta Tijuana."

"What? And what about us? The dance?"

"What about it?"

"Uhhh, I mean, dontcha wanna big wedding?"

"Yeah, I guess so. But darn it, all my moola is going to pay for the dress, the food, the cake and all the other stuff . . . and I still ain't picked me a Junior Bridesmaid. My cousin Gloria who works at Pennys gots a kid, a girl called Porky. So I think I'll ask her. And me and Cricket still gots ta go see the priest, and I don't even know what he charges . . . "

Chapter Twelve

The Junior Bridesmaid

The idea of having a Junior Bridesmaid in her wedding was not something Blanca had thought up. Mostly, it was Lucy who insisted Blanca include a young girl as Junior madrina, just like the Americans. While trying on dresses at La Mas Popular, Lucy had heard a customer ask to see dresses for teenage attendants, or Junior Bridesmaids. Blanca was very impressed. It sounded like a real hep thing! Lucy went to work on Blanca, who finally tired of the whole thing and her to forget it. But once Blanca got used to the idea, she began to scout around the neighborhood for a madrinita. She settled on Porky, the spoiled daughter of a distant cousin. Mariana, nicknamed Porky by the neighborhood kids, was short, fat and ate like a pig. She was related to Blanca through Gloria, a cousin who worked as a stock-clerk at Pennys in San Cristobal and was known to give nice wedding gifts, many of which were bought at a discount. At a friend's wedding Blanca eyed the electric coffee-pot given to the bride by Gloria. Blanca decided right then and there to invite Gloria to the wedding. Better yet, she would ask Porky to be in her wedding. Instinct told her this was a mistake; but the thought of a gleaming two-slice toaster won out.

Porky was a stubby girl of twelve who wore size 14 Chubby dresses bought exclusively at J.C. Pennys in San Cristobal, the only department store in the Valley that catered to overweight girls. She liked nothing better than to eat. Throughout the day and night she munched to her heart's content, stopping only to sleep. She could polish off an entire loaf of French bread covered with oleo at one sitting. Often she cut the bread in the middle, added cheese, pickles, baloney and whatever else was to be found in the family ice-box. Then she would sit on the back porch, with a half-gallon of milk at her side, and indulge her expanding stomach.

"Porky was born fat," her mother often told people. "She weighed all of ten pounds! She can't help herself . . . that's how she's always been. I let her eat all she wants, except when she gets sick, then she takes Milk of Magnesia and in two days eats more than ever. She's healthy, so what do I care if she's fat? Just look at her! Fat and sassy! That's my baby!''

At twelve, Porky weighed more than her mother, a slight woman with soft pink skin. Porky's thick, round arms, which literally burst from her dress sleeves, were almost the size of her mother's thighs. All of Porky's dresses had elastic waistbands to accomodate her round belly, which each year grew more prominent. Her thighs, like huge pink hams, bulged from beneath the summer shorts (Size 16 Chubby) she wore, even in the cold of winter. Her round face was a healthy olive. Her squinty eyes gleamed wickedly above a small snout. Her short curly hair was worn parted in the middle, then held down with large barretts. As the leader of a group of kids that hung around the corner store, Porky always had spending money. She was allowed by her indulgent mother to charge ice-cream and candy at the store. At the end of the month the bill was paid by Porky's robust father, who weighed in at 200 pounds.

Porky could smell meat frying a mile away. She especially liked the carnitas made by her grandmother, with whom she stayed once school was out. The carnitas, smothered with onions and tomatoes, were eaten with hot, flour tortillas made each afternoon by the grandmother in time for assorted sons and daughters to eat them or take them home for dinner. When no carnitas were to be had, Porky ate the hot tortillas sprinkled with salt. Later at home she feasted on warm French bread.

When told by her mother that she would wear a pretty dress at Blanca's wedding, Porky tried to cut down on her eating, but found it hard. She then decided to eat only a half-loaf of French bread and at her grandmothers limited herself to three warm tortillas thinly spread with oleo.

Porky hated being fat, and often got into squabbles when the neighborhood kids made fun of her "spare tire" and ran after her calling, "Oink! Oink!"

When teased too much about looking like a pig, Porky hit out at small, thin boys and then stood on the sidelines, smirking while they limped home, victims of a swift kick.

In the weeks before the wedding, Porky swore not to eat too much. She wanted to look pretty and slim. For weeks she had stood in front of her dresser mirror to practice putting her arms at her sides so as to look thinner. But after playing kick-the-can with the kids who lived on her street, she once more treated the neighborhood kids to candy and ice cream, forgetting about her image and diet. She devoured two little cupcakes, an ice cream sandwich and two boxes of Milk Duds. Two days before the wedding her mother was once more forced to adjust the waistline of her Junior Bridesmaid dress.

Chapter Thirteen

The Dress

Once it was agreed that the marriage would take place in September, Blanca and Lucy took the bus to Los Angeles. The day was hot the, sun was bright when the two women walked to the corner to await the bus. Blanca, clad in a fuschia dress, her wide feet encased in sling-back pumps, briskly walked next to Lucy, who was dressed to the nines in a pink suit with wide shoulder pads, a short peplum jacket and matching skirt. Lucy had dressed with care, aware that the chicks from "Los" looked down on those from the Valley as hicks. Lucy was determined to look hep, even if it killed her.

Blanca was tired, sleepy and irritable. Worse, her feet were killing her! The night before she and Lucy had gone to a surprise birthday party for Sally and they had danced their feet off. The two girls were also hung over, but as Lucy put it, "dammed if I'm gonna show it." Uppermost in blanca's mind was the thought of the dress she was going to buy. It could not be too expensive, or she would have to borrow money from her mother. And Blanca was not about to do that. But to Lucy it was important to keep Blanca from buying a piece of shit or a dress that lacked style.

Everyone in Taconos expects me to buy a simple dress, Blanca was thinking. They think I'm stupid, but I'm not as stupid as they think. I'm gonna buy me a real purdy dress, then let's see what they say, especially them stuck-up chicks from San Cristobal. I'll show them." She stopped to straighten her stocking seams, slid another bobby pin under her lopsided pompadour, then climbed aboard the dank, smelly bus and settled down for the long ride. Next to her, Lucy, flipped through a comic book, bored already with the days events, or so it seemed to Blanca.

"Gee, Lucy, thanks a lot for coming to Los with me. I'm so nervous!"

"Yeah? Well, I been in lotsa weddings already and, I tell you man, you gotta do things right. Otherwise why gets hitched."

"Yeah."

"You gotta buy your dress en Los. They gots the latest!"

"Yeah. Hope Cricket don't mind helping out."

"Shit, that guy is so goddam cheap. If it was me . . . "

"We're here. Come on! I can hardly wait!"

Blanca's heart was set on buying her wedding dress at La Mas Popular, a bridal store in Los Angeles patronized by most Mexican-American brides-to-be. The small store, smack in the middle of Broadway near Spring Street, was easy to reach by bus. The store owner, Sadie Solomon, extended credit to brodes-to-be on meager salaries with an interest rate that was not written in, merely tacked on and initialed in red. The store was usually full of customers.

Lucy and Blanca stepped off the crowded, smelly bus on 3rd and Broadway. Around them traffic was picking up. Shiny Fords, Chevies and dusty pickups slowly went by. Shoppers with assorted boxes and packages in their arms jostled each other, others stopped to look at the merchandise in the windows.

Inside department stores, harried clerks afixed the latest fashions to pale, skinny mannequins and, with nimble fingers, stacked merchandise on wide counters. At a corner drugstore a dark man in overalls wiped off the windows, his hands moving up and down in the pale sunlight.

Blanca, her eyes wide, stared at the huge buildings that towered over her and at the crowd of shoppers that went past her. "Gee, I'd forgotten L.A. is so big," she gushed to Lucy. "It is so big and . . . "

"For God's sake, anyone would think you had never been to town. You acts like you was born in the sticks."

"I was."

"Well, don't act like it, be hep, esa. Come on, let's go in."

La Mas Popular, housed in an old building which from afar looked like all the other stores, except for the pink paint peeling off the walls and a huge pink and black sign with a picture of a bride and groom above the door. Inside was a tiny lobby wallpapered in pink cabbage roses with ornate mirrors set at strategic points. A faded green carpet, worn thin and full of indentations from high heel shoes, covered the floor. Along one wall sat dainty satin chairs. Next to the entrance and beside a full-size mirror a small counter supported a filebox, assorted papers and a shiny cash register. Small cubicles separated by flowered curtains were designated as dressing rooms. One room, larger than the others was the fitting room. Here, a short, wide-hipped woman pinned and adjusted bridal dresses on blushing girls. On this Saturday morning, as Blanca and Lucy entered, dark eyed females swished in and out of the dressing rooms wearing an array of bridal gowns sewn during the week in a dusty back room by a Mexican seamstress.

Blanca, her eyes wide, her mouth agape, walked into the store and timidly stood to the side until Lucy yanked her towards the front counter to greet Mrs. Goldie Solomon, a plump, effusive red-haired woman with bright blue eyes and a heaving bosom. Goldie immediately put one ring-laden plump hand on Blanca's husky arm to murmur, "September? Perfect weather my dear!"

"Yeah?"

"You'll want something lacy, delicate."

"Yeah?"

"The dress of your dreams."

"Yeaaaah."

Goldie Solomon made it a practice to personally greet each customer. Her success, she knew, lay in making these backward and awkward girls feel comfortable, important. Once she greeted each potential customer, she or Rufina, her assistant, escorted the giggling girls to the fitting room, where they undressed were measured and fitted. Rufina now bustled around the numerous cubicles, a measuring tape looped around her round neck and a pinchusion full of straight pins strapped onto her wide wrist.

As Blanca undressed, Lucy stood looking at the dresses on the mannequins in the window, all of which had tiny breasts and no hips. Lucy gasped, they ain't gots no tits! Or ass either! Man, I sure wouldn't wanna look like that. They look like gringas all right, all faded and with tits that look like mosquito bites. She tucked in her waist, stuck out her small, ripe breasts and glanced at her reflection in the mirror, then took out a plastic compact, smeared Tangee Red on her thin lips, adjusted her bra-straps and waved her index finger at Mrs. Solomon to come close.

"We wanna look at the latest . . . "

"Oh, but of course!"

"No matter how much . . . "

"Why of course, my dear. Money should be no . . . "

"I'll tell ya which ones to . . . "

"But of course!"

Inside the fitting room Blanca frowned at her mirror image. Her wide face had lost it's morning freshness. "Dammit," sighed Blanca, "just like I thought. Lucy's gonna take over again. First with the flowers, then the Best Man and now she's gonna tell me which dress ta buy. I shoulda come alone."

Earlier, worried about having to shell out all her money, Blanca had hinted to Lucy, "I only wanna spend . . . "

"Man, don't be so goddamn cheap!"

"But . . . "

"You gotta look mellow, sister."

"Mellow?"

"Yeah! Hep."

And now here's Lucy asking for the most expensive dresses! Just 'cause she ain't paying for nuttin. The minute my back is turned, Lucy tells Goldie to bring out the best. Ain't I the bride . . . or what? "Shit," hissed Blanca, yanking at her snug slip, "I shoulda come alone." She slumped down on a velvet chair, staring at a crack in the ceiling. The dressing room was cold; she shivered slightly, as from afar came the strains of "Stardust," the most popular song in the barrio. Blanca leaned back, closed her eyes and sat waiting to be measured, after which she would be fitted with sample wedding gowns by the ever-busy Mrs. Solomon, who now approached the cubicle, a satin dress in tow.

The first dress chosen for Blanca to try on was of heavy white satin with a sweetheart neckline and puffed sleeves that tapered down to the wrist. Both neckline and sleeves were edged with Chantilly lace. Each shoulder seam was pleated so that when the bride moved, the pleats appeared to open and close. The skirt, cut low at the waist, gathered in huge ruffles that hung to the floor. The dress went over Blanca's head easily, then slid over her generous breasts where it now clung. "This dress sure is purdy," Blanca admitted, her brown eyes aglow, "especially the sleeves. But there's something wrong. The sleeves are too tight!" She tried to squeeze her round arms and husky shoulders into the dress, but afraid of tearing the material and having to pay for the damage, Blanca yelled out, "Hey, Mrs. Solomona . . . "

"Goldie."

This one doesn't fits me!"

"Nonsense, my dear! All it needs is a little adjustment and . . . "

"My arms are too fat . . . and it's starting to . . . "

"Oh! Well, don't you move, now. Let me bring you a wider, uhhh, another current favorite, an eyelet gown with a large hoop and . . . "

"Gosh! That's so pretty. And that one? How much . . . "

"My dear! This is your wedding dress! Don't think of money, think of the wedding, your parents, of . . . "

"Cricket."

"Oh, hi, Lucy. Whatcha think of this one?"

"Neh, too plain. You need something with class."

"Oh yeah?"

"Yeah."

Blanca, her face flushed a bright pink, pushed back her drooping pompadour, then called out once more, "Hey Miz Salodom!"

"Goldie to you, my dear!"

"Lemme see the other dress, okay? Them eyelet ones."

After inspecting an array of satin, taffeta and lace encrusted dresses, Blanca selected a "colonial" style dress, then the current rage, similar to that worn by Scarlett O'Hara in "Gone With the Wind." The low-cut dress of creamy satin was nipped in the waist and gathered in swirls at the front from where it ballooned to the floor in a cascade of white froth. Attached to each shoulder and swirl were tiny clusters of pale wax flowers. The dress back was cut in a low V with fifty-two satin covered buttons. The sleeves were huge puffy masses of lace; the bosom was modest, cut neither too high nor too low, but just right for shy young brides.

"This is one of our most popular, uuuh, prettiest dresses," exclaimed Goldie Solomon, pushing back a gold curl, "and you look lovely in it! Now, if you want something distinctive, uhhh, really different, we can add more lace at the hem . . . for a small sum of course."

"Yeah?"

Goldie Solomon felt it her duty to encourage young women, especially timid, unworldly Mexican girls from the small barrios, to think big and keep in mind that the most important day of a girl's life was her wedding day. She advertised in *La Opinión* and in Spanish radio, kept her own books and was meticulous about each entry, making sure each prospective bride who wanted credit produced a current check stub before signing on the dotted line. She kept the back room stacked with sodas and played the latest tunes on a record player hidden behind the fitting room. Goldie was also determined to sell any and all accesories to the blushing, chattering horde of girls who frequented her shop, and she kept an array of petticoats, shoes (or slippers, as she preferred to call them), bras, garter belts and misty-light pegnoirs on hand. Much of this was bought at discount in the garment district on Los Angeles street. Now and then Goldie bought rejects which Ramona, the seamstress, would disguise with pink rosettes. She now pulled back the flowered curtain of Blanca's cubicle. Bosom heaving, blue eyes shining, Goldie scooted off to find the eyelet dress in size sixteen large.

Blanca stuck her head out of the dressing room to look for Lucy, who had disappeared. She was fascinated by the young women who scooted in and out of the steamy cubicles, arms modestly crossed above sweaty breasts bursting out of worn, mended slips. As the girls went by Blanca, they smiled as if to say, I'm gettin married too! Blanca smiled back, anxious to find out what things were gonna cost.

Damn, that Lucy's not doing nuttin, sighed Blanca to herself, adjusting her stocking seams, all she does is stare at herself in the mirror! She's too damn conceited . . . She parted the curtains, glanced to the right, then to her left, angry not to see Lucy nearby.

When she realized that Blanca had liked the colonial dress, Mrs. Solomon, her flowered dress swishing to and fro, moved in for the kill. "My dear, here are some petticoats. You'll need one, you know."

"Oh yeah?"

"Yes! And undergarments and . . . But don't let me overwhelm you, my dear! Let's begin with this, shall we?"

"Yeah."

Mrs. Solomon handed Blanca what resembled a huge lamp-shade that was actually a petticoat made of layers of white nylon net edged with thick wire, trimmed in wide lace and garnished with tiny pink rosebuds. With a smile and a wink of her baby-blue eyes, Goldie urged Blanca to slip on the tentlike garment.

"My dear girl, a wedding dress is not complete without the correct petticoat, uhhh, the right brassiere and garter belt!" Arms clasped in front of her heaving bosom, Goldie took a deep breath, then hurried on. "Foundation garments are soooo important! They can make or break a dress. Here." She laid the petticoat on a pink satin chair, then stood back, her head tilted to catch a Tommy Dorsey refrain, and awaited Blanca's reaction.

Inside the cramped cell-like room, a nervous Blanca stared at the array of petticoats, slips and dresses strewn over the chair of rose velvet. The dressing room was stifling. Her armpits were start-ing to smell, her mouth felt dry. Darn, Blanca groaned, the morn-ing's dragging and still I ain't bought nuthin! She wanted the colonial-style dress, that she knew, but hated to think how much all this was going to cost. I'm not gonna have enough money, she grumbled, looping the petticoat around her wide waist, then twirl-ing it around. Everything costs so much in Los.

For the past three months Blanca had worked every Saturday. She now felt exhausted. It was getting to where the dead turkeys, whose feathers she was hired to remove, were appearing in her dreams. In her dreams the turkeys all looked like Cricket, espe-cially when he yelled at her. In one especially bad dream, a night-mare really, a big Tom turkey had attacked a small, white cat that was too dumb to run away.

"But this is the most important outfit I'm ever gonna buy," Blanca told her reflection. "I don't wanna make a mistake. If I gets the colonial dress, I gotta buy a slip or petticoat. But this one makes me look fatter." She pushed back her limp hair, feeling ner-vous, apprehensive. "Gosh, all them dresses are so purdy, even the one that didn't even fits me! What am I gonna do?" Blanca looked around, then spotted Lucy fingering a purple satin gown splattered across the front with shiny sequins. Suddenly Blanca slumped down on the chair and put her head down between her knees, as the petticoat grazed the faded carpet and fell around her. She felt nauseous. Just then Lucy stuck her head into the dressing room. In a voice hoarse with emotion, Blanca whispered, "Lucy, everything costs too much. I ain't gonna . . . "

"I told you, man! Dresses costs more in Los. So, get Cricket to pay for it. I'm telling you, man, that guy is too goddammed cheap. You shoulda told him right from the start. For a guy who thinks he's hot stuff, he sure is chip. Shoot! When I gets hitched, my old man better know he's gonna pay for everything, even my undies."

"I shoulda eloped," groaned Blanca, pulling the petticoat over her head. "I'm tired of killing myself just to pay for a wedding dress. I shoulda got a dress made of sacks, with some of them birds and butterflies. But I gotta make my Ma proud. Shucks! And I still gotta buy me some shoes and . . . "

"Shoes? Why, my dear, we have a special selection of satin slippers right here," gushed Mrs. Solomon as she thrust her hand underneath the curtain. "Why, just look at these!" She held up a tiny satin shoe, and handed it to Blanca, who took one look at the shoe and in an embarrassed voice said, "I wear 9, double D."

"Double? Oh my, that is a bit wide, but never you fear. We'll find something for your . . . for you." Goldie Solomon thrust the satin shoes aside, made a mental note to restock shoes in wide sizes, then returned once more to the business at hand, that of selling the shop's most expensive petticoat to the friendly, stocky girl now trapped inside the flowered dressing room.

Inside the hot, humid room, Blanca sat on the faded pink settee, her wide hips overlapping the tiny seat. She tried to remember, where did I see white sandals for $2.99? Pennys? Karls? Man alive! I gotta find me some cheap shoes, she concluded, or I can't buy the other stuff. If only Lucy was here! She could tell me . . . But again Lucy was nowhere to be seen.

With Goldie's help, Blanca tried on the Scarlett O'Hara dress once more. The nylon petticoat spread the dress to it's ultimate fullness. Blanca stared at herself in the mirror. She twirled around in the small room. Mrs. Solomon beamed her approval. "Already I look like a bride!" Blanca giggled. She swished from one side to the other then, unable to see the back of the dress and the fifty-two satin-covered buttons, she walked out to the lobby straight to the full-length mirrors, all the while smiling at the half-dressed women who dashed in and out of the dressing rooms. Lucy joined her once again.

"Gosh, I look just like a bride, Lucy! Lookit me! Gee, Cricket's gonna like this!" Blanca's eyes sparkled; beads of moisture clung to her upper lip. "This dress is really hep! But it makes me look shorter . . . and fatter," Blanca admitted. Maybe I better not buy it. I look more like a big fat tub, than Scarlett O'Hara. She frowned, pulling at the swirling puffs of material. Next to her, Mrs. Solomon, alert to sudden shifts in taste, moved in close. She pressed Blanca's warm, sweaty hand, then looked to Lucy for support. Goldie smiled into Blanca's soft brown eyes and exclaimed, "My dear! You're as pretty as a picture! Don't you agree, Miss, uhhhh."

"Yeah."

Blanca heaved a sigh of relief, "At last," she beamed, "at last I have the perfect dress. A dress just like Scarlett O'Hara's! Man alive! Wait till them chicks from San Cristobal see this . . . they won't call us from Taconos hicks. Ha, ha." With Lucy's smiling approval and Goldie looking on, Blanca signed a purchasing contract for the dress. "First I'll order the dress," Blanca decided, "then I'll charge the other stuff, if I gotta." She reached into her worn purse, counted out five ten-dollar bills, handed them to Mrs. Solomon and slumped down on the rose settee, weary of the whole thing.

"I shoulda gone to Penny," Blanca sighed as next to her Lucy burst into a loud laugh. "I shoulda gone to TJ." From the shocked look on Lucy's face, Blanca knew she had said something stupid. Again. She sat up, took out her cracked Max Factor compact, dabbed rouge on her pale cheeks and smirked at Lucy. "Not really."

"Yeah. I knew you was only kidding."

"The wedding is important," Blanca admitted, "at least to me and my Ma. I gotta show people in Taconos that our family is just as good as the Sotos and Sierras. Ain't nobody worn a colonial-style dress yet. I'm gonna be the first one . . . unless Lucy opens her big mouth and blabs about it. I'll just work more overtime so I can pay for everything. Even though my sister married a guy whose always in the can and our house is falling apart, I gotta leave by the front door, in a white dress. Yeah, I don't want my cousins from up north to say my wedding was a drag. Maybe I can still get some money from Cricket, but I ain't gonna beg. No way am I gonna let my family down."

In the small lobby, before Blanca had second thoughts about Goldie's best-seller, Goldie quickly brought out a pink-striped box with filmy lace garters and soft latex girdles, including the very latest thing, a Playtex rubber girdle which was guaranteed to squash all protruding bellies. Each girdle was accompanied by a small sales tag. Goldie handed the box to Blanca, then stood back.

"Lucy, lookit this. It ain't gonna fit on my butt," cried Blanca, holding a tiny latex girdle encrusted with lace and pink satin rosettes. "Ha, ha, ha. It's only gonna fit on one leg. Shit, I better look at . . . "

"Uhhhh, here are some nice linen drawers," suggested Mrs. Solomon, handing Blanca a pair of wide leggy bloomers.

"Man alive," squealed Lucy, doubling over in laughter. She picked up the bloomers, held them aloft, then waved them at Blanca. "Look, Blanca these ougtha fit you!"

"Your mother too," snapped Blanca, tired of Lucy being so damn bossy. "Buy them for your mother, Lucy. And when she's through with em you can put them on too!"

"Come on, I was only kiddin. Can't you take a joke? Let's look at other stuff, okay?"

"Okay."

Once confident that Blanca and Lucy were through scrapping and hopeful Blanca would not change her mind about the dress contract, Mrs. Solomon signaled to Rufina to bring out what she called "underthings," which included assorted strapless bras. Goldie then slipped to the back room, took an orange soda from the small refrigerator and gave it to the bride-to-be.

From past experience, Goldie knew it was the small courtesies she extended to her Mexican clients that ensured La Mas Popular would continue to be the most popular bride's store in all of Los Angeles. And if on occasion she sold the coy, uneducated senoritas a dress worn before by another bride, so what?

Inside the curtained room Blanca fingered the strapless brassieres, which were engineered with thick wire and covered in seam binding. Most resembled a harness. Around the sides extra panels and wiring were added. Thick elastic wound around the bottom of each bra cup and around the back, making them cumbersome, hot. Huge snaps, stitched onto the elastic at the back, ensured that once on, the bra would not shift.

"I hate them strapless things," hissed Lucy once Mrs. Solomon was out of earshot, "they make me look flat as a pancake."

"Yeah? Well try on some padded ones."

"Yeah? Maybe I will, for the wedding. That way I can . . . "

"Padded bras? Why of course my dear!" As though by magic, Mrs. Solomon reappeared, blue eyes flashing. She took the orange soda from Blanca, put it on the floor, then quickly wound the tape measure around Blanca's ample breasts and asked, "How much more do you want?"

"Want?"

"You did say you wanted to see padded bras, did you not?"

Blanca burst out in a giggle. "She wants them padded bras," she cried, pointing at a red-faced Lucy. "She's almost flat. I gots too much already. Ha, ha, ha."

Once she was able to stop laughing, Blanca tried on various brassieres, including the very latest thing, a harness-like support called a Merry Widow, which was similar to one worn by Jane Russell in a movie. The bra of white taffeta which came to the hips, and although it resembled a harness, it pinched in the waist a good three inches. Once squeezed into the contraption, Blanca took a deep breath and examined the bra which thrust her ample breasts almost to her chin. The Merry Widow, disguised with ivory lace, pale pink ribbons and tiny silk rosabuds, literally took Blanca's breath away. She stood in front of the mirror, trying not to laugh.

"Lucy! This thing is squashing my tetas. I gots my tits up to my chin almost. But lookit my waist! Don't it look lots smaller?" Blanca read the price tag, then took a deep breath. She felt faint. The pull of the elastic and the hot room was making her sick. With a swift glance at the closed curtains, Blanca unbuckled the hooks, thrust loose her full breasts, then slipped on her threadbare bra and slip. She stifled a yawn, then sat down to drink the orange soda.

I'm gonna gets home late and won't even have time to gets ready for the party," Blanca grumbled, sipping on the cold drink. "I don't even wanna go, but then Cricket will go by himself. And I don't trust him." She stretched her thick, short legs, then ran a hand through her limp hair.

The trouble with Cricket is he likes too many chicks. And they like him too. And he knows it. Last time we was at Angelinas, he kept putting his arm around her. He thinks I ain't seen him, but I did. Sometimes I don't know howcome he liked me. I ain't shapely like Lucy, and I can't even tell jokes like Sally. All I gots is a job pulling feathers off turkeys. And that don't pay so good. But . . . Cricket's my honey . . . and that's that.

"I better forget about all," Blanca decided as she adjusted her dress, them petticoats and bras . . . I'll just do what other girls do when they wear them low-cut blouses. I'll pin my bra up with seguros. Them safety pins are okay. That way I don't gotta squash my tits. Better yet, I'll save some moola! She took a deep breath, then once more slouched on the settee. From the dressing room came the sound of loud trumpets. Artie Shaw! Blanca stuck her head out between the curtains, sipped on the soda, then waited to see what was next.

Within minutes, Rufina, Mrs. Solomon's efficient assistant, discreetly entered the small cubicle and handed Blanca a pretty pink box in which lay garter belts, nightgowns, pegnoirs and sets of Baby Doll nighties. Blanca held the box in her wide hands and gaped at the nightgowns in the box. She could feel her face getting hot as her calloused fingers caressed feather-light garters and lace panties. "Gosh, they sure are suggestive," Blanca whispered to Lucy, who had slipped back into the dressing room, a cherry soda in her hand. "Man alive! Them things don't cover nuttin! Lookit this! Blanca held up a short, satin nightgown. "This don't even cover my tits!"

"You're supposed to wear em around your neck," giggled Lucy, holding a peach-colored lace nightgown to Blanca's throat.

"On my neck?"

"That's a joke, stuped. Look," Lucy continued, "you put it on . . . then later it winds up around your . . . "

"Gosh! You're so filthy!"

"And you're so lame."

"And have you decided on a gown for your first night?" interjected Mrs. Solomon, peeking in between the flowered curtains. "The First Night is so . . . a night to . . . Mine certainly was! Why, I still remember . . . "

"What night?" asked Blanca, straining to hear Stan Kenton's "Peanut Vendor." "What night she talking about?"

"Your wedding night, dummy. Uhhh, the first time you and Cricket, uhhhhh . . . "

Blanca, her face a bright pink, quickly looked away, then began to jam the lacy pegnoirs into the box. She handed it to a flustered Mrs. Solomon, who realized she had just lost a sale. Lucy took one look at Blanca's red face, then left the dressing room and edged her way towards the racks holding bridesmaids dresses or "formal gowns," as Mrs. Goldie Solomon preferred to call the long, flowing dresses worn by bridal attendants. Now and then she glanced across the way to where Blanca sat.

Poor Blanca, Lucy thought, she looks like shit. But that's what she gits for getting mixed up with a guy like Cricket. He's too cheap, just like I told her. Ain't no way he's gonna pay for nuthin. All them Tacones are the same. Out for one thing only. They think they're so tough, just 'cause they beat the Planchados. But they ain't gots a steady job. No pachucos gots a good job. Shit, for somebody who works in the garbage, Cricket sure thinks he's tough. He's just mean. Mean, mean, mean. He gave Blanca a big line and she swallowed it whole! And now lookit her. But that ain't gonna happen to me. I ain't gonna be that stupid. A chick's gotta watch out for herself, or the guys will throw ya to the dogs. Lucy twitched her hips, tucked in her stomach, then wandered back to Blanca.

Inside the stifling room Blanca counted on her fingers the amount she had to spend to look good on her wedding day. Her thick, sweaty fingers clutched the now empty wallet. "God," Blanca sighed, "the whole thing is gonna cost almost two hundred dollars! Golly Moses! Two hundred smackers! And I still gotta buy me the veil. And shoes. And . . . "

"It's time to try on wedding veils," announced Goldie Solomon, "and I have just the thing for you." She smiled at the awkward-looking girl standing in the brightly lighted cubicle and handed her a frothy white veil. Goldie knew that for most brides-to-be selecting the right veil could be a problem. Veils did not come with a wedding dress, but were sold separately, usually at a high, high price. They were made in various designs and materials: lace, off-white shades of satin, taffeta or chiffon, materials not easily matched.

"I know what I want, Blanca whispered to Lucy, "and I ain't seen it yet." She looked around her, humming softly, hoping to find the veil of her dreams.

Ever since she could remember, Blanca had envisioned her wedding veil. It had to be made of azares, orange blossoms made of wax, the traditional headpiece worn by most Mexican-American brides. It was a sign of purity. As a kid Blanca had delighted in twisting the orange blossoms into a crown, then placing it on her head. She liked to play bride-and-groom! She especially enjoyed hearing her mother and her friends describe weddings in Taconos: the dress, presents and attendants. Most times these discussions centered on the bride and the question of purity.

"The bride wore rhinestones on her veil!"

"No?"

"She must have a reason not to wear azares."

"Well, they say she . . . "

"Ay no!"

"Well, she walks kind of funny, don't you think?"

"I'm gonna have orange blossoms," Blanca had assured her mother, "even if I have to make the veil myself." She now balanced herself on one tired leg, waiting for Goldie Solomon to return with more wedding veils.

A grumpy Goldie Solomon was tired of extending herself to the awkward-looking girl who was now standing in front of the oval mirror. Goldie rummaged in a back room, sensing she should find something special for this timid, husky girl.

"She doesn't know what she wants,' Mrs. Solomon hissed to Rufina, the assistant. This customer has no taste for the finer things. If I don't find a bargain for her, she'll be here the whole day." She began to poke through boxes of wedding veils made-to-order, determined to recoup her losses by selling a veil made for another bride.

In front of the steamy mirror Blanca ran a comb through her hair, careful not to disturb the limp pompadour. Once more she glanced at her reflection in the gold-leafed mirror in the lobby, then at the array of wedding veils: headpieces made of lacey caps, sweatheart crowns, chiffon ruffles, pearl seeded Juliet caps and Spanish mantillas. Once again she felt hungry, irritable. "All my hard earned money is going in one shot," she moaned. "Gee whiz! Six months of slaving at the turkeys! Darn!" She stared back at her tired face and smeared mascara, trying to focus on the creamy white headpieces that kept slipping off her straight hair. "How much is this one? And that one?" But she could not concentrate. All she thought of was how much everything was costing. "I don't want to make payments on nothing," she whispered to Lucy.

"Why not? Shit, everbody makes payments. How else you gonna have a big wedding? Rob a bank?" Once more in command of things, Lucy lit a Lucky Strike, took a sip of her cherry soda and then glared at a rumpled Blanca.

"You just gotta do it," Lucy advised, puffing on the cigarette. "You'll pay it in a year, anyhow . . . "

"A year?"

"Well, maybe two."

Suddenly Blanca stood up and moved toward the bathroom, her face pale in the soft light. Mrs. Solomon, knowledgeable of the fainting spells and dizziness that accompanied many bridal fittings quickly ran to get a glass of water for bride-to-be. On the way back she swept up the boxes with underwear and pegnoirs, handed them to Rufina and turned up the record player. Once Blanca returned, the fitting continued.

"Why, just look at this garter belt," pealed Mrs. Solomon. "It's perfect with you dress and only $19.95!"

"Uhhhh, I dunno . . . "

" . . . and this . . . " she handed the mute Blanca a baby blue satin robe. "For the morning after! Why just feel the lace . . . And mules to match!"

"Mules?"

"Slippers. For the boudoir."

"Yeah, real purdy." Her tired eyes glazed over, Blanca tried to once more focus on the flimsy nightgowns with matching pegnoirs and slippers. "Man, she sure don't give up for nuttin, Blanca groaned. She wants ta sell me the whole store!" Suddenly she stood up, handed the boxes to Mrs. Solomon and said, "I don't want nuttin but a veil. Get it?"

Mrs. Solomon, taken aback by this chunky, sweaty girl, quickly recovered her composure and said; "Oh, yes! Of course my dear. I thought you had already picked one."

"No. You showed me them Merry Widows and some other stuff, but . . . "

"Well, no wedding is complete without a veil, now, is it?" Goldie's eyes glistened, her small blue-veined hands fluttered back and forth. Soon, soon. She picked up the box of bargain veils and patted Blanca on the head.

"Just you sit and rest, honey." Then, noticing Blanca's sweaty brow and pale face Goldie added: "You do feel alright, don't you?"

"Yeah, I'm okay."

"Weddings are so much work," trilled the owner of La Mas Popular, 'Oh yes! I still remember mine. Why I was . . . . Oh, here are the veils. Why don't we begin with this one." She glanced at the price tag, then added: "Why this one's been marked down to . . . "

"To what?" asked Blanca, suddenly alert.

"Why it's only $29.99! A real bargain, I assure you."

Blanca eyed the veil suspiciously, then with a firm movement pushed it onto her dark head and called to her Maid-of-Honor."

"Lucy, c'mere. Whatcha think of this one?"

"It's purdy."

"Yeah?"

"Yeah."

"But I wanted azares. Orange blossoms."

"Oh, but of course, we have veils with orange blossoms," cried Goldie, her ample chest heaving. She pulled at a stack of boxes behind the counter. "Here, take your pick of these slightly, uhhh, slightly wrinkled veils. She handed Blanca the box, then stood back to await her cue.

Blanca sifted quickly though the boxed contents, her expert

fingers plucked first at the price tag then the headpiece. Finally, her fingers came to rest on a cluster of creamy-white wax flowers shaped like an inverted V.

"This ones kinda purdy. But it's wrinkled!"

"That's why it's marked down. But if you iron it . . . "

"Yeah. I can do that." Blanca took the azares, laid them on the wispy veil selected earlier, then carefully put the headpiece on her head. Perfect! Just perfect! And cheap. Her quick mind calculated that this was the one headpiece she could afford. "I'll take it,' she told the shopkeeper. "This is the one I want."

Mrs. Solomon quickly wrapped the headpiece, aware that the veil had been worn once before by another bride who had then sold it back to the store. "I'll just add it to your account," she gushed. "Once I add the tax."

"Are you gonna buy that?" asked Lucy, wrinkling her small nose. Don't you want something with rhinestones?"

Blanca, too tired to answer, merely shrugged her shoulders. "If I buy this I'm gonna have to forget everything else," she sighed, smoothing down her dress, "the strapless bra, garter belt and fluffy petticoat," she concluded. "I can't buy everything and I ain't gonna postpone my wedding. I'm not gonna work for six months more for a lousy petticoat. She heaved her tired body to the counter, picked up the veil, now boxed, and silently vowed to get some money from Cricket to pay for half of everything. Other guys do, so why can't he? As they left the store, Blanca heaved the pink cardboard box that contained the veil with the orange-blossom headpiece onto her sturdy hip. She walked alongside Lucy, content with her purchase, content with herself.

Part II
Chapter One

The Wedding Morning

The wedding day dawned bright and clear. A fresh breeze from the nearby foothills rustled the leaves on the trees. From her small bedroom Blanca could hear birds twittering outside the window and a neighbor's car start up. She stretched her husky legs, then suddenly chilled, reached for the chenille bedspread twisted near her feet and threw it over her thinly clad body. She laid back once more. I wish I could stay in bed, she thought, but I am so hungry. My stomach is growling! I gotta get up and eat!

During the last few months Blanca had awakened each morning thinking only of food. She was now in the habit of keeping a piece of sweet bread wrapped in wax paper on top of the chipped maple dresser. The first thing Blanca Muñoz did on the morning of her wedding day was stuff a piece of stale bread into her wide, expectant mouth. She lay in bed, munching contentedly as breadcrumbs fell onto the still warm sheets. She finally got up and wandered into the kitchen, where the smell of chorizo made her nauseous. She bolted to the bathroom, her face pale, where she remained for some time.

When she felt better, Blanca splashed her face with cold water, then rubbed it dry with a towel hanging from a nail. She stared into the small bathroom mirror and saw a round, full face with puffy brown eyes. The arched eyebrows gave her face a serious, brooding look. The nose was short, flat. The full mouth, devoid of color, looked wider than usual. Above the cotton nightgown her neck was thick and wide. Already her armpits were damp with sweat.

"I sure don't look like a bride," Blanca told her mirror image. "Not yet, anyhow. Mostly I look like hell. I shoulda gone to bed earlier . . . and taken an aspirin. Now I'm gonna look awful in the pictures. Darn!" She wandered into the small living room, where an assortment of clothes and boxes and a trunk reminded her that this indeed was her wedding day. "Gee whiz," Blanca giggled, "after all them stupid meetings and all the fuss with Lucy over the bridesmaid's dresses—and all them fights with Cricket, my wedding day is finally here. Gosh!"

Fully awake now, Blanca began to remove the bandana wrapped over the pink net that was wound around her hair. She shook her head a few times, secured the loose bobby pins around stray pincurls and then walked back to her room. She rubbed her eyes and yawned, then slowly opened the closet door and stood staring at her wedding dress.

"This dress is perfect! Just perfect. Everything I always wanted!" Her eyes misting, she touched the dress sleeve, which felt soft, warm. "Gosh, it's the prettiest thing I ever had. Just like I always dreamed. Ain't nobody in Taconos gots married in one like it. A Cinderella-Scarlett O'Hara type dress, white and fluffy. And expensive!"

Blanca gently fondled the milky white material, then held it up to her face. Ummmm, it even smelled good! She put it back in the closet, arranging the folds carefully. She bent over, scooped up the pink striped box that contained the wedding veil and laid it across a bent chair. She reached for the shoe box from underneath the dresser, where her white baby-doll pumps lay wrapped in white tissue paper. She laid the shoes next to the veil, then took out panties, a bra and the lacy wire petticoat that resembled a lampshade. Gosh, Blanca sighed, pushing back a stray bobby pin, I'm getting excited! Pretty soon I'm gonna put on all this stuff . . . and really look like a bride! But it's too hot for stockings . . . and the garter belt Lucy gots me is too darn tight. I'm not gonna wear no stockings, she finally decided, throwing aside the pink garter belt. Anyhows, nobody's gonna see my legs.

She lounged on the bed, adjusting the numerous bobby pins that held the pincurls and curlers in place. She got up and reached into a drawer, took out an emery board and began to file her short, crooked nails. She moved quietly around the small room getting her things in order.

Blanca smiled down at her bed and thought, Beginning tomorrow I'm gonna wake up in bed with Cricket! God! He's gonna see me without makeup. Without nothing! Gee whiz, I hope he don't get scared. From today on I'm gonna be Mrs. Sammy-the-Cricket Lopez. Hitched. An ole married lady. Man alive! She sat down again and enjoyed the moment, until her growling stomach drove her toward the kitchen.

Blanca was determined to eat very little on this day. I'll wait till the reception, she vowed, pressing down on her stomach. Already my dress is too tight. She had twice moved the buttons to accomodate her expanding waistline; there was no more room left around the seams. She sighed, stuck a piece of Juicy Fruit in her mouth, hoping it would make her stomach stop growling.

"If it gets hot today, I'm gonna sweat like a pig," Blanca groaned. "I don't wanna ruin my pretty dress." She ran her hand under wet armpits. "Shit, I don't wanna sweat today. I want everything to be perfect! I been waiting for this day ever since . . . for a long time. Ain't nuthin' gonna ruin it, not even Cricket."

A wedding day was supposed to be the beginning of a new, exciting life for a girl. From that day on she would be with her honey. The guy of her dreams. Ever since she could remember, Blanca and her friends in Taconos talked of nothing else but guys, weddings and babies.

Few girls in Taconos thought of working for a while, then getting married. What for? Why not get hitched right away? Few of Blanca's friends wanted to stay single. All their plans were tied up with a guy, with falling in love, going steady, getting engaged and, if everything went okay, getting married in church with lots of bridesmaids and the whole town watching. They spent hours talking about the guys in Taconos. Which one had a future? A steady job? Which one would wind up in jail? Or knifed in a street fight? Blanca and her friends separated guys into two categories: those with steady jobs and cool cars and those who didn't have a pot to piss in. Of all her girlfriends, it was Lucy who swore she had been engaged two times who was the most practical. "No way I'm gonna get hitched with some dumb jerk," Lucy often chanted. "There's a lot of fish in the ochean . . . and I gots plenty of bait." Still, most of the chicks wanted to get hitched to a guy with a steady job . . . and live happily ever after.

Blanca hurried to bathe, aware of the growing excitement around her. Her Tio Ernie stuck his head in the door, said, "Hallo," then left to rake the yard. In the small kitchen, her mother bustled around.

Inside the bathroom, Blanca sat in the cracked bathtub, staring at the ceiling, letting the warm water relax her. Now and then she dipped a washcloth in the water, then rubbed it over her thick arms and legs. A piece of Palmolive soap floated in the water. She scrubbed her armpits once more, rinsed her face and arms, then reached for the fluffy towel on the bent aluminum rack and began to dry off. I better hurry up, Blanca told herself, as she gently removed the net from her head and adjusted the aluminum curlers. I still gotta do my hair. It's gotta look just right, Blanca vowed, bending down to unplug the drain. I gotta look really fine!

The night before, Lucy had rolled Blanca's hair into tight pincurls, wound the longer sections on aluminum curlers, saturated each curl with wave set and finally placed a pink net on Blanca's head in hopes that Blanca's straight hair, which usually lost it's curl within the hour, would hold up on her wedding day. "You worry too much about your hair," Lucy advised. "Lemme show ya how ta set it."

Weeks before, with Lucy assisting and Sally watching, Blanca had been given a Toni Home Permanent. The permanent kit was on sale at Thrifty's in San Cristobal, and all the chicks were buying it. But the permanent did not take. Neither did the henna pack Sally swore would give Blanca's hair gold streaks. All it did give Blanca was a rash around the hairline that drove her nuts, and also a headache from the stench of henna mixed with peroxide. And then the two women who worked with Blanca at the turkeys had come to work with kinky hair. They urged Blanca to try the Toni once more.

"Just lookit Sadie's curlies. Cute, huh?"

"She looked better with a pompadour."

"No? Well, how come you gots rid of yours?"

"'Cause my boyfriend's too chort . . . and I wanna make him feel good."

"Well, buy him some high heels! Ha, ha, ha."

"Gosh, Petra, you're so mean!"

"Ha. Lissen, anytime you wanna know how ta make a guy feel good, just ask me."

"Oh, yeah?"

"Yeah. And it ain't got nuttin to do wiz a pompadour."

And now here I am, still struggling with my straight hair, thought Blanca on her wedding day. I'll just havta do the best I can. I sure don't look like no Toni Twins! I'll just pour on lotsa wave set and stick a pack of bobby pins inside my rat. I better hurry it up too. Wrapped in her chenille robe, she remained sequestered in the cramped, steamy bathroom to take down the numerous pincurls and the awful aluminum curlers that had kept her awake most of the night.

Blanca spent the last night tossing and turning. I'm gonna look like hell in the morning, Blanca groaned as she scrunched against the pillow. I'm gonna gets bags under my eyes and look like shit. I'm nervous, she admitted, pulling the pillow over her aluminum covered head, then turning over for the tenth time. Darn it, anyhow! What if Cricket shows up with a hangover? What if the dance is no good? Will there be enough food? She now paced the room, angry at Cricket, angry at herself. After once more dousing her face and neck with cold water, she was happy to see that she did not look tired, after all, but alert and ready for the big day. Now, if only my curls hold . . .

Slowly Blanca combed the tight curls, her knees rubbing against the dressing table. From the living room came the sound of a mellow tune. Delighted with the way her hair now fell in thick waves and tight ringlets, she smiled into the fogged mirror. Now and then she dipped a comb into the green wave set and readjusted the bobby-pins.

From outside came the sounds of neighbors shouting to each other and of cars going by. In the kitchen, Blanca's mother and Aunt Chonita argued over something. Blanca sat in front of the dresser, engrossed in plucking her eyebrows, and did not hear Lucy come in. An excited Lucy, preceded by the fragrance of Evening in Paris, barged in the door, her dress swishing to and fro.

"Man, aren't you ready yet?" she asked, twirling around the bed. "I've been up since five!"

Surprised to see her Maid-of-Honor, Blanca slowly put down

the hairbrush, rubbed her hands across her swollen eyes and stared at Lucy. Lucy's wasteline in the new purple dress looked especially small. Her breasts were suprisingly full. Determined not to show how pissed she was, Blanca began to smear Ponds Cream on her round face. Lucy sure looks pretty in her bridesmaid's dress, Blanca admitted to herself. Prettier than I'll ever look. But I wish she'd go home. I don't wanna hurt her feelings, but I wanted to fix myself up. Just me. Just today.

It was a Mexican tradition for the Maid-of-Honor to help dress the bride, and in some things Lucy was no slouch. More than anything, Lucy wanted everyone in Taconos to know that she, Lucy Matacochis, had dressed the bride! After all, she was the the most hep chick in town.

I better not let Lucy see I'm mad, Blanca decided, or she'll tell everybody. But I still wish she'd go away. She pulled the thin robe around her thick shoulders and continued to smoothe Ponds Cold Cream on her round face. Maybe if I play dumb she'll go in the kitchen and beat it. She rubbed Mum deodorant on her armpits while Lucy buffed her nails and re-arranged her rhinestone brace-let. Once more Blanca adjusted the rat inside her pompadour, jammed three more bobby pins inside each curl and put the comb down. Satisfied that the curls would hold, Blanca took a tissue and began to clean her face.

"Gee, I sure wish I could do something different with my face," she lamented. "I always wind up looking the same. Darn it! I shoulda shaved my eyebrows like Sally. Except she looks like shit. Or bought false eyelashes at the Five and Dime. Something besides putting on lotsa rouge and making my pompadour higher. Except that I don't know how to do my face. And I wanna look so fine!"

Blanca knew the bridesmaids would try to outdo each other. Sally had bought new pancake makeup two shades lighter and Tangee Ripe Blossom lipstick. Josie had touched up her hair with peroxide and Rosie had taken the bus to San Cristobal to get a permanent at her cousin's beauty shop. Gosh, I wish I wasn't so plain looking, thought Blanca, and had a tiny waist like Lucy, or dimples like Rosie. Everybody's gonna look better than me. And I'm the bride! Shit!

But I ain't gots money for more stuff. For makeup or stockings. I'm almost broke. All I gots is fifty bucks under the mattress. And that's for the honeymoon. And I can't borrow from my mama, 'cause she ain't got nuthin either. She strained to look at her reflection, at the wide face and dark brown hair, eager for the cream and makeup to transform her into a radiant beauty.

Most of Blanca's makeup came from the Five and Dime. She bought only what she needed. She scraped lipstick from a tube with a bobby-pin, then packed it in a small jar kept on top her dresser. She used each cake of maybelline until there was no color left. Even then she added more water to the small brush. But Blanca allowed herself one luxury. Once a month she bought a large jar of Ponds Cream. She applied this to her round face each morning and night, then waited for results.

Lucy now looked down at Blanca's smiling face, then without asking took out her compact and began to smear rouge on Blanca's pale cheeks.

"You gotta put on lotsa rouge, babe."

"Yeah?"

"Yeah. You're the bride, man! You gotta look hep!"

"Yeah, but I don't feel so good."

"Well, put on more rouge. You'll feel better! Come on!"

Lucy dusted powder on Blanca's nose, patted her hair with swift, expert fingers, then stood back, satisfied with how Blanca now looked. She went towards the door, saying, "I gotta gets my bouquet. I'll be back in a jiffy, okie dokie?"

"Uhhhh . . . "

"Then we can puts on your dress."

Once Lucy was out of sight, Blanca went into the bathroom and took two aspirins. She had a headache, one that came and went each time she thought of Cricket or money.

In the next room Blanca's mother was hurriedly dressing. She put on a dress of challis that she had bought on lay-away at Pennys in San Cristobal. The mauve dress had a high neckline, long sleeves and lace collar. On her feet were the sensible black shoes worn every day. Heavy cotton stockings were wrinkling around her knobby ankles. Earlier that week Blanca had suggested to her that she have her hair styled.

Although Aunt Chonita was in her sixties, she still worked in a packing shed during the grape season and made what she and Blanca's mother thought was good money. She now came out of the bathroom wearing a light-grey gabardine dress that came to her ankles. In the bright light, her tinted hair shone blue-grey. Two spots of pink rouge gave her sallow cheeks color. Her shiny patent-leather shoes had a modest heel and gold buckle. She smiled at Blanca, who was still sitting in front of the dresser. All in all, Aunt Chonita was pleased with her appearance.

Chapter Two

The Wedding Mass

At exactly seven-thirty, a transformed and excited Blanca Muñoz alighted from the gaily decorated car in front of St. Stephen the Martyr Catholic Church. She stood gazing around, as though in a dream. While Lucy adjusted her train and fluffed her veil, Blanca scanned the church entrance, looking for Tudi. If Tudi's here, then so is Cricket, she reasoned. She looked around at the wedding party, at the shiny, decorated cars and at her friends decked out in tuxedos and formal dresses. She was getting more excited by the minute. "Gosh! It's happening," she gushed, squeezing Lucy's arm. "I'm really getting hitched!"

Within minutes Blanca was surrounded by squealing bridesmaids and tuxedo-clad ushers, most of whom looked like black crows, especially El Pan Tostado, whose face shone blue-black in the bright sunlight. The flower-festooned cars, mostly Chevies and Fords, were lined up along the side of the street next to the chainlink fence that separated the church from the street. While everyone watched, Lucy pulled at and puffed up Blanca's billowing dress train and fussed over the bride, letting everyone know that not only had she told the bride which dress to buy, but early that morning she had dragged herself out of bed to dress her! "After all," Lucy hissed to Sally, "ain't I the Maid-of-Honor, or what?"

Lucy wore a purple taffeta and chiffon dress with a sweetheart neckline and small cap sleeves. Elbow-length gloves of purple net clung to her skinny arms. From her slender neck hung a delicate gold cross. On her pompadour sat a heart-shaped nylon hat with a ruffled edge that partly hid her small, dark eyes. Purple satin shoes peeped from beneath her taffeta skirt. On Lucy's ears dangled long, rhinestone earrings.

Next to Lucy stood a smiling Sally, decked out in a chartruese dress similar to Lucy's, but three sizes larger. Unlike Lucy's, Sally's hat did not have a ruffle nor veil. This was something the bridesmaids and Lucy had bickered about until Lucy had won out. "After all," she had snarled, "I'm the Maid-of-Honor. I gotta look different!"

Rosie, dressed in a hot pink dress, her hair a mass of light-brown curls, smiled at everyone to show her dimples. Unlike Lucy's dress that nipped in at the waist, Rosie's dress clung to her slender frame. The seamstress at La Mas Popular had not measured correctly and had made the dress too big! This had upset Rosie to no end. Still upset, she pouted every five minutes to show both her anger and dimples. "Now I can't show off my twenty-one-inch waist," Rosie sighed, "but at least my chooz looks better."

The bridesmaids had at first agreed to wear baby-doll pumps, dyed to match their dresses, until Sally spotted Lucy at a local shoe store, trying on purple shoes with gold trim. She then alerted the other chicks. Josie said she didn't care, but Rosie, fit-to-be-tied, took time off from her job at the pottery factory to buy pink satin sandals with rhinestone clips, which no one in Taconos had ever seen. There, she told herself, let's see what Lucy's gonna do when she sees my pretty chooz. Now, as they crowded in front of the church, Rosie glared at Lucy, who was encased in a purple dress that showed off her nineteen-inch waist.

Soon the street began to fill up with cars and people. Old, middle-aged and young were dressed to the nines! Young children elbowed each other, as they crowded around the church entrance, trying to get a look at the bride. Inside the church the altar boys dashed around lighting candles, turning on lights and making sure to lay out the right vestments for a nervous, pale Father Ranger. From the back of the church Blanca stared at the confusion up front. "Why ain't the church ready? Man, I coulda slept some more," she groaned.

Like most brides-to-be of Taconos, Blanca resented getting married at such an early mass. "Eight o'clock is too early," Blanca had groaned to Lucy. "We gotta get up with the chickens! That Father Ranger is so mean. I mean, just on accounta the choir only sings at this mass. If you ask me, who cares about a stupid choir?"

Blanca took a deep breath. Already she felt hot . . . and sticky. The stench from the gardenias clutched tight in her sweaty hands was suffocating. The bobby-pins were beginning to slip. The pimple on her chin was itching and her dress was pinching at the waist. "I shoulda got orchids instead of gardenias," she hissed, "at least they don't stink so much. And my dress is just too tight!" Just before leaving for church, Blanca and her aunt had reinforced five of the 52 buttons near the waistline with huge safety pins that now pressed into her tender flesh.

She now stood poised at the church door, the warm September sun on her round, happy face, her armpits damp with sweat, beads of perspiration on her upper lip. Ahead of her, Lucy and the brides-maids stood in a semi-circle, adjusting their long net gloves, running a comb through hair raised high in elaborate pompadours or securing a rat. At one side of the church, now bathed in sunlight, the young bridal attendants giggled as they tore rose petals from a nearby bush to toss at passing friends, but making sure to save those inside their wicker baskets for the recessional. From behind a dusty blue Chevy, Petey, the snot-nosed ring-bearer, stood still as his mother cleaned his nose, hopefully for the last time. Next to him, Porky munched on candy bought at the store across the way, then walked towards the bride. Inside the church, Cricket and Tudi stood at the communion rail. In the church sacristy, the altar boys giggled and nudged each other. In the choir loft the nervous organist checked her watch, waiting for the signal from Father Ranger. When finally she saw him leave the sacristy and walk to the middle of the main altar, she released her foot from the organ pedal. The church filled with the strains of the "Wedding March."

When she first heard the "Wedding March," Blanca's eyes filled with tears. She quickly dabbed at her eyes, fearful of smearing the dark mascara, fearful of having Lucy make fun of her running make up. But for once Lucy understood and gave her a swift hug before moving into line.

Blanca stood inside the church vestibule, smiling at Tio Ernie. In front, the bridesmaids and ushers began to march towards the altar as Lucy barked orders in a low, hoarse voice. Blanca tried not to laugh or cry, but the familiar sight of Lucy giving orders was getting to her. Damn that Lucy, she sighed, she's taking over again. But this is my wedding day and nobody's gonna ruin it. At the front, a solemn Tudi, the Best Man, stood next to Cricket as Lucy slowly came up the aisle toward them.

And then all of a sudden the music became louder, the tempo picked up. Everyone stood up. At the back of the church stood the bride, dressed in her Scarlett O'Hara-colonial-style dress. On her dark head sat a crown of orange blossoms with a misty white viel. In front she carried her gardenia bouquet. The music filled the church as warm sunlight filtered in through the windows.

Here I go, Blanca whispered to herself. Here I go. She put her husky arm through that of Tío Ernie, wet her dry lips with her tongue, brought the gardenia bouquet to her waistline, just as Lucy had instructed, and began the walk towards her husband-to-be, her future. Cricket.

Shortly before, a tired and irritable Father Ranger had stood in the quiet sacristy waiting to begin the wedding mass that would unite Blanca Muñoz and Sammy-the-Cricket Lopez in holy matrimony. He adjusted his stole and chasuble for the third time and tried to focus on the ceremony he was about to perform. The church altar looks pretty, he thought, gazing at the white gladiolas on the main altar. He yawned. The drive to the Hollywood Bowl the night before had exhausted him, as had the crowds screaming for Oscar Peterson. Worse, he was forced to sit between two loud blondes, one of which wore very little on top and who during intermission had turned to him to say, "Buy ya a drink, honey?"

"No, thank you."

"Whatsa matter, think you're too good?"

"Well no, it's just that I'm a priest and . . . "

"Yeah? My uncle Tim is a priest. And man, does he booze!"

"Hummm."

He had then found a new seat, away from the dizzy blonde. On the way home he had gotten stuck in traffic just past Sunset Boulevard, so he did not get to bed until late, and then he slept fitfully with the intricate musical arrangements perfected by Peterson flooding his weary mind. Rather than count sheep, he counted musical notes: eighths, sixteenths. He could envision the perfect fingering of the Negro artist. He hummed softly and willed himself to sleep. It seemed that he had just dozed off when the sound of screeching tires woke him up. He jumped out of bed, ran to the window and threw aside the threadworn drapes in time to see a car he just knew belonged to Los Tacones slow down. A rock was thrown from the car. As soon as the rock hit the rectory, the car sped off and away. Cabrones, he hissed, certain the pachucos were at it again.

Inside the church, people shuffled in and took their seats. On the main altar the tapered candles waited to be lit. In nearby pews restless children shoved each other as their parents growled at them. Father Francis was still in a bad mood. All morning he had snapped at the altar boys, especially at Marcos, whom he once caught swigging the consecrated wine. He usually hid the small liter of holy wine underneath the main altar. This morning he had smelled Marcos' breath and realized he would have to find a new hiding place. Again. Damn squirt, Father Ranger thought, brushing imaginary dust off his stole. I'll teach him! This time I'll tell his grandmother. She'll take care of him. He thought back to the many times he too felt like taking a sip of wine so as to relax while performing on the main altar. But he knew the dangers of sipping too much vino. The problem is, Marcos is so efficient, so fast, Father Francis thought. He can light candles, flip on lights, ring the bell and sip wine all at the same time. And when he's had a good gulp of wine he moves with the speed of lightning! Who can I get to replace him?

Father Francis was angry for another, more serious reason. The cleaners had not returned his favorite outfit, one made by Belguim nuns and given to him by the people of Thorpe. The chasuble was made of light chartruese silk with red and yellow embroidery. He wore it only on special occasions. He had planned to show the pachucos that he too owned cool "threads." More than anything, he liked to put on a good show. "Simple-minded people always appreciate fancy costumes," the seminarians had learned, "as they respect power. The power of the church!" Now, as he stood at his full height of just under six feet, dressed in full regalia, Father Ranger did indeed exsude power. He fiddled with the golden rope around his waist, angry at the numerous delays that accompanied most Mexican weddings. As he paced back and forth across the marble floor, he caught sight of Cricket and Tudi approaching the main altar. He hated to think of the last time he had seen Cricket.

Some weeks back on the night before Blanca and Cricket were to discuss the wedding banns, Father Ranger was entertaining his good friend Father Micheal Pius Murphy, who was visiting from the San Francisco diocese. Happy to be with his buddy, he had put on a Duke Ellington record and hummed along, sipping a cold beer. He prided himself on not being a racist, as were many of his Texan friends, and he particularly liked music played by Negroes. He often said of them, "one thing about Negroes, they sure make some good music."

During the two days that Father Murphy had visited, they had been to the beach, to Olvera Street and to the Natural History Museum. The two priests were sipping cold beer as a record began to play. The doorbell rang and Father Ranger reluctantly got up from the comfortable sofa to go to the door. Just before he undid the doorlatch, he put his beer glass behind a huge Bible, then slowly opened the door. He was shocked to see Cricket standing before him, dark glasses riding on his hawk-like nose, wearing his best pin-stripe jacket with huge shoulder pads and pants so draped that to the startled priest they resembled a skirt.

Cricket, nervous as hell, could only mumble, "Uhhh, Blanca and me, we . . . Me and my chick, uhhh my girlfriend want ta . . . "

"Yes?" Father Ranger fought to control his growing anger. He clearly remembered having told Blanche to come alone and was now fit-to-be-tied. He put his hand to his mouth, afraid the pachuco standing outside the door might smell the beer on his breath.

"Ohhh," Cricket began once more. "Blanca and me we wanna gets hitched, and we wanna see about the bands."

"Bands? You must mean the banns."

"Yeah. Them bands for the weddin."

"Can you come back tomorrow. I think your appointment was for . . . "

"Well, we was just riding around, and thought if ya wasn't doing nuttin, maybe we could . . . " Cricket squinted up at Father Ranger, the dark glasses shining in the bright porch light.

Just then Father Murphy, who was standing behind Father

Ranger, opened the door and extended his hand to Cricket saying, "Hello there. I'm Father Murphy. Well, well, getting married, did you say?"

"Yeah. Well ya see, my chick and me we wanna gets going wid the bands."

"Well, come right in! Come right in!" Father Murphy, his voice oozing Irish charm, opened the door and ushered the startled couple into the softly-lit room, lowered the record-player and turned to Father Ranger, who was speechless with fury. Father Murphy broke the silence.

"How wonderful to know young people today still seek to marry in the Holy Mother Church. Saint's be praised! How fortunate for you, Francis! Ever since the war, far too many couples elope to Las Vegas and are denied the sacraments. You are indeed to be congratulated." Father Murphy asked Blanca and Cricket to take a seat on the plaid sofa, then settled into a leather chair and said, "Come now Francis, get the forms."

Father Francis Ignatuis Ranger, his German blood flooding his face, knew he would burst a gasket. Outraged as he was at Father Murpy's impertinence, he dared not interfere, nor suggest to Blanca and Cricket they return another day. He knew that Father Murphy, as secretary to the archbishop, was expected to report all he saw and heard to His Eminence. Father Ranger recovered his composure, slid behind his desk, pulled open the middle drawer, selected a gold pen and began to fill out the marriage forms. Cabrones, he thought, as his shaking fingers fought to control the pen. Cabrones.

The wedding march was about to begin. From the choir loft the organist waited for a signal from a woman who now peeked out the window and would tell her when the wedding party was lined up and ready to march. Inside the sacristy Father Ranger fingered his chartruese stole and prepared to approach the communion rail to begin the show. His eyes still hurt; he could barely focus on the candles that flickered on the flower-bedecked altar. The sun shining through the stained glass windows made a pretty pattern on the marble floor as Father Francis moved forward. "Saint Francis help me," he prayed. "Help me get through this pachuco wedding." He pulled in his stomach, took a deep breath, adjusted his chasuble and slowly walked to his accustomed place at center stage.

All through mass Blanca thought she would faint. The small church was stifling hot. The smell of incense mixed with that of the pungent gardenias in her bouquet and the drooping altar flowers. Twice she tottered back and forth in the tight baby-doll shoes. Lucy grimaced at her with eyebrows raised in alarm. Blanca's face was bathed in sweat, her tight curls now hanging limply on her broad shoulders. Her mascara was running; her eyes were stinging. She had licked off most of her lipstick while waiting for the march to begin. The only thing that kept her from falling apart was knowing that without her support, Cricket would keel over. Blanca, her plump elbow stuck under his thin arm, literally held Cricket up! Although he now knelt, Cricket had twice slumped toward her, almost knocking her down. She had had to jab him in the ribs and glare at him as if to say, you better stay awake, buster! And now she was literally stuck. If she took her arm away, Cricket would slump over the communion rail and ruin the wedding. "I just gotta hold him up," Blanca told herself. "I just gotta."

Blanca was furious at Cricket. Intuition told her he had been out drinking with the guys the night before and was now hung over and falling asleep. On his wedding day! "This ain't how it's supposed ta be," sighed Blanca, on the verge of tears. "He shoulda stayed home." She remembered trying to tell Cricket not to go out. In a sweet, soft voice she had whispered, "Honey, you gotta go to bed early. Remember what the priest said."

"Yeah?"

"Yeah. He said the mass is gonna start at . . . "

"Yeah?"

Cricket, his eyes narrowing from behind the dark glasses, had given Blanca a dirty look. "No priest is gonna tell me what ta do," he hissed, flexing his large hands. He looked at his pale, nervous wife-to-be and added, "And no chick is gonna tell me not to go out, get it? I gotta be with my buddies, and show my cousins from Fresno a good time. Get with it, man!" Blanca said nothing more.

Inside the stuffy church Blanca glanced back and saw friends and relatives seated behind her and Cricket. She took a deep breath, steadied herself on the communion rail and smiled at the tall, gangly man next to her, whom she was restraining from falling over. His dark hair was plastered above his thin, gaunt face. The pock marks on his homely face looked larger than usual. The eyes behind the dark glasses were half-closed.

When Blanca had suggested he leave his dark glasses at home, Cricket had almost had a fit.

"Just this once, honey," Blanca had pleaded. "Please! We gotta look nice and . . . "

"No way," Cricket had screeched. "I'm gonna get hitched how I want. With my boppers, and that's it. Get it?"

Lucy had come to Blanca's rescue and told Cricket he had to take off the dark glasses during communion. "You gotta show some class, Cricket."

"That's why I wanna wear em."

"That's not what I mean."

"You got something to say?"

"Noh."

As the priest droned on in Latin, Blanca stared at the flickering candles on the altar. Everything looks so pretty, she sighed, except for Cricket in them dammed glasses. I know why he wore them! So he could fall asleep during mass. God, I hope nobody else notices. But I'll bet Tudi can tell. Lucy too. Just so he don't pass out! I'll pretend it's okay, she decided, and maybe nobody will see. She took a deep breath, adjusted her veil, glanced down at the offensive gardenias and swore to let Cricket have it once mass was over. But for now, she and Cricket had to act right. After all, everyone in the church was watching them.

This mass sure is long, Blanca thought. That Father Ranger sure knows a lot of prayers. He ain't stopped talking since we started, except when the choir sings. I wish he'd hurry it up before Cricket passes out. Twice Blanca tried to get Lucy's attention to ask for the time. Lucy was the only one who wore a watch, a gold Elgin bought at the Easy Credit. But Lucy, busy looking at the guys from out of town, ignored her.

While Blanca struggled to keep Cricket from keeling over, Lucy let her eyes wander slowly through the church. She arched her slender back, threw out her round, full breasts and heaved in and out. She turned slowy to the left, then to the right, determined not to be too obvious. From past experience Lucy knew that weddings were a good place to meet new guys. She also knew that she looked especially pretty this day, with her new, full chest that pushed against the purple taffeta of her formal. Now, if only I can latch onto a guy with a steady job and a nice convertible, life will be perfect, Lucy thought. She wet her lips, smoothed a wrinkle off her dress and once more looked around. Suddenly she spotted Willy, Cricket's cousin from Fresno. His brown eyes met her dark, slanted eyes. "Gosh, Willy sure is cute," whispered Lucy to Sally, who stood next to her. "I think he likes me! I can hardly wait till the dance!"

During the long wedding ceremony, Porky, the flower girl, began to get a stomach ache. She held her hand to her belly as if in pain, her pudgy face pale, her squinty eyes shut tight. Porky looked around for her mother and then, unable to stand the pain, she yanked at Blanca's sleeve. "Blanca, Blanca, I'm gonna be sick."

Blanca looked at the Junior Bridesmaid in disbelief. "Try to wait till we get outside," Blanca whispered. "Sit down and try to wait." Once Porky moved away, Blanca took a deep breath, adjusted her flowers and looked out the church window. I wish I could give her a piece of my mind right this minute. Damn little pig. That's what she gets for eating all them cookies right before mass. She better not get sick. That's all I need! First Cricket and now her. Shit! She leaned across Cricket, hoping to catch Lucy's attention, but Lucy was busy adjusting her bra.

The mass dragged on. Now and then the choir sang, waking those who had dozed off. In a front pew, Blanca's mother beamed with pride. At last she too could brag about her daughter's white wedding, the beautiful gown, the ivory-white veil with the traditional organge blossoms and the lovely gardenia bouquet, which when dry would be preserved forever. Blanca's wedding would be a topic of conversation that would occupy her for the next five years, barring the birth of grandchildren, of course. Blanca's mother wiped a tear off her lined, brown cheek. Sí! My daughter is a lovely bride. My pretty, pretty daughter. Ahhh, if only the groom was not such a rat!

The bride and groom knelt down at the rail as the priest prepared for communion. Blanca tried to concentrate on the mass, but nothing made any sense to her. She dreaded having to sit through the communion service, which she thought was next. She knew it was customary for the bride and groom and all their attendants to recive communion. Most of Blanca's friends had made it a point to go to confession so as to join the bride and groom at the communion rail, to offer them not only their best wishes, but also a communion prayer. But Cricket and the guys never went to church.

Blanca had hinted to Cricket that they should both receive communion at their wedding mass. But Cricket had thrown a shit fit, screamed at her and told her where to go. Now, as she watched Father Ranger come near the communion rail, Blanca felt uneasy. She sat back to allow Lucy and the others approaching to receive communion. Blanca felt ashamed at not being able to receive communion on this terribly important day, but had broken the mandatory fast by eating sweet bread. But it's more than that, Blanca admitted to herself, I never really wanted to, unless Cricket did too. And since Cricket never went to confession, then there's nuthin for me to do but sit here and watch the others. But, dammit, it sure would be nice to do everything right."

Darn Cricket, Blanca grumbled. He could have gone to confession if he'd tried. But no, all he wants to do is be tough and make sure the guys don't see him in church. Damn, he spoiled everything for me. Now people are gonna talk. I hate to admit it, but Cricket sure is stubborn. What about when we have kids? We won't be able to baptize them? Blanca knew Cricket was already calling the shots, making the decisions. What will he be like later? she wondered. What will I do then? As she stood for the benediction, Blanca saw Porky moving toward Lucy with her hand held to her mouth.

"Lucy, I'm gonna throw up! I'm gonna . . . " Porky, her small face twisted at the mouth, pulled at Lucy's dress.

"Shit," hissed Lucy, her eyes bulging, "you better not . . ." She jerked back, teetering on her high heels seconds before Porky, hands clutched to her round stomach, leaned over and promptly vomited on the satin cushions made by Aunt Chonita.

"Sona-va-beesh," grumbled Cricket, now fully awake. He stepped back quickly, holding his dark pants aside.

"Jesus, Maria y Jose!" exclaimed Aunt Chonita from her pew.

"I'm gonna pass out," cried Blanca, suddenly dizzy. "I'm gonna pass out." Her eyes glazed over, her heart thumped loudly. She swayed backwards but managed to stay on her swollen feet. The thought of having to face Father Ranger kept her from fainting, as did knowing her mother and Aunt Chonita were watching. She took a deep breath and turned to face the priest, who was staring down at the bride and groom, his steely eyes narrowing on the cushions. He took a deep breath, then continued with the blessing. He raised his arms high and wide, prayed "Dominus Vobiscum," then sprinkled Blanca and Cricket with holy water as he intoned the special blessing reserved for newlyweds. He turned to face the tabernacle. When the priest's back was to the congregation, Aunt Chonita reached across the front pew and handed Blanca a handkerchief. Trying hard not to look at Porky's mess and making an effort not to gag, the pale-faced bride frantically wiped at the cusions. She avoided smearing the blue-birds entwined with red flowers. When Blanca finished, her stomach heaving, she bunched the hanky into a ball, then gave a sudden jerk to the silk lasso on her shoulders that bound her to the groom, hoping to alert Cricket, who was once more asleep behind his glasses.

Right before the final benediction, as she turned her head to adjust her orange blossoms, Blanca saw Petey was crying. "What now," she sighed, her hands shaking. "What now? I'm sure sorry I let my relatives choose my ring-bearer and flower girl. Shit, everything is going wrong."

"I gotta pee," whispered Petey to Blanca as he edged around the damaged cushions. "I gotta makes chi."

Blanca, her mouth wide open, stared at Petey, who tugged at her sleeve. She felt her head would burst. The tight headpiece that pressed against her thick hair was making her see double. She squeezed her eyes tight, hoping the fainting spell would go away, and then she stared hard at Cricket, who glared back. Just as Blanca turned to speak to Lucy, Petey went past and tripped, brushing his face on Cricket's pantleg, and leaving a trail of snot on Cricket's black pants.

Cricket, trying not to stare at the cushions being picked up by Sally, moved to let Petey pass, forgetting that he was roped to Blanca by the white silk lasso. He stuck out his hand to adjust the rope only to brush against the snot.

"Son-ava-beesh," hissed Cricket, his hand on his pantleg.

"Go in peace," sang Father Ranger. "Amen," responded the congregation.

Father Ranger closed the tabernacle and adjusted his stole while below him the bride and groom removed the rope that had connected them throughout the mass. He noticed the cushions being picked up by a bridesmaid and saw the ring-bearer dash out a side door. He approached the newlyweds, said "Congratulations," in a tight, clipped voice, then walked toward the sacristy. Just then the organist began the recessional and everybody stood up. It was time to march out. "It's almost over," whispered Lucy, adjusting Blanca's bouquet. "Try not to . . . "

"I'll be okay!" answered Blanca Muñoz, now Mrs. Sammy-the-Cricket Lopez, as she smiled at the congregation. She took a deep breath, adjusted her veil, cupped the gardenia bouquet in her wide hands and, arms entwined, she marched down the aisle with her new husband.

Once outside Saint Stephen the Martyr Church, Cricket yanked a handkerchief out of Tudi's pocket and wiped at his pants, swearing softly at Petey, who had suddenly disappeared. Blanca stood smiling while her friends and relatives gathered around her to offer congratulations. Lucy secured her bra straps once more while Rosie checked her Tangee Blush lipstick. Porky, now fully recovered, snuggled against her mother. In a corner Petey surrendered to his mother, who gently cleaned his nose.

Cricket, his dark glasses glinting against the hot sun, grinned at Tudi. The pants incident was now forgotten. Behind the dark boppers his eyes were once more alert. He turned to Blanca and said, "We dids it. We gots hitched!" Blanca stared at Cricket, happy at the change in her new husband, then joined the reception line that, according to Mexican custom, formed outside the church. After a little while the wedding party piled into the gaily decorated cars and took off down the street. Honk, honk, honk. Up and down the streets of Taconos went Los Tacones. Honk, honk, honk. The kids playing in the street watched the parade of Chevies and Fords go by and ran after them shouting, "Here they come!"

Chapter Three

The Wedding Breakfast

The Wedding Breakfast, or el almuerzo, as it was popularly called, was held in Lucy's house, three blocks away from the church. Although the breakfast was only for the wedding party, already there were numerous hangers-on, friends and relatives who immediately after the ceremony had followed the crowd. They made themselves at home, knowing full well that because of Mexican courtesy, they would not be asked to leave but could remain to eat sweet bread and chocolate. By the time the wedding party left the church—after signing the marriage certificate and receiving Father Ranger's gruff congratulations—and had arrived at Lucy's house, the small living room was jam-packed with people. Noisy, boisterous children ran among their elders, most of whom were standing because ther was no room to sit.

Lucy did not bother to ask her mother's permission to have the breakfast at home. Long used to having her way with her easily intimidated mother, she merely told her. What Lucy most wanted was to impress the bridesmaids and ushers with the new furniture now sitting in the cramped living room: a blue velvet sofa and matching chairs bought recently at the Credit Now Furniture Mart in San Cristobal. She had saved the tips earned at Tottie's Place for some time, then gave what she thought was a good down payment. She enlisted the help of two burly customers of the cantina who owned a pickup. They lugged in the furniture, which smelled of newly sawed wood and mothballs. It was Lucy's pride and joy.

And when they see my new sofa they're gonna know I gots class. Two days before the wedding Lucy directed her mother to clean the house. Wash the curtains! Mop the floor! Hide anything that looks bad under the bed!

"Put some clean towels in the toilet."

"Sí, m'ijita."

"And hide them ugly shairs."

"Where will people sit?"

"Let em stand!"

"Ay, Dios!"

"And make chure you gots enough stuff."

"Ay, sí!"

"And keeps the shocolate hot. Get it?"

Once the velvet sofa and chair were installed, Lucy put starched doilies on their back rests. She stepped back to admire her possessions. Everything appeared in order. The curtains of maroon and beige flowers looked clean enough. Not even the worn seams showed. The small windows shone squeaky clean. The green linoleum still had marks from Lucy's high heels, but the blue sofa and chair were what stood out. Next I gotta gets a coffee table, thought Lucy, them plastic ones like a kidney or somethin with skinny legs. I seen some at the Easy Credit . . . And when I pays all that off, I'll charge me two lamps and some fancy ashtrays. Last of all I'll get me a hope chest of the wood that smells so good and start puttin stuff in it. Anyway, when I get hitched, I'm gonna take all my stuff wiz me . . . and if my mama don't like it, tough. Once satisfied that the plastic sheets covering the blue velvet sofa were in place, Lucy concentrated on her dress and makeup, leaving her mother to prepare the wedding breakfast of sweet bread and chocolate.

After the mass the wedding party, paper flowers blowing in the early morning breeze, cruised the streets of Taconos. Up and down they went, honking aloud, taking the corners slowly, alert for kids and dogs. Inside the lead car, the bride smiled at the world, her wide face radiant beneath the creamy azares and misty veil. In the trailing Chevies and Fords, the bridesmaids and ushers stretched out, adjusted outfits, lit cigarettes, and tried to appear bored with the whole thing. After all, this wasn't the first wedding of a Tacones guy.

For most of the ushers, all members of the Tacones, the day was just beginning. But the worst part was over: the long wedding ceremony with Father Ranger presiding.

Inside the car with white flowers sat Blanca, staring at traffic. Next to her sat the pale-looking groom, his thick Indian hair reeking of pomade. In the front seat Tudi lit a cigarette. Beside him huddled Petey, the ring-bearer. Against the door sprawled Porky, munching on small fruit-filled pies slipped to her by her mother. As though told to be quiet, the kids in the front seat remained silent.

The parade of cars, now covered with a fine film of dirt, finally screeched to a stop in front of Lucy's house. The bride and groom had arrived! Inside the house, Lucy's mother and the neighbor women scrambled to re-light the old stove, their voices rising with excitement, aware that the newlyweds and their attendants would soon be inside.

Inside the house the wedding party, including the young attendants, squeezed their way past others into the small living room, where the new sofa and chair covered in large plastic sheets awaited them. They stood around talking loudly, trying to look sophisticated, as cigarettes were quickly passed around.

"Man, whatta long mass. I almost passed out," giggled Sally, hitching up her long dress.

"Yeah, man! I'm so hot already, and it's only nine-thirty!" added Rosie, looking enviously at Lucy's tiny waist and newly formed breasts.

"Pass me the Maybelline," said Josie to Sally. "My mascara is smeared. I wanna look good in the pitchers."

"Gimme the comb first. My rat's falling out."

In the tiny kitchen, the women wearing brightly colored aprons stirred the chocolate in the blue pots and they arranged the Mexican sweet bread in large, colorful platters.

The ushers, being men, were served first. El Pan Tostado, grabbed two pieces of bread and a mug of chocolate. Then he popped the bread into his generous mouth, swallowed the chocolate, belched aloud and went back into the kitchen. He returned with a plate full of ginger-flavored sweet breads shaped like pigs. Across the room Sally nudged Rosie.

"Man, look at Paulie eat. He's finished the ones I like."

"He's such a pig! He used to work with my uncle. He said Paulie takes two lunch boxes ta work!"

"No?"

"Yeah, his momma packs him three sandwiches and six tacos in one. The other one's fer little cakes and cookies."

"What a pig! I chure wouldn't want him for my husband."

"Don't worry. I hear he likes Tencha's sister."

"Bubbles?"

"Yeah. Bubbles the whale. I hear all they do is cruise around and stuff themselves with taquitos."

"What pigs!"

"I'm telling you!"

Tudi stood against a window, nibbling on a soft bread seasoned with anise. Unaccustomed to his new teeth, he was having trouble chewing. He already had turned down the pumpkin turnovers, his favorites. As he chewed, he kept looking toward the window, hoping that if his teeth fell out, nobody would see. I coulda been havin a good time, Tudi sighed, if only Lucy didn't makes fun of my teeths. Nobody said I looks like a Jack o' Lantern until Lucy started that shit . . . and didn't wanna be my partner. Now I gots to make payments . . . but at least I can smile for the pichers. Too bad Cricket don't wanna help me pay for em. After all, it was his fault I gots them knocked out.

Across from Tudi, Cricket slouched against the porch, sipping hot chocolate. Disgusted with Paulie, Cricket puffed on a Camel, his eyes half-closed behind the dark frames. Cricket was anxious to get going to L.A. There was a rumor going around that the Planchados were gonna jump Los Tacones sometime today. Right before mass Topo had approached Cricket to say, "The Planchados are getting things ready."

"Yeah? What things?"

"Chains. And Skippy's been talking . . . "

"What he say?"

"He wantsa dance at yer weddin . . . "

"Yeah? Well, let them come, I'll show em how ta dance!"

Cricket, amused with how things were going, took a long drag from his cigarette. He sauntered to the alley to check things out. Although it was still morning, it paid to be alert. I gotta be ready for the cops or the Planchados. Ain't nobody gonna catch me sleepin. He now looked to the right, then across the narrow alley behind Lucy's house, but saw nothing, so he started back to the wedding breakfast.

When finished gorging on sweet bread, the ushers joined Cricket. They puffed on fresh cigarettes, combed messy ducktails, then checked out the cars, looking for damage done to the shiny chrome during that morning's ride through the rock strewn streets of Taconos. They lingered outdoors, smoking Camel cigarettes, anxious to get going to the photo studio. And to L.A. where things were always jumpin!

The bridesmaids ate quickly but daintily, fearful of spilling chocolate on their pretty dresses. There was no time to change hair styles for the photo session. But they did have time to add another layer of pancake makeup or some rouge. The brightly-clad bridesmaids squeezed into the tiny bathroom, leaving makeup streaks on the thin cotton towels. When she saw they were alone, Rosie whispered to Sally, "Gosh! Lucy sure gots big tits all of a sudden!"

"She bought them."

"Huh?"

"They're falsies. She gots them in L.A. when her and Blanca got the dresses. But don't say nuthin, 'cause she'll get you."

"Oh yeah?"

"Yeah. She wants the guys from outta town to think she's got a real cool chape. Big tits, a little waist and . . . "

"Jeez, who she trying ta fool? Yesterday she had two fried eggs and today . . . "

"I'm tellin ya!" Giggling to herself, Sally heard movement near the door, so she covered her mouth with her hand. She gave her dress a pat, straightened her hat and walked out the door. At least I don't need falsies, Sally smiled, throwing out her chest. I gots too much already!

Lucy held court in the small living room. Aware of how impressed everyone was with the sofa, she now felt it safe to go outside to see what was happening. She especially wanted to see what Sally had to say about the new furniture, being that Sally thought she was so hot 'cause her house was bigger and had a big front porch.

"Gosh! Whatta purdy sofa."

"Yeah! Pure velvet!"

"Where did she gets it? In L.A.?"

"No, in Sancristofas. At the Easy Credit . . . "

"No kiddin?"

"Yeah. She gots it for nuthin down."

"Man! How suki."

"And the payments . . . "

Fully aware of her sudden rise in status, Lucy re-entered the room and joined her friends sitting gingerly on the sofa arms. Most of them were not quite sure of how to sit on plastic. Only El Pan Tostado was sprawled out on the blue velvet chair. His sister owned an identical sofa set, except hers was green velvet. El Pan Tostado felt comfortable amidst such luxury. He leaned back, lit a Lucky Strike and waited to be served another helping of sweet bread.

Chapter Four

The Pictures

The cortege of brightly decorated cars headed down San Cristobal Road past the towns of Razgo and Burbank towards Los Angeles. In the lead was Tudi's '46 Chevy draped with huge white flowers. In the back seat sat Mr and Mrs. Samuel Lopez. Petey, the reluctant ring-bearer and Porky, the Junior Bridesmaid, were sitting up front. Behind them followed six other cars festooned with crepe paper flowers. In a snazzy maroon Merc rode Tere and her partner Topo. Lucy sat alone in the back seat. Tere and Topo puffed away on Camel cigarettes and now and then swigged from a bottle of Jim Beam which earlier had been passed around by other Tacones. Lucy felt happy. Already she had caught some guys looking at her newly formed breasts, their eyes narrowing slightly. Let them stare, Lucy grinned, pushing down on the falsies that now and then shifted. Let them stare. Look but don't touch is my motto and ain't nobody gonna change that.

Every time the lead car reached an intersection, the others would line up behind it and honk loudly. Down the highway they flew, passing every car on the road. Everyone who heard knew it was a wedding procession. Everyone loves a wedding; everyone loves the bride and groom! As the cars wove in and out of traffic in perfect rythmn, they made a pretty picture. Tudi's car, the only one with white flowers, shone from three coats of wax. Topo's maroon and white convertible was decorated with purple flowers made by Lucy. The other cars had assorted colored flowers.

Traffic was heavy. Tudi, his warm brown eyes squinting against the sun, tried to concentrate on his driving. Next to him Petey and Porky jostled each other against the door, until Tudi hissed at them, "Whatcha think you're doing? Ya want us to gets in a crach?"

Damn, I wish somebody else was leading, lamented Tudi. I forgets where to turn. He leaned over to change the radio station, aware the music was too square. Any minute now Cricket would begin to cuss up a storm and tell him to change it. I gotta keeps cool, Tudi grumbled, as he smiled down at Petey. Tudi was determined not to aggravate Cricket this day. Not that it would take much to do it. I gots ta play it cool, Tudi vowed, or Cricket is gonna shit all over me. He glanced around at the moving traffic, twirled the radio dial back and forth, and was so intent on changing the radio station that he missed the Hill Street exit for Los Angeles. By the time he straightened out and turned to look out the rear window, the other cars were heading for the Hill Street exit towards Chinatown and the Los Angeles Photo Studio.

In the backseat Blanca smiled at Cricket. She felt happy. When leaving the church she had spotted her mother near the back. In her eyes were tears of happiness for her Blanca, her youngest daughter, who had redeemed the family honor by having a big church wedding.

It was worth all the trouble, thought Blanca, stifling a yawn. Now my mama gots somethin to brag about. And pretty soon she's gonna have the wedding pichers and . . . Suddenly Blanca looked out the window. Shit! They had passed the Hill Street turnoff! She flipped her veil aside, then glanced out the back window and between two crepe paper flowers. What she saw gave her chills: a parade of flower-bedecked cars that zoomed right, horns honking and disappearing.

Darn, Blanca thought, sitting up in the seat. Tudi's lost again and Cricket's gonna be pissed off 'cause he took the wrong turn. How can he be so dumb. He shoulda listened to Sally, or Lucy. Man alive! Now we're gonna get separated and be late for the pichers. Oh darn it! She slumped back onto the seat, trying to avoid Cricket's scowl.

Tudi drove on, his small mouth moving up and down as he chewed a wad of Juicy Fruit. He was perspiring like never before, partly from the heat, partly because he could feel Cricket's eyes burning through his thick skull. He kept his brown eyes on the asphalt road and continued to drive straight ahead as though he knew where he was going. Just then he spotted a familiar landmark, made a swift left turn and went careening down a steep street that ended in an empty railroad yard.

"Where the hell ya going, Tudi?" screeched Cricket. "You

gonna take a train or sumthin?"

Tudi, his throat suddenly dry, took a breath and squeaked, "I thoughts Main was right here, man. Uhhhh, it used ta be around here. I knows it."

"Well, find et. We gotta gets to them pichers."

Just then Petey pressed his hands against his crotch and began to wail. "Tudi, Tudi, I gotta make chi. I gotta piss."

"You what?" exclaimed Tudi, mopping his brow. You what?"

"I gotta pee."

"You gotta wait," Tudi answered, eyes glued on the rearview mirror. "You gotta wait."

"Son-of-a-beesh," hissed Cricket, his eyes bulging behind the big boppers. He flung his arms across the back seat, his duck-tail flipping in the air, then glared at Blanca, trying to make up his mind who to yell at first. "Whatcha gonna do, man, take the kid to piss or get us to the pichers? Man, whatta lota jive shit this is." Then, in a sudden change of heart, Cricket shifted in his seat, moved close to Tudi and in a calm voice said, "Give a U-turn so the kid can go to the toledo."

Tudi quickly grabbed the steering wheel, relieved at Cricket's tone of voice, then gave a fast U-turn off the main road and turned into the first gas station he saw, a tin-roofed shack with several gas pumps and a water fountain. As the flower trimmed car came to an abrupt stop, Petey jumped out and ran to the bathroom located in the back. Inside the stuffy car everyone sat quietly. Tudi's nerves were shot, Porky felt sick and Cricket was pissed off. Blanca could feel her wet armpits; the sleeves of her dress were pulling. She looked out the car window at the quiet street, the slow hum of cars going by.

Gosh, I sure hope them guys don't gets mad, Blanca sighed, twitching at her hem now caught on her baby doll pumps. Especially Lucy. I chure don't wanna get to the pichers all messy 'cause then I'll look like shit . . . and everybody else is gonna look better. That Petey is a pest. I shoulda gots Joey instead.

Just then Petey ran out, trotted to the car, yanked open the door, pushed Porky aside and made himself comfortable.

"Ya? Ready?"

"No." The sharp retort came from Porky, who without asking

Blanca's permission, scampered out of the seat so swiftly she almost fell onto the sidewalk. "I gotta go too," she squealed, making a face at Petey. "Me too!"

"Jezus," grumbled Cricket. "How come everybody's gotta go piss? Shit, if we keep stoppin, we ain't ever gonna make et to the peechers."

Within minutes Porky, a piece of chocolate clinging to her mouth, came out of the bathroom and took her seat in front. She elbowed Petey, grabbed her flowered-basket off the floorboard and sat back, ready for the ride. They sped off; in the front seat a relaxed Tudi turned on the car radio, lit a Camel cigarette and turned the radio dial in time to hear, "I Want a Sunday Kind of Love."

"Turn it up, Tudi," asked Blanca. "That one's my favorite song. They sure sing it good! Don'tcha think so, honey? I sure hope Gato plays it at the dance, don'tcha honey?"

Cricket, busy adjusting his dark glasses, responded with a snort, stuck out his big feet and lit up a Lucky Strike. In the front, Tudi frantically looked around for a street sign, aware that the small quiet street he was on was taking them nowhere. He slicked his hair back, stuck a Juicy Fruit into his dry mouth and took a deep breath. His stomach was in a knot. Twice he had ignored Blanca's suggestion that he stop and ask for directions. He now looked at the gas indicator which was below the half-way mark. I sure am stuped, Tudi thought. I shouda filled er up. I shoulda asked Frankie to take the lead. That way Cricket could shit all over him. He drove on, his sweaty hands gripping the steering wheel, as he held on for dear life.

"Are we lost?" asked a repentent Petey.

"You're stupid," barked Porky, adjusting her dress sash. "We're not lost, are we Tudi?"

"Uhhhhhh. Justa liddle." Tudi stepped on the gas, adjusted his bow tie and gave a right turn, humming along with the music. Just as the song ended, he realized they had just passed the gas station again.

In the back seat Blanca moved close to Cricket. Her hands twitched in her lap, nervously pulling at her dress. She was trying hard not to cry, but her brown eyes were overflowing. We're lost and everybody at the pichers is gonna be waiting. And Cricket's gonna get all pissed and drink too much and . . . She leaned forward to whisper something to Tudi, but Cricket's heavy hand pulled her back.

They drove in silence for what to Blanca seemed like hours until Blanca, on the verge of tears, shouted to a beleagured Tudi, "Go down Main."

"Yeah, okay," answered Tudi as he manuevered the car around to where Blanca indicated. He made a fast turn, then slammed on the brakes. "Shit, we're back in the railroad tracks," Tudi groaned, mopping his damp forehead. "How could I be so dumb, dumb?" He put the car in reverse, smiled weakly at Cricket, patted Petey on the leg and once more turned left.

In the car the newlyweds sat contemplating the quiet street and the railroad yard they were now familiar with. Blanca, her face pinched and white, bit her lips to hold back the threatening tears. Next to her, Cricket stretched his long legs the length of the car. Near the window Porky played with the door handle, aware that the newlyweds were nervous and angry at Tudi and Petey . . . and probably her too. She smiled at Tudi who kept glancing around hoping Hill Street would materialize.

Porky was hungry. Her stomach was beginning to growl, a sign that it was almost lunch time. The three pieces of sweet bread and four cups of hot chocolate gulped during the breakfast had only whetted her apetite. Even the chocolate candy eaten in the bathroom had not satisfied her. She pulled her stomach in and out, testing to see whether it could hold out until she got food. Finally, unable to stand it any longer, she pushed Petey aside, moved across the seat and said to a startled Tudi, "I'm hungry."

"Whatcha say?"

"I'm hungry," Porky repeated, her mouth turned up in a pout. She twirled her flowered basket and once more said, "I'm so hungry! I wanna eat something."

"Shit," hissed Cricket from the rear. "She just ate a candy. No wonder they calls her a . . . "

"I wanna eat," Porky insisted, her mouth beginning to pucker. "My momma says I gotta eat or I'll get sick." She shifted her plump bottom, jabbed Petey in the ribs, then crunched against the lumpy seat where she continued to whine. Just then Tudi gave a sharp turn right. Porky almost flew out the door, saved only by an alert Tudi who grabbed her by the dress sash, which almost tore in two. Frightened by the near miss, Porky put her plump arm around Petey. After that she remained silent, sullen and hungry.

Tudi, his eyes on the gas indicator, was in a sweat. Not knowing what else to do, he stepped on the brake and came to a screeching halt. He waited till a dusty brown car came alongside the Chevy, then said to Blanca, "I'm gonna ask this guy which way ta go, okay?"

"I'll ask him," volunteered Blanca, fearful Tudi might once more forget the directions. "Let me, okay?" She swiftly rolled down the car window, stuck her veiled head out and shouted, "Hey mister. Which way to Main?"

"Go back to the gas station and turn left at the light."

"Thanks a lot."

Blanca closed the car window, smoothed down her dress and smiled sweetly at Cricket. "Gosh, whatta mess, huh, honey?" She moved close and carefully pulled at Cricket's lapel. "Honey, honey. Did you hear what I . . . " But Cricket only grunted. His eyes behind the dark glasses were half-closed, his thin mouth half-open. Blanca stared down at her homely bridegroom, a tender smile on her face. My honey's hungover, she realized, and don't even know we're still lost. Tanks, God! She pulled at her white veil, secured the orange blossom crown, took a deep breath and smiled at Tudi, who smiled back. Next to her, black boppers dangling from his hawk nose, the groom sat stretched across the length of the seat to sleep off the hangover.

By the time the car bearing the bride and groom arrived at the Los Angeles Photo Studio on Main Street, most of the parking places were taken. The bride and groom were forced to park a block away in an alley across Main, where sleepy winos smiled at Blanca's clumsy attempt to cross the busy street in her long, flowing gown. Blanca looked tired, yet she smiled at the moving cars. But Cricket, dark eyes hidden behind the boppers, looked really shot. His greasy duck-tail askew, pant legs wrinkled and black bow-tie coming untied, he lagged behind the perspiring bride. Behind them trudged an embarrassed Tudi with Petey and Porky at his side. Once clear of traffic, they fielded their way past cars and trucks parked alongside the street, then walked the short block to the studio.

In the lead, Blanca walked briskly toward the studio. She could smell her wet armpits and the velvet-like gardenias. I sure hope I don't stain my Scarlett O'Hara dress, she moaned. I don't wan spots ta chow in the wedding pichers. And my feet are gonna kill me. Man, them chooz chure pinch. She flipped back her veil, wet her dry lips and tried to appear calm, in control. Now and then she smiled at Cricket, who looked the other way. They walked into the studio, smiling as though nothing had happened, not the least bit apologetic for the delay. They were the stars of the show. After all, Blanca had whispered to Cricket, we're the most important peoples in the weddin. Ain't nuttin anyone can say, not even Lucy. Can't gets no pichers taken without us. Ha, ha, ha.

Inside the unventilated studio, the photographer's assistant, a tall, skinny woman, was busy lining up the wedding party. She yanked at Sally, then at Paulie, trying to fit everyone against a backdrop of climbing vines and tropical flowers. "We're gonna look like Tarzan and Jane," snickered Lucy, tugging at her head-piece.

"Yeah," hissed Sally, bending her head close to Rosie, "and Lucy can be the monkey!"

"Whatcha saying, Sally?" asked Lucy, hands on hips. "You gots somethin ta say? Come on esa, you and me are gonna . . . "

"She wasn't saying nuthin," cried Rosie, alarmed at the start of yet another argument between Lucy and Sally. "But I don't like them vines. They look too creepy."

"I can change them," volunteered the assistant, looking more nervous every minute. "Stay still and I'll change em."

"Well, do it, man," snarled Lucy, "ain't that whatcha gets paid fer?"

"Oh look! Here come Blanca and Cricket," cried a relieved Sally. "Now we can really start the pichers."

Everyone began to talk at the same time. Where was you? Whatcha do, get lost? It's about time. We was getting ready to call the cops.

"Hey, Tudi," chortled Frankie, "where was ya? We was

afraid the Planchados had gots you. Topo and me was gonna come and look for you in a minute."

"Shut up, Frankie," whispered Rosie, leaning back into the vines, "don't say nuthin or we're gonna be here all day."

Just then the photographer asked everyone to be quiet, so he could get started. Sally nudged Rosie, then stopped giggling.

All talk stopped. Everyone tried to look serious, even Mudo who giggled at everything. The bored assistant pushed a button near the door. Instantly a screen depicting a wide meadow with blue skies and small white clouds descended in front of the vines. From below, Blanca sighed in relief. Rosie elbowed a nervous Sally. Lucy smiled her approval. Cricket frowned. Once more Lucy was in charge.

While waiting for the bride and groom to show up, the photographer, a balding man with thick bifocals and a round behind, and his assistant had lined up the wedding party, leaving a wide gap in the middle for Blanca and Cricket. The ushers, beginning with Topo, were lined up first. Then the bridesmaids were positioned, each girl in front of her partner. Everyone was cautioned to stand up straight, look up, smile, look to the left, look to the right. While the photographer adjusted lights, rechecked the camera and crawled underneath the hood attached to it, his assistant went around offering the perspiring group Kleenex from a box kept nearby. Once the bride and groom arrived, the group settled down. The bride and groom were told to stand in the middle. Blanca's dress was spread out like a fan; her bouquet raised to hide her bulging waistline. When at last Blanca and Cricket looked picture perfect, the assistant signaled to the photographer. Blanca smiled wide; Cricket grinned. Lucy tried to look glamorous, while Sally smiled her usual smile. Rosie pouted, Porky too. Everyone breathed a sigh of relief. At last!

But before the camera lens clicked, the harried assistant, sensing a problem, immediately signaled to the photographer. All movement ceased. From the top row Topo rolled his eyes, a sign that he was bored stiff. Next to him, Paulie fidgeted with his bow tie, tired of the delay, anxious to sip from the small flask hidden inside his jacket.

"Now what?" asked Lucy, stepping down to the floor. "What

the hell's. . . . "

"You don't fit," wailed the nervous assistant, moving quickly aside. "There are too many of you for the . . . I mean, we have to rearrange you all and . . . "

"Whatcha talking about, man?" hissed an irritable Lucy, "Aint't this a studio? Just whatcha mean?"

The thin woman did not answer, but instead lifted a latch from underneath the last row of steps removed several small stools, then stood back to see how she should arranged them. "You'll have to step down," she intoned. "All of you will have to . . . "

From behind a dark curtain she and a young man, busy ogling the bridesmaids, hauled out more steps, which they arranged around and in-between the other stools. Then the entire process of lining up the wedding party was repeated. The sweating ushers were shown to their places; the disheveled bridesmaids followed, including an irritable Lucy, who was fit to be tied. The ring bearer and flower girl were positioned in front of the bridal couple. Petey's nose was wiped clean by the alert assistant. Once more the rotund photographer crept under the camera. "Smile, please," urged the skinny assistant. "Look this way please," hissed the photographer, holding up a card in his left hand. "Everyone look straight at this . . . "

"Blanca," cried Petey, his hand to his crotch, "I gotta make chi."

"Shit," hissed Blanca, pulling at her bra strap with one hand. "Double shit." She moved back as Tudi, who felt responsible for Petey, tapped her on the shoulder, then quietly moved to the front, yanked Petey with one hand and prepared to take him to the bathroom.

"Son-ava-vichi," groaned Cricket, "that kid sure can piss."

"We'll take a short break," shouted the assistant, holding a tissue to her forehead. "Then line up again, okie dokie?"

Blanca caught up with Tudi and Petey, remembering that Petey was her nephew. She wanted to spare Tudi from putting up with more of Cricket's shit. She took Petey's hand and led him to the women's bathroom.

Inside the women's bathroom, which reeked of Pine Sol, Blanca tried not to retch while she waited for Petey to finish. She felt sick. The dark, stuffy studio had made her sleepy and the stench coming from her bouquet made her want to throw up. But I better not let Lucy know it. Or anyone else. I wish I could tell Cricket, but he don't care about nuttin. Except for the dance goin on tonight. I better keep it to myself. She hurried Petey out of the toilet stall, then tucked in her growling stomach, wet a Kleenex and held it to her sweating neck. She felt a little better. With a slight tilt to her head, Blanca walked toward the darkened room, only to find that it was almost empty. The wedding party had disappeared! Only Sally remained near the water fountain, talking with the pale assistant.

"Where's everybody?" cried an astounded Blanca, gripping her bouquet tight. "Where's Cricket?"

"They took off," grumbled Sally. "Lucy said we could.."

"Lucy?"

"Yeah, them photographer was taking too long . . . and we're tired," finished Sally, trying not to look at Blanca.

"But . . . "

"They had to change the lights . . . and put on more steps. And then Porky thought she was gonna throw up . . . so Lucy decided we needed a break, that's all," finished Sally, looking contrite. "I'm sorry, Blanca, but . . . "

Sally did not have to explain that the group was tired, hungover and that to a person the wedding party had decided to take a break. While the photographer and his assistant looked helplessly at them, the men dressed in black tuxedos had strutted out the front door. And the chicks in pastel formals had then scooted off to the women's bathroom. She looked at Blanca, who was swinging her white satin purse to and fro, trying not to scream.

Outside the photo studio, Cricket and Tudi checked out the cars going by, then took off towards Main Street. From past experience, Cricket knew there were plenty of bars around. Fully awake now, he threw back his shoulders, kicked out with his black shoes and walked briskly towards Ernie's Bar, a place he had spotted on the way over. Paulie, Frankie and Mudo followed their leader. Tudi and Topo brought up the rear, having first stopped to take a fast piss. Once inside the dark bar, Cricket chose a booth near the back, checked the door leading to the alley, then ordered beers for everyone. Cigarettes were passed around, as was Frankie's flask. Cricket puffed at the cigarette that dangled from his thin mouth, flexed his hands, stretched his long legs and grinned from behind the dark glasses. He felt good now, in control of the situation. Sitting in a dark bar having a beer made him feel sophisticated, suave. The Big Cheese. Visibly relaxed, Cricket looked around at the Tacones, his buddies. He raised his glass and in a gruff voice said, "Here's to the dance."

The reason for being in Los Angeles, the pictures, was soon forgotten as the ushers sat down to enjoy a break from the wedding activities. When Tudi and Topo finally drifted in and squeezed into the dim-lit booth, everyone smiled. Los Tacones were together at last! Everyone drank. Toasts to Cricket and Blanca were made. Behind his dark glasses Cricket could barely see the outline of his beer glass. The party was getting good and everyone was finally relaxing, when the bar door opened and in stormed Lucy.

When Lucy realized the guys were heading for a bar, she decided to say nothing to Sally or Rosie. Why look for competiton? Instead, she told Tere she was going to get her purse from the car. Once out the studio door, she took off for Ernie's Bar. After all, she reasoned, this was L.A. and there were bound to be a lot of guys just waiting to meet her. The very idea of walking into a strange, dark bar made her heart thump. Just before entering the bar she assumed a pose, just like Joan Crawford in the movies. She wet her thin lips, puffed up her falsies and made her entrance.

Lucy stood silhouetted against the bar until sure the guys had seen her. Then she walked over to the back booth, sidled up to Cricket and took a sip from his beer. She dusted off imaginary dust from Cricket's lapel, then in her brassy voice, just like Ava Gardner's, said, "Come on, you guys. We're gonna be late for the food. It's almost two o'clock and we ain't even taken the pichers. Them old ladies like to serve the food hot."

"And how do you like it?" asked Topo, leering at Lucy. "Do you like it hot?"

"Like this," answered Lucy, as she whacked Topo across the mouth. "Like this, you asshole."

"Man, I was only kidding," screeched Topo. "Can't ya take a joke?"

"Keep your jokes to yerself, jerk. I ain't anxious to hear them, okay?"

"Okay."

The guys, mellowed by the beer and scared to death of what Lucy might do next, drank up, put out their cigarettes and dashed to the can to take a fast piss. They finally made their way back to the picture studio. They entered the dark studio and were about to take their places on the bleacher-like steps, when they realized the chicks weren't around. "Damn," groaned Paulie, "we left Ernie's Bar for nothing! Them chicks are still in the can. They're stuck in the toledo!"

"Whatcha want us to do?" asked Tudi of the photographer. "Line up or what?"

"Uhhhhhh."

"Tell them dames in the crapper ta make it fast," yelled Cricket, his loud voice like ice. "Nobody's gonna look at them no how. Man, that Lucy pisses me off," Cricket hissed to Topo. "She thinks her shit don't stink. I gotta chow her whose the boss."

"I ain't about to tangle with Lucy, brother. She's small, but she sure can hit." Topo rubbed his cheek. "She chure can hits."

"Shit, that chick ever lays a hand on me, I'll smack her in the kisser. You gotta show wimmen whose the boss or else . . . "

"Hey you," Cricket called to the pale assistant, "go tell the bride, uhhhh, my wife, to get out here or . . . "

Inside the small bathroom, Blanca waited for the bridesmaids to finish with their primping. She leaned back onto the faded brocade chair, her wrinkled dress pulling tightly at the waist. Her stomach was aching again. The wilted gardenias, once a creamy white, were beginning to brown around the edges, but the orange blossoms on her head still looked pretty. Blanca stifled a yawn, then stood up, smoothed her dress and called to the women lined up in front of the mirror. "Hurry up, you guys. Let's finish with the pitchers so we can go eat."

Inside the small, cramped bathroom with one leaky faucet that worked, Lucy and Rosie hitched up their garter belts, adjusted their stocking seams and added Tangee Ripe Red and Pink Frost to lips already caked with color. They finally dashed out the door to once more take their places. The young male helper reappeared, and with his delicate hands, hands that to Rosie appeared to slide over her hips, helped the young women line up. Now and then his small dark eyes, like those of a weasel, riveted on Lucy's pointed breasts that appeared to pop out of her purple dress. Once everyone was in position, the helper held out a white card and asked the wedding party to focus on it. From his vantage point at center stage, Cricket adjusted his dark glasses, then, remembering where he was, took them off and put them inside his tuxedo jacket. He stood still, fighting to keep his bleary eyes open, while on the stool below him Porky smiled shyly into the camera. Next to her, Petey grinned through a film of shiny snot.

When finally the wedding party exited the photo studio, Blanca took Lucy aside and whispered, "Tell Topo to stay in front. I don't trust Tudi to get us home. He's too goddamn stuped," she concluded, pulling at her white veil. Lucy, who liked to give orders, but hated to take them, stalked off towards the bunch of men in tuxedos and to Tudi. She asked him for a puff of his cigarette, then in a low voice told him, "Ya better let Topo go in front, or else Cricket's gonna . . . "

Once they were inside the decorated cars, the wedding party started to leave. First they waited for Tudi, who while backing up the car through the narrow alley had almost hit Topo. His kind face flushed red, Tudi leaned out the car window and stuttered his apologies before stepping on the gas and leaving Topo behind. In the back seat, a nervous Blanca grabbed Cricket's hand, aware that Tudi was once more in the lead. But Tudi was not all that nervous, not anymore. He turned on the radio, then lit a cigarette. He felt good. The morning's escapade was now forgotten. He stepped on the gas and careened down Main Street towards Chinatown and onto the Hill Street ramp that led to the main highway. But, as he approached the next stoplight he slowed down, afraid to burn out the brakes. Just then the light changed and on came Topo, careening down the road and toward the ramp that led to San Cristobal Road, grinning broadly as Lucy, sitting next to him laughed aloud at the dummies.

In the back of Tudi's gleaming Chevy, Blanca held a hand to her mouth, trying not to vomit. The sudden jerking of the car pitched her back and forth. The sickness she had controlled all morning long was gaining on her. Just then Topo cut in front of Tudi. The car screeched to a stop. From the back seat, Cricket, warming to feelings of impending danger, quickly looked around. "Shit," Cricket snarled, "Tudi almost missed the turnoff. Man alive, what a jackass." He fought to control his temper, while in front Tudi shifted gears and eased the car forward. Next to the groom, his bride of one day held her wide hand over her mouth. Unable to make out the cars around him, Cricket removed the dark glasses from his jacket, then with the tip of his tongue spat on them and wiped them off on Blanca's dress. He put them back on. They flew down the highway towards Taconos, their bright streamers flying in the warm September breeze. They arrived at Blanca's house just in time for the food.

Chapter Five

The Reception

On the wedding morning, Blanca's Tio Ernie and his two boys
walked over to Blanca's house to get things ready for the reception.
Tio Ernie carried a large rake in one hand. Wound around his arm
and shoulder was a patched garden hose. Perched on his greying
ducktail was a tattered baseball cap. He walked in short, brisk
steps, his kids lagging behind. He was in a hurry to get the job
done, so that he could get home and dress in a shiny tuxedo for the
wedding. After all, he was giving the bride away. As a former
pachuco, he wanted to do it without mud on his shoes.

The day before he had hauled benches borrowed from friends
to Blanca's yard. He had also made another trip to the outskirts of
Taconos to rescue an old picnic table that his boss had thrown away.

It was now mid-afternoon and everything was in place. The
back yard had been swept, then hosed down and decorated with the
bright paper flowers made earlier by the bridesmaids. Two small
trees stood like sentinels over the odd-shaped tables scattered
throughout. In the back alley, little kids who were dressed in
church clothes ran about shouting and hitting at each other. They
also started shoving each other out of the way to peek between
clumps of nopales, hoping for a glance at the bride who had not yet
arrived.

"Quit puchin."

"I got here first."

"Lookit the flowers! They sure growed fast . . . they wasn't
there yesterday."

"They're made of paper, stupid."

"If you stick your hand through here you can touch them."

"I want the purple one."

"No, I saw it first!"

In the kitchen, Blanca's mother became alarmed at the rowdy
kids about to steal a purple flower. She wiped her hands on her

apron, bounded out the porch steps and in a high squeaky voice shooed them home. The kids, most of whom would later return with their parents, left, vowing to return later for a paper flower and piece of wedding cake. Once the kids had taken off, Sunday clothes now wrinkled and stained, Blanca's mother re-arranged the paper streamers, fluffed up the wrinkled purple flowers and went inside the house to prepare for the wedding party and guests.

Earlier that week Blanca's mother, grey hair rolled in a bun, dark dress to her ankles and worn purse clutched to her chest, had taken the bus to San Cristobal to buy the food for her daughter's wedding reception with the wilted dollar bills hidden for months in a coffee can by Blanca. Her first stop was at the Five and Dime, where she bought the long, black hairpins she used in her bun. From there she walked briskly to the butcher shop to buy chickens. She knew that often the meat was not fresh at all, but beginning to smell, and so was sold at half price. Once it was rubbed with lemon juice, then smothered with chile and onions, few could taste the difference. Once the chickens were wrapped in white butcher paper and stuffed inside a brown shopping bag, she took the bus back to Taconos, content with her work for that day.

In order not to offend Don Macario, who owned the Taconos Mexican Store where she shopped and who was the only grocer in the barrio to extend credit to Mexican families, Blanca's mother bought the other foods there. She loaded up on rice, beans, lard, chile, garlic and fresh tortillas. Last of all she bought bunched green onions so fresh they still had dirt clods. She fondled ripe avacados, then, seeing as how she had money left over, bought several cans of big black olives to be used in the salad. She approached the counter, ready to pay.

On the Friday before the wedding, Blanca's mother and some neighbor women began to cook the food. First they cut up the chickens, setting aside the wings which would be served to the children. The chicken liver and giblets, disliked by everyone, were put away for another time. The chicken skins were removed, the parts rewashed. Then the women filled huge pots with water, threw in cloves of garlic and several Spanish onions, slid in the chicken parts, then put the heavy pot on the cast-iron stove to cook, making sure to save the broth for the mole. Once cooked, the chickens were removed, cooled, then cut up into smaller pieces and put aside. Next the women prepared to make the mole. Each woman had her own recipe; each wanted to cook it her way. Finally, when the señoras could not agree on what spices to use for the mole, they stuck to the usual Mexican recipe, agreeing to use pumpkin seeds, peanut butter and bits of chocolate. Blanca's mother sighed with relief, brought out a thick skillet reserved for the mole and once more tied her apron on her skinny frame.

By mid-morning the women were ready for the mole. In the small kitchen the women peeled the garlic cloves, then threw them into the cast-iron skillet. They stirred them until brown, then removed the cloves and put them aside. Next they toasted flour in hot lard, added powdered mole and slowly stirred in the chicken broth, taking care not to spill anything on the kitchen linoleum. Once seasoned with oregano, cumin and salt, they added the pumpkin seeds, crushed peanuts and dark chocolate. Once each woman had tasted it, mole was declared ready.

Soon the smells of garlic and mole filled the small kitchen. Satisfied that the mole was the right thickness, the women removed their aprons, heated stale coffee, then wandered outside to talk and smoke. From her apron pocket Doña Remedios removed a small tobacco pouch and cigarette paper. She licked the thin brown paper till wet, then spread it on her hand. She poured a thin line of tobacco onto the paper, rolled it tight, then once more licked it. She then lit it with a big wooden match and inhaled.

"Ummmmm."

"Bueno?"

"Sí, muy good."

"I like los Camels."

"A mí los Philip Morris."

"They gives cupones?"

"Sí! I'm going to buy a radio!"

"Eees too much money!"

"And lots of cupones!"

Once ready, the mole was cooled, put in big pots and taken home by the women to be stored in their kitchens until Sunday, at which time the señoras would bring it to Blanca's.

The pinto beans were left for last because they took longer to cook. They were parceled out to the women to be cooked in their own homes. Early Sunday morning they were carried slurping inside blue enamel pots to Blanca's back yard, then set on the linoleum counters in the small kitchen to be warmed up. They would be served directly from the pot and also smothered with thick yellow longhorn cheese. The fluffy rice, made the night before by Blanca's mother and Doña Remedios, was still moist and needed only to be rewarmed. All it lacked were the cooked eggs on top for a garnish.

Last of all the women made the salad that would compliment the heavy food. The señoras washed the lettuce, sliced tomatoes, trimmed the green from the onions, then mixed everything in a big wooden bowl. Last of all they added the black Italian olives and juicy radishes. When done, the women stood back to admire the salad, which made a pretty picture on the flowered linoleum tablecloth. The food, chicken mole, beans and rice, now covered every corner of the kitchen. In the back yard, assorted dishes of plastic and thick china, and select pieces of Blue Willow that came in soapboxes, sat on makeshift tables waiting for the wedding party. Inside the small kitchen, Blanca's mother and the neighbor women, wearing crisp, cotton aprons, laughed and recalled other weddings, other brides.

The wedding party arrived just past noon. The once shiny cars, now dusty from the long ride to the photo studio, were heard from afar. Honk, honk, honk. In the lead car sat Blanca with Cricket slumping back against the seat, his dark glasses hanging from his large beak. In the front seat Tudi took a deep breath, dusted cigarette ashes off his jacket and felt relieved to be back in Taconos. Petey sat next to a pouting Porky, who stuck her chocolate-covered tongue at kids in Sunday clothes.

When the wedding party had driven up, Cricket and Blanca got out first. Tired from the long ride, they dismounted from the decorated cars, stretched out, then stood around talking, waiting for what was to come next. In the back of Topo's car, Lucy sat alone, waiting for everyone else to go inside so then she could adjust the falsies that kept shifting.

From behind the kitchen window Blanca's mother wiped her eyes on her apron, then smiled at her daughter, who from afar looked dewy-fresh and so very, very pretty. Blanca, sleepy and irritable, but determined not to show it, grinned at her mother, waved at the neighbors, picked her way between scampering kids and bounced up the stairs. I gotta look happy, she vowed. After all, I'm the bride. She handed her gardenia bouquet to her mother, who held it to her nose and inhaled deeply.

"Yeah, huh. I'm so glad I gots them gardenias."

"They're gonna be so good, Ma! Just wait. Everything . . . I mean everybody's gonna come out so fine!"

"Y Cricket?"

"Even Porky und Petey were so good. Gosh, the food sure smells good. I'm so hungry, Ma!"

Blanca hitched up her colonial-style dress and squeezed her way past friends and relatives to the tiny bathroom, hoping to reach it in time. I sure don't feel so good, she groaned, leaning over the bowl. But I can't let anybody knows it. I'm gonna make this a day to remember. Ain't nobody gonna spoil it. Not Lucy, nor Cricket. I owe it to myself . . . and to my Ma.

The smell of delicious hot food filled the back yard, as did the shouts and laughter from the kids running around. Near the alley stood three scrawny dogs, salivating at the smell of chicken, waiting for a home. At a table beneath a large pepper tree sat the newly-weds, smiling into hand-held Brownie cameras. The bridesmaids and ushers were free to chose a table at random; no one felt obligated to sit with a partner. Tudi set his dish down next to Lucy, saw her make a face and turn up her nose. He quickly sat next to Sally, who welcomed him with a wide smile and a steaming dish of chicken mole.

Beneath a fragrant orange tree drooping with waxy orange blossoms sat Lucy, small teeth bared as she nibbled on a chicken thigh. Now and then she looked around to see who else had come by, then continued eating. She stopped eating long enough to wipe her purple fingernails on a paper napkin, being careful not to tear them, for the day was only half-way through. She still had tonight to look forward to. She wanted to look picture perfect. Across from Lucy sat Rosie, Paulie and assorted friends.

The bride, feeling better and looking revived, stood looking out at the throng squeezed into the small yard. She leaned against the porch, squinting against the sun that was now burning. She took a deep breath and smiled at the world, at her friends. Starving since before mass, Blanca picked her way across the yard, the points of her white baby doll pumps barely touching the ground. She lifted her heavy dress, laid her bouquet on the table, then slowly sat down on one of the two chairs decorated with white flowers and pink crepe paper.

Gone was her concern with weight. She ate heartily of the mole, trying to take small bites of the chicken, aware that as the bride, she should not eat like a pig. She rolled a hot tortilla, stuck it inside the mole, then licked her lips. She helped herself to another helping of beans and rice and then polished off a serving of salad. She felt the buttons of her dress straining and thought she heard one pop off, but ignored it until she finished a second tortilla. She got up slowly, wiped her hands, adjusted her voluminous skirt and once more made her way past well-wishers to the bathroom, which, thank goodness, was empty. Once inside the room, now littered with wet towels, bobby-pins and assorted combs, Blanca loosened the safety pins she was able to reach. She dusted her flushed face with powder, wiped at her melting mascara and then returned to eat another helping of rice.

At a nearby table, Paulie, El Pan Tostado, leaned back. Already he had eaten three servings of mole, four of rice and five tortillas. That was still not enough. He waved at the women serving beans to fill his dish. When his dish was once more overflowing, he took a hot tortilla given him by Blanca's mother. From across the way Rosie snickered, then poked at Sally.

"Lookit El Pan Tostado eatin like a pig!"

"God! He's eating enough for ten people."

"I'm tellin ya. Somebody oughta tell 'im it ain't polite ta eat all the food. Ain't gonna be none left for . . . "

"But he's so happy when he's eating . . . "

"So is a pig!"

From the back porch Blanca's Tio Ernie glared at the groom. He could tell that Cricket was either hungover or full of marijuana. He stationed himself as close as possible to the bride; if Cricket started something, he could hit him in the kisser. "I ain't afraid of that guy," Tio Ernie had told Blanca's mother earlier. "He ain't nuttin but a piece of chet."

"Ay Dios! But he's my daughter's husband now and . . . "

"Don't cut no ice."

"We have to be nice to him Ernesto, or . . . "

"Or what?"

"He might take it out on Blanca . . . and then?"

"He'll havta tangle asses wiz me first."

"This sure is good, Ma," cried Blanca, wiping mole from her wide, generous mouth, as her mother went by to serve more hot tortillas to the guests.

"Yeah," echoed Cricket, remembering his manners. He raised his head, alert for any sudden moves, then glanced down at his new wife, who was busy munching on a tortilla. From beneath the dark glasses riding across his beak, Cricket made out the two small forms sitting directly across from him. Damn, it was Petey and Porky eating as though starved. "What brats," hissed Cricket, flexing his long legs. "Them little fu . . . "

"What honey?" Blanca asked, blushing a bright pink. She smiled at Cricket, then at her mother. This was the first time she had called Cricket honey in front of her family. But now that she and Cricket were hitched, as a real married couple, it was okay to call Cricket honey in front of others. Still, it felt funny. "Whatcha looking at, honey?" Blanca repeated, smiling coyly at her new hubby.

"Nuttin."

When everyone, including kids and dogs, had been served, and once Paulie, El Pan Tostado, had stopped munching, the women gathered up the dirty dishes and went indoors to put up the leftovers. Later, once the cake was eaten and the presents opened, they would wash, dry and sort out the dishes. In the alley, dogs whining for chicken bones were sent running by a shower of small rocks from Petey's slingshot.

Just before he was forced to sit down next to Porky, Petey had spotted the big black dog in the alley. It was the same damned dog that a few days before had chased him home from school. He could barely concentrate on the food put in front of him by his doting mother. Instead, Petey looked about the yard, kicking the dirt with his feet, hoping to dislodge the rocks he knew were beneath the surface. "I'm gonna knock the chet outta that black dog," he vowed. "Just as soon as I finish eatin. First I'll gets lotsa rocks, then . . . " He chewed furiously on a radish, spat it out, then took a sip of Kool Aid and waited.

As the warm afternoon progressed, the men moved away from the women and gathered over by the fence, where they smoked, swapped jokes and drank beer iced in a zinc tub. Others stood in small groups, talking about their current jobs or lack of jobs and who was hiring at the labor hall. They teased Tudi for having got lost that morning on the way to the photo studio. Mostly they discussed the dance later that evening.

"I hear Gato gots some good sounds."

"You bet."

"Think them Planchados will . . . "

"Neh. They ain't chickenshit."

"Shit, I seen em beat up guys in funerals!"

"Oh yeah? Well, let em try it. We'll be ready."

"Yeah."

To the Tacones, tough as they claimed to be, the dance was a different matter. After all, Cricket was their leader and the Planchados knew it! This was their chance to call the shots, to let the guys in the entire San Cristobal Valley see that they, Los Tacones, knew how to throw punches and were'nt about to take no shit from the Planchados. Let em come!

Some gangs, the Planchados among them, had a code of honor that held them back from fighting at baptisms, funerals and weddings. This did not keep them from beating up the guys as they left a funeral; it just meant that they didn't crash right in. Sometime back, when the Planchados had got wind that some guys from L.A. were coming to the Valley for a funeral, they decided to leave them alone during the funeral, but chase them outta town afterward. Once the wake was over, the Planchados had parked along San Cristobal Road where they knew the funeral cars would go past on their way to the cemetery. When finally they saw the big black hearse go by, they chased not only their rivals, but also the black hearse. "Them guys don't got no class," Sapo said after that. "They ain't gots no respect for nuttin."

But a dance, everyone knew, wasn't really good unless somebody threw some punches. Still, the guys knew they should be careful. Now, as they waited for the reception to wind down, they spoke in low voices, heads together, not wanting the chicks to hear. They guzzled beer, cracked jokes and looked across the yard full of people to their leader, Cricket, aware that among Los Tacones Cricket called the shots.

Cricket leaned on the rickety fence and watched the others eat and talk. He could barely keep his eyes open. His head ached and behind the dark glasses his bloodshot eyes were half-closed. The night before he had stayed out late. Now he felt and looked like shit. As the leader, it was his duty to show he was tough, that he could drink and party until late and not gripe about sleep. Even though this was his wedding day, it was important that he act tough and not take off before the others, like a wimp.

The night before, while the moon moved across a starry sky, Cricket and the ushers had parked in front of Tudi's house to drink beer and whiskey and to smoke marijuana. They had accompanied the bridesmaids to Tudi's to decorate the shiny cars used in the wedding with the paper flowers made at one of the other endless meetings. Once finished with their part of the job, that of stringing the flowers across the hoods and trunks and tying them to the front and rear license plates, the Tacones killed a fifth of Hill and Hill and a case of beer. After the chicks split, the Tacones went into Tudi's to listen to records and sing along. They prided themselves on how well they could imitate the popular crooners of the day, like Frank Sinatra and Frankie Laine. Feeling no pain, they sang along with Billy Eckstine, Blanca's favorite singer.

Paulie, El Pan Tostado, feeling hungry again, left around two. He was followed by Mudo, who could outtalk and outshout everybody. Frankie took off in the maroon Mercury he had just bought to go get more beer and cigarettes. Cricket stayed outside on the porch with Sonny and Wimpy, his cousins from Fresno, and the ever-faithful Tudi, who tonight looked more rumpled than ever in a pair of stained overalls. Cricket closed his bleary eyes and hummed along with Billy Eckstine, determined not to act like a small-town hick. Inside Tudi's car, Topo and Sapo snapped their fingers, puffed on thin brown cigarettes and blew smoke out the window. They were tired and wanted to go home, but knew that real men should be tough, which meant staying up with the guys until some-body passed out. Tudi smoked a Camel, chewed on Juicy Fruit gum and looked up at the sky that to his bleary eyes appeared full of clouds.

"Shit, it's gonna rain, ese."

"It don't rain on Sunday."

"Oh yeah? How come?"

"'Cause it's Sunday. Sun-day, get it?"

"Ha, ha. For a minute I thought you was kiddin. Man, if it rains, them flowers are gonna . . . "

"Who gives a chet 'bout da flowers," growled Cricket. "What I gots ta worry about are dem Planchados. That Skippy and me, wees gonna get somethin straight soon or . . . "

"Yeah?"

Topo and Sapo moved in close to Cricket, eyes alert, hands at the ready, as Sonny and Wimpy, scared to say anything, gaped at them. Cricket took off his dark glasses, wiped them, then leaning across the car hood, lit a Lucky Strike and took a long drag. It was going to be a long night.

"Yeah, like I seez it, them guys operate in the dark . . . even when it's raining."

"Yeah, the last time da Planchados tangled wiz Maravilla they jumped them when there was tunder."

"I told ya."

"Right."

"Pass the bottle . . . and put on the Ink Spots."

"I gotta chow my buddies I ain't no square," vowed Cricket to Tudi, taking a swig from the bottle of Hill & Hill, "but just as tough as the guys from Los. Taconos ain't so hot . . . but I chure wish it wasn't so far from L.A. Man, that's where things are really happenin. The real action. The guys from there really know how to dress . . . and fight. They gots some good bailbondsmen . . . and don't havta go to the can." He leaned along the back on the car, his long, thin legs kicking out. He looked bored. Now and then Cricket took a drag from his cigarette, pursed his thin mouth and tried to blow smoke rings. Unable to impress the guys, he adjusted his dark boppers, punched Tudi in the arm and hummed along with Billy Eckstine. Now and then he cracked his knuckles and balled his hands into a fist. Just in case.

Twice that night Cricket had forked out money for booze, aware his cousins would call him cheap if he didn't keep the liquor flowing. "Dis wedding's gonna make me broke," he snarled, his thin lips sucking on a limp Camel cigarette. "Them dudes guzzled all the booze, just like they was in the desert. Especially that Paulie. Man, that guy gots a wooden leg. He killed a fifth by hisself, and almost a case of booze. But no way them guys gonna call me a chipskate or say I don't gots class. I showed them tonight."

From behind his dark boppers Cricket glared at his cousins and at Tudi, Topo and Sapo. Man, I coulda used all the cash on some cool threads from Bunny's, he thought. Or gets me some heels for my chooze.

"Them guys all drinks like fiches," Cricket hissed to Tudi, who dared not answer back. "And I still gotta come up wiz money for the band. That Gato Cortez wants me, uuuuh, us guys to give im halfers."

"Halfers?"

"Yeah, half the moola before he starts."

"Ain't ya gots it? I already paid, ese!"

"Yeah? Well I used the money to buy some new churts. Wanna make sumpin outta that?"

"Neh."

Towards dawn, Cricket staggered home supported by Tudi. Once in his room, he flopped down on the bed, dressed in his pin-striped pants and shoes with the thick soles, and passed out. He vaguely remembered Tudi helping him into the car and later being half-carried up the wooden steps past the quiet kitchen to his cramped room.

Cricket was soon lost in a drunken stupor. He tossed and turned in his sleep, but was later awakened by the barking of a neighbor's dog. "Goddammit," he grumbled, pushing his black hair out of his bloodshot eyes. "Fuckin dog." Suddenly his eyes popped open at the sight of his wrinkled pants. He quickly sat up. "Sonavavichi," he mumbled, "my drapes gots dirty." He smoothed his crumpled pants leg, his hand lovingly fingering the material of his custom-made pants.

Now, as the reception continued, Cricket sat with a rumpled Tudi and the still neat-looking ushers and tried to focus on what he should be doing and saying. I gotta play et cool, he thought, I gots my reputation ta tinks of. None of the other guys gots any class. Especially that pig Tudi. I gotta chow the Planchados who's the big shot of Taconos. They wears churts ironed by chinamen, but we gots more balls. He flipped cigarette ash at Tudi, took a drag from his cigarette, then suddenly stood up straight, as a big, black dog ran in through the back gate and came straight at him.

Once he had enough rocks in his tuxedo pocket, Petey had walked toward the back alley, opened the chain link fence and slowly edged his way past the nopales to where some dogs stood. He put the chicken wing stolen from Porky's food in his hand, then moved towards the big black dog that looked at him. He put his left hand out, thrust the chicken at the dog, then, just as the black dog opened his mouth, Petey kicked out at it and let loose with a rain-fall of rocks. "Here, ya damned dog." He began to back off, eyes steady on the dog, but just then his foot slipped . . . and he fell.

The black dog looked at the boy who fell in front of him, then, with a wave of his long tail, loped over to him and began to lick his face. "Mama, mama," cried Petey, "the dog is gonna eat me up." He scrambled to his feet, pushed open the gate and ran to the back yard, screaming at the top of his lungs, straight to Tudi. The dog followed him into the yard.

When he first saw the dog coming straight at him, Cricket closed his eyes, thinking he was dreaming. After all, dogs usually ran from him! He pushed himself straight up, glanced over to Tudi, then nearly fell over when the dog jumped on top of him. "Sonava-beech," screeched Cricket, his face dark with anger. "Gets that fuckin dog offa my tuxedo," he hissed to Petey, as he moved back against the fence.

"I'm scaaaared," sniveled Petey, his small face turned into Tudi's chest. "He's gonna eat me up."

"Shhhh, here doggie," cried Lucy, getting off her chair. "Come 'ere." The dog, swayed by the sound of Lucy's voice, turned away from Cricket and Petey and ran towards Lucy. Just as the dog got near her, Lucy kicked out with her purple high heel shoes and sent the dog flying. The dog turned tail and ran toward the alley. Delighted with herself, Lucy smiled all around, then once more fluffed her dress, stuck out her pointy chest and sat down.

Cricket stared down at his pants, now full of dirt from the dogs's paws. He glared at Petey, at Petey's mother (now holding her son on her lap) and at Tudi. "If that was my kid I'd beat the chet outta him," he said to Tudi, surprised at how calm he felt. "Yeah," answered Tudi, busy wiping his hands. "Well, ain't nuthin else gonna happen," Cricket added, slicking back his hair. "Whatcha say we goes ridin?"

"Okay," agreed Tudi, relieved to see that Cricket was smiling. "I'll get the car, you tell the guys." He took off at a fast trot, climbed inside his blue Ford and brought it around in front of Blanca's house. Honk, honk, honk.

Chapter Six

The Presents

The six wedding presents, individually wrapped in pale tissue paper with bright silver designs, sat on a small wooden table in the back yard, where minutes before the cake had been cut. Around the table and in between the guests who sat nibbling the remnants of the cake, ran little kids led by Petey, whose tuxedo jacket now sported pieces of white frosting. His straight hair falling across his snotty nose, Petey ran in between his mother Lola and the guests, then stopped long enough to punch Porky in the ribs and then careen out the back gate and into the alley.

Blanca, worn and hot from a day spent on the run, and stuffed inside the creamy Scarlett O'Hara dress that literally took her breath away, had insisted the gifts be opened out back. She still had the headache brought on that morning in church when she had seen Cricket was hungover. But it was now worse, due mostly to the heavy bridal crown balanced on her head. Although most of the day was now gone, Blanca still had the evening's events on her mind. Not just the dance, but Cricket and their honeymoon. Blanca, brown eyes squinting at the sun, squeezed her mother's arm. She knew that what bothered her mother most was the embarrassment of her having received only six wedding gifts. But I ain't about ta worry about that, sighed Blanca. Besides, ain't nuthin I can do about et. Ain't as though anybody's countin. Besides, I ain't rish, and my friends ain't either. Neither are the bridesmaids. Ain't no way I'm gonna ask em ta buys me somethin if they ain't gots no money. She put her hand through her mother's thin arm, smiled at the guests drinking Kool Aid and beer, then waved at Cricket who was standing with the ushers. "Don't go too far, honey. We still gots to open the presents." Blanca knew that few people in Taconos gave more than one wedding gift. And nothing fancy at that. "Nobody gots ta put on the dog fer me," she had often told Sally. "Not for me." She smiled at her mother and at Cricket, who appeared to be ignoring her, and thought back to her other shower. Weeks be-

148

fore, she had been given a bridal shower by Lucy and the bridesmaids. She had received towels, doilies and sheets. She felt content with that.

When Blanca called to Cricket to help with the presents, he began to edge across the chain link fence and grumble. Shit, we only been hitched a liddle while and she already wants ta boss me around. He stared at the remaining guests, lit another cigarette and ignored Blanca, who called out to him once more, "Honey, it's time for the presents." From behind the dark glasses, his insolent gaze shifted from the bridesmaids to Blanca to Tudi. "Man, whatta drag," Cricket sighed, "whatta drag. I ain't gonna get up in front of all dem people! I ain't no woman!"

Next to the wooden table, Blanca's mother watched Cricket. Her dark eyes narrowed as she took in the scene. She twisted her dress belt into a tight knot. My Blanca's husband is full of marijuana. Next to the porch steps, Tudi whispered to Topo, "Jeezus, Cricket's high again! I thought I smelled somethin in the can. Man, I tell ya, that guy don't even act right on his weddin day! Always gotta start sumthin. I ain't lookin forward ta tanight."

"I ain't eeder." Topo snarled, looking the other way. Tudi pulled his tuxedo jacket tight. The sun was slowly disappearing and the slight breeze gave him a sudden chill. He edged towards Sally and the bridesmaids who silently watched as Blanca pulled Cricket toward the table and the gifts.

Suddenly the wedding guests heard the screeching of tires. Everyone froze. Cricket, his eyes glowering behind the boppers, pushed Blanca aside and then stormed toward the alley. Topo jumped up from his seat, nearly upsetting Tencha and ran to join Cricket. In the bathroom and about to take a piss, Tudi zipped up and ran out the door. Just then Paulie, his stomach heaving underneath the black tuxedo, walked away from the alley where he had been checking his car. "Ain't nuttin," he stammered. "Just some guys chasing eesh udder."

Grateful it wasn't the Planchados, Blanca pulled Cricket towards the pile of gifts and handed him a box. The bride and groom then began to open their wedding gifts. The first box, wrapped in two shades of tissue paper, contained a glass pitcher with six matching glasses. "Ummmm, tanks a lot," smiled Blanca as she handed the box to Lucy. "Tanks a lot."

"Shit," hissed Lucy, "another of them sets from the Thrifty. That makes three."

"Shhh," whispered Sally, tugging at Lucy's sleeve. "Blanca don't mind."

"Gosh!" sighed Rosie, pouting to show her dimples, "some people are so cheep!" She ignored the snickers made by the others around her. "People like Blanca," Rosie whispered to Sally, "but they hates Cricket." Rosie knew people were not about to give an expensive gift to a guy who at one time or another had kicked the shit out of friend or relative.

The next gift, a plastic tablecloth with purple and yellow flowers, was followed by a set of white sheets. Everyone clapped loudly as the box was passed around to sighs of "Ohhh" and "Ahhhh." A bright pink blanket wrapped in silver wedding paper, topped with a huge white bow and tiny silver bells, came next. This was from the Maid of Honor, who smiled modestly from the sidelines.

"So she can keep warm," laughed Rosie, munching on a potato chip.

"She ain't gonna need nuttin," said El Pan Tostado, as he popped a second piece of cake into his mouth. "She ain't gonna need nuttin."

"Don't be so dirty," scolded Sally, as she passed the blanket around. "It ain't polite."

"But it chore is funny," chortled Tudi, "Ha, ha, ha."

Blanca tried not to mind the jokes, fully aware this too was part of a wedding. The sly and suggestive remarks about the first night were expected. At least they aren't as bad as them told at my other chower, she thought. Them guys at the turkeys sure take the cake!

Three weeks before, Blanca's co-workers, Sadie and Petra, had given Blanca a wedding shower at work. Right before lunch, they swept clean their work area, cleaned the table of turkey feathers, threw on a plastic tablecloth, set stools and benches around the worktable, took out cold sodas kept next to the frozen turkeys, set out sugar cookies, tacos, salami and baloney sandwiches and began to eat. Last of all they took out the brightly wrapped gifts, which had been hidden under the table, and plunked them next to the bride-to-be and urged Blanca to open them.

The first box held a pair of black lace panties with a matching top. Called "baby dolls," these were very suggestive to Blanca. "Man, they don't hide nuthin," gasped Blanca, her face a bright red.

"That's whatcha gettin married fer," offered Sadie, bobbing her henna-red hair.

"Wait till ya see the rest," giggled Petra, a tall, skinny woman with short, curly hair, dressed in dark slacks and a polka-dot blouse.

"Yeah," cried Myrtle, a freckled, jolly woman, "ya ain't seen nuthin yet." She grinned at the women, adjusted her jersey turban and munched on a sugar cookie.

The brightly wrapped packages were opened to squeals of loud laughter. One small box held an alarm clock, another Tabu perfume. Still another box, oblong in shape, contained a blue ceramic vase etched with pink roses. Two boxes held kitchen towels and one, bath crystals. Blanca, smiling all the while, breathed a sigh of relief, grateful that so far the gifts had not made her blush. She was about to begin her thank-you speech when Sadie handed her another box.

"Here's somethin yar gonna use a lot," Sadie giggled. "At least I hope so."

Blanca took the package, opened it and stared at a huge jar of Vaseline. "And what's this for?" she asked, turning the jar over in her hand. "I ain't gots no diaper rash."

"It's for the first night," screeched Sadie, "so Cricket won't have ta push too hard!"

"God, how filthy you are," protested Blanca, pulling at her bra strap. She took the Vaseline and put it underneath the other gifts, trying not to giggle. "I never heard anybody say so many dirty things," she cried, her face a bright pink.

"They ain't dirty," snickered Tere, "they're a lota fun, huh Sadie?"

"Well you oughtta know," retorted Sadie, "youz had more men than anybody I knows."

"Oh yeah? Shit, you ain't no saint. What about . . . "

Blanca, knowing full well that Sadie and Tere were at it again, banged on the table with her wide fist, got their attention and then in a sugary-sweet voice thanked them for the party. And the Vaseline.

Now, on the afternoon of her wedding day, she opened the last gift. Blanca sighed with relief. At last, a set of dishes! The white plastic dishes with orange flowers were just what she and Cricket needed. Blanca had seen them at Thrifty's the week before, but knew she couldn't afford to buy them just yet. The dish set was passed around, then everyone clapped and began to yell, "Speech, Speech."

Just then Blanca's mother took her daughter's hand and in a low voice whispered, "There's still one more."

"Where?" asked Blanca, looking around.

"There." Blanca's mother pointed to a large zinc tub that sat under the table. "There."

"That's not a present," hissed Blanca. "Its a tub!"

"Sí," answered her mother, pulling the shiny tub towards Blanca. "Ees a tub and presente."

"Man, all she needs is the washboard," chortled Rosie, holding her hand over her mouth. "And some Purex."

"Shame on you," chided Josie from the kitchen door. "Whatcha think, we are all rish?"

"Man, whatta purdy tub," cried Tencha as she doubled over in laughter. "Just right for the diapers."

"Huh," grumbled Lucy, dabbing on lipstick, "all that fuss over a tub. God!"

"Well say something, Blanquita," ordered her mother. Go tell Doña Panchita the thanks."

"Ahhhh, gracias, muchas gracias," grumbled the embarrassed bride as she walked over to Doña Panchita. She put her arms around her and hugged the lady tight.

"Son-uva-beesh," hissed Cricket, adjusting his dark glasses. "Now I gots ta lug the tub too. Shit!"

"Shhhh," cautioned Blanca, taking her place next to the groom. "Shhhh."

"Fill it up," suggested Rosie as Tudi picked up the tub and set it next to the gifts.

"You're mean!" cried Sally, giving Rosie a dirty look and staring at the retreating figure of Doña Panchita, a woman she knew well. "You're so damn . . . "

Suddenly from behind the alley came the sound of shots. Bang! Bang! Bang! Tudi, his face a greyish color, dashed to the gate, then ran towards the noise, followed by El Pan Tostado, still munching on food. Inside Blanca's house, Lucy gave her new falsies a pat, shoved them a little to the left, then, assured they would stay put, ran out the door towards the crowd.

"It's only Petey," gasped Sally, hanging on to the fence. "He was popping some firecrackers."

"Thanks God," groaned Rosie, holding her hand over her beating heart, "we thought it was the Planchados."

"What?" cried Lucy, throwing out her chest, "all that fuss for nuttin. Come on, Blanca, it's time to get ready . . . "

"Yeah, it's time to take a break, then get ready for the dance." Blanca smiled at her new husband, Cricket, her brown eyes shining in the afternoon light. "Okay?"

"Chure!"

As if given a signal, the bridesmaids began to gather their things and make ready to leave. Tencha dashed indoors to get her purse, while Josie searched for a lost bouquet. Josie picked her net gloves off a table, stuck them inside her purse and went off to find her coat. Cries of "pick me up at seven," filled the night as the wedding party ran to the waiting cars and sped off. In the darkened yard, Porky lingered, licking at cake frosting stuck to a plate. Blanca's mother walked Doña Panchita to the alley, then took the gifts inside. Behind the alley, Petey wiped the snot off his pants. Inside her room, Blanca and the bridesmaids that had stayed behind closed the door, kicked off their shoes and squeezed together on the sagging bed. Only the tub, shoved next to the fence, still remained in the backyard.

Chapter Seven

The Rumble

Tudi slicked down his duck tail and prepared to chauffer Cricket and the guys around Taconos.

"Get with it, man! I gotta cruise before the dance."

"Sure!"

"Where ya wanna go, Cricket."

"Go down San Cristobal Road."

"To Sancristofas? You kiddin me or what?"

"I ain't kiddin ya. Give it some gas."

"What if the Planchados . . . "

"Ya got sumthin ta say? Step on the gas . . . before the chicks come out and wanna go too."

"Okay."

Tudi put the car in first gear and eased the car forward, taking care not to scrape other cars parked along Honeysuckle Street. In the back seat Cricket stretched out, adjusted his dark glasses and lit a Camel. Next to him Paulie, El Pan Tostado, munched on a stale piece of tortilla while Frankie took out a small flask which he first offered to the irritable groom and then passed on to Tudi. The driver took a fast gulp of whiskey, wiped his mouth with his tuxedo lapel, then popped a piece of Juicy Fruit into his mouth.

As he drove, Tudi chewed furiously on the wad of gum. Now and then he hummed "Stardust," while watching out for stray dogs and running kids. He first drove around Taconos, hoping to distract Cricket from wanting to invade the Planchado's turf by cruising to their barrio in San Cristobal. He drove up and down Main Street, then turned right onto Progress Street and back to Honeysuckle Street and once more to Main. Tudi wasn't too anxious to invade a rival gang's territory. He often told Sally, "I wanna live to be an old man, but if this shit keeps up between the Planchados and Los Tacones . . . and if I keep palling around with Cricket, I ain't gonna live to see twenty-five! Shit, if it was up ta me, I rather ferget them Planchados was our enemies. Don't mean I'm gonna go shake hands, or kiss their ass, but all the fightin ain't gonna get us nothing. Sometimes it pisses me off just to be around Cricket. All he wants to do is get high and look for trouble."

Finally Tudi was approaching San Cristobal's main street. He popped a fresh stick of Juicy Fruit into his dry mouth, pulled a handkerchief from inside his coat pocket and began to wipe his steamy brow as the car radio played "One More Time."

"Where shall I give it?"

"Give a U-turn."

"All right!"

Tudi turned the flower-festooned car in a neat U, then slowly drove back through the main drag. He could feel the sweat gathering underneath his armpits; his bow-tie appeared to be choking him. "Cricket is asking for it," whimpered Tudi to no one in particular. "We're gonna get jumped." He glanced in the rearview mirror, trying to get Paulie's attention, but Paulie looked the other way. Tudi's brown eyes looked troubled as he glanced to the left, then to the right, trying to guide the car through San Cristobal Street, half-empty on this Sunday afternoon. He cruised up Fifth, then right on Independence Avenue, picking up speed, twin pipes blasting. He was going like hell when he reached an empty intersection. Tudi swept through San Cristobal Street as if he owned the road. As he approached a stoplight, Tudi looked across the street and spotted a familiar navy-blue car with gleaming white walls. It was the Planchados! At the wheel was Skippy, their leader and Cricket's mortal enemy.

"Jeezus Christ," groaned Tudi, a lump in his throat, "theyze gonna jump us! We're all gonna die. Suddenly the light changed to red. Tudi brought the car to a screeching halt, slumped back against the seat and took a deep breath, relieved to be out of the Planchado's sight.

"Hey Cricket," squeaked Tudi, his brown eyes bulging, "I just saw Skippy and the Planchados near the corner. Whatcha wan me to do?"

"Chet in yar pants."

"I'm serious man, whatcha want me to do?"

"Step on it, man," suggested Paulie, slipping on a pair of

brass knuckles borrowed from Frankie just for the ride. "Give it some gas."

From the back seat Cricket leaned forward, grabbed Tudi by the shoulder and hissed, "Keep going straight, get it?"

"Straight? Shit, man, dem guys are gonna . . . "

"Chut up and give et some gas."

Cricket, a Lucky Strike dangling from his thin lips, grinned at Paulie. He waited till Tudi was next to the car full of Planchados, then rolled down the window, stuck out his big hand with its middle finger out and screeched, "Here, ya mudder fuckers."

Tudi could hardly control the car. His sweaty hands slipped back and forth from the steering wheel. His heart was thumping like mad. He stepped on the gas; the car sped forward, barely missing an old man leading a kid by the hand.

"Jeezus, man, you trying ta kill us or sumthin?" screeched Paulie, smoothing down his jacket. "Whatcha doing, anyway, drivin or sleepin?"

"Yeah, Tudi," added Cricket, taking a drag from his cigarette, "ya wanna get us ta the dance or to the cemetery?" The sudden screeching of tires, as the Planchados came after them, drowned out anything else Cricket had to say.

Tudi could feel his heart pumping, the blood racing through his bluish veins. His brown eyes bulging with fear, he turned into an alley, hoping the Planchados would not turn around, but go past on the main street. Aint' no way we're gonna get outta this one, he grumbled to himself, scanning the back mirror, afraid of what he might see. Them guys gonna surround us from all sides. Just like in them war movies! Shit! And all on-accounta Cricket. He drove furiously, knowing their lives were on the line. I gots ta lose them Planchados, Tudi swore to himself, I gots ta. He turned left at the next corner, riding on two wheels only, then slammed on the brakes.

"Shit! It's a one-way street," Tudi moaned, looking at Cricket for confirmation. "Es one-way!" He put the car in reverse, then in first gear, waiting to see what Cricket wanted to do. "This street ain't the one I wants," Tudi hissed, "it ain't goin nowhere." He sat with his foot on the brake, sweating like a pig, waiting to be told where to go next, but Cricket, taking a swig from Paulie's flask, ignored him. Desperate and scared shitless, Tudi put the car in reverse and, paper streamers blowing, the powder-blue Chevy roared backwards down the one-way street. Once clear of the alley, Tudi set the car forward and drove slowly down the street. He had just turned the corner towards the boulevard, when he looked up to see not one, but two cars full of Planchados. One car pulled up beside them.

"Hey, Cricket," shouted Skippy from the navy-blue Ford, "ya wanna throw some punches?"

"You bet! Where ya wanna meet," yelled Cricket, flexing his big feet. "Where ya wanna tangle? Here?"

"Nel! Tell ya what, we'll race ya to the railroad tracks. If ya wins, we call it quits. If we win, then we gonna tangle asses. Ooooooo, watch et."

"Shit, Cricket, we ain't gonna make it to them railroad tracks," screeched Tudi. "We ain't gonna makes et."

"Hit the gas, Tudi," growled Frankie, "they ain't comin yet."

"This car gots eight cylinders," yelled Paulie, "so get the chet outta yer pants and drive!"

Tudi thrust the car into first gear, almost stripping the gears, released his shaking foot off the brake, and off they flew, the Planchados right behind them. They ran two red lights, missed hitting a garbage truck and almost jumped the curb. The Planchados, jeering and laughing, followed close behind. Now and then, when they got real close, they taunted the Tacones, yelling, "Weez gonna gets ya, mudder fuckers," and "Up yer ass, Cricket."

Inside the stuffy car, Cricket was sprawled out next to Frankie, bored with the whole thing. "That Skippy wants ta get me," he said to Frankie, "but his car ain't worth a shet. Just give it some gas, Tudi. And watch where ya going."

They careened down the street, Tudi's hands gripping to the steering wheel, his ducktail flipping in the wind. The Planchados, tail pipes roaring, appeared to be getting closer and closer. Tudi could make out their jeering faces, especially Skippy's light-blonde hair that in the fading light shone like gold. Now and then the Planchados honked, just for the fun of it. The navy-blue car came closer. Just as they hit the main drag, Tudi looked back and almost slammed on the brakes! Through the car mirror he could see two

black and white cars were chasing the Planchados and Los Tacones! They were gonna get the whole bunch of them at one time!
Jeez! He pulled to the right, scraping against the sidewalk, then
slammed on the brakes.

"Whatcha stoppin fer, stupid?"

"Cricket, lookit behind us, man! The coppers are pulling the
Planchados to the side. And it looks like theyze comin fer us too,
man.

"Neh," cried Frankie, "they ain't comin. They gots who dey
wants. Hee, hee."

" . . . They gots them cuz of them red lights. Ain't no way
theyze gonna let 'em go without stripping the car. Now we gonna
make it to the tracks!"

"Turn around."

"Whatcha sayin, Cricket?"

"Ta turn the goddam car around."

"But . . . " Tudi swallowed hard, slicked his hair back,
looked at Paulie for help, then reluctantly and slowly turned the car
around. He slowly drove back to where the Planchados, now lined
up against the side of the navy-blue Ford, were being frisked by the
cops. As the Tacones came close, Cricket rolled down the car window, stuck his head out and yelled, "I ain't fergetin this, ya punk.
Next time we gonna tangle asses, or else."

They reached Blanca's house in record time. In the back seat
Cricket leaned against the plastic car seat and dusted off his pants
leg. Then he took a swig of whiskey from Paulie's flask. Behind the
dark glasses, he appeared to be asleep, except for the clenching of
his wiry hands. Frankie wiped his thin moustache, jammed the
empty flask into a pocket, adjusted his tuxedo jacket, buttoned his
shirt cuffs and took a deep breath. Before getting out of the car, he
slipped the brass knuckles loaned to Paulie under the car seat . . .
for later. Tudi parked the car, his face a sickly grey, then ran inside
Blanca's house to take a fast piss.

Chapter Eight

Girl Talk

For Blanca and the bridesmaids who stayed behind, the interval between the reception and the dance was for relaxing. They threw off their hot, wilted dresses that by now had lost their freshness. They talked and evaluated the day. The worst was over, but the best was yet to come. And for the bridesmaids now inside Blanca's small bedroom, this was the time to take a nap and intermittently gossip about who had come to the wedding, and who had not.

"How come Suki ain't showed up?"

"Topo sez she went by with her kids."

"Yeah? How many she gots now?"

"Three, and another on da way."

They exchanged jokes about the kid at the picture studio who was trying to grab Rosie's behind, and giggled about the skinny assistant who, when it was time to rearrange the steps, appeared to be going out of her mind. Now and then when the bridesmaids weren't looking, Blanca stifled a yawn, trying desperately to stay awake.

"Come on, let's go outside and see what the guys are doing," suggested Sally. "Let's go outside."

"What for?" asked Blanca, swinging her swollen feet onto the bed. "The guys ain't around . . . they went riding."

"Shucks! I wanted to go too," wailed Sally as she threw off her shoes and laid back against a pillow. "I wanted ta go."

"Well, beat it, man," smirked Lucy, licking at her teeth. She jumped up on the bed, pushing Sally to the side and once more said, "Well beat it, man!"

"Well, I would if I knew where . . . " Sally laughed nervously, then got off the bed, aware of whom she was sparring with. She and Lucy had tangled more than once. Just that afternoon while chasing a dog, Lucy had kicked Sally in the shin and then pretended not to have done it. Yeah, Sally sighed, Lucy's out to get somebody. Better not be me. Sally knew it didn't take much to get Lucy's dander up, especially when drinking. I better watch it tanight, Sally thought, her pleasant face suddenly bleak.

Blanca reached over to turn on the radio that was on the dresser. As the bride, she would have to ignore the fight now brewing between her Maid-of-Honor and Sally. Blanca slid off the rumpled bed and reached underneath it for the dusty baby doll shoes that she had worn all day. She dusted them off with her hand and turned them over to examine the damage. "Darn it," she softly sighed. "My chooze ain't no good no more." The white shoes, bought on sale at Karl's, were a mess of dirt and scratch marks. They now looked old and worn, not at all like what a bride should be wearing to a dance. Well, ain't no good ta cry over spilled milk, Blanca knew. I'll just rub them wiz a rag and see if they look better. She smiled at the women in the room, then put the shoes back under the bed and sat down to join in the gossip.

"So what's so funny?" asked Sally as she plopped onto a nearby chair. "How come yer laughin?"

"She's thinking of tonight," snickered Lucy as she chewed on a wad of Dentyne gum. "She's thinking of what she's gonna do tonight when Cricket gets her and . . . "

"Aha!" laughed Sally. "I bet she can hardly wait."

"Well, thats what she gots married fer," added Rosie matter-of-factly as she gazed out the window. "And to have kids."

"Shit, I'm not gonna have no ten kids when I get hitched," snapped Lucy from the bed, her beady eyes shining bright. "I wanna have fun."

"Well, don't get married, esa," advised Rosie, squatting on the floor, legs crossed beneath the pink ruffles of her petticoat.

"I'm only gonna have four kids," announced Sally in her low pitched voice. "Two boys and two girls."

"How perfect!" laughed Rosie, shaking out her petticoat, "how perfect."

"Ha, you'll probably have ten kids, like your ma," snickered Lucy as she adjusted her bra strap. "You're gonna end up like your mama, just wait and see."

"Oh yeah? And what about your mother?" Rosie asked, her

face a bright pink. "How many she hads?"

"Uhhhh, she had seven . . . the rest died. But not me," Lucy continued, running her hands along her stockings. "I'm only gonna have two."

"Two? Ha, ha," screeched Sally. "Two in two years, you mean. Ha, ha ha." She rocked back and forth on her hips, brown eyes dancing. "Ha, ha."

Blanca looked up at the cracked ceiling and said nothing. She knew that what Sally was saying was true. The four girls now sitting in the room would probably give birth to at least twenty kids. At least four each, or maybe five, starting with me, she thought, shivering at the very idea. There ain't no way to keep from having kids. None that me or any of the girls know about, other than for the guy to use something, or pull out. It had never entered her mind to see a doctor before the wedding. Nobody she knew ever had. What if somebody saw her? They would think she was doing something, then the whole town would talk. She decided to do what other women in Taconos did. Once she was sure she was pregnant, or when she had had enough kids, then she would go. That was how women of the barrio did things. But by then, many were used to large families.

Blanca had often heard her friends say, "after I have four kids I'll see the doctor, so he can give me something." Or, "once I have me a boy, I'm gonna quit." Even Lucy's Aunt Tortie, who had an answer for everything, had had five kids, although not one had the same father. Still, trying to keep from having lots of kids was a big problem for women. As Blanca wiped off her tired feet with a damp towel, the conversation continued with Lucy heatedly stating, "There ain't no way in hell I'm gonna have ten kids."

"I'll have me an operation first," Lucy announced to the startled group, "instead of so many kids."

"Yeah?"

"Where?" asked Blanca, sitting straight up. "Where?"

"Uhhhh. Well, I dunno know . . . "

Lucy, at a loss for words but determined to keep the bridesmaid's attention, turned around to face Rosie, who had never before been so friendly. Lucy was almost sure that the girls in the room all knew something about birth control, stuff passed down from mothers, aunts or sisters. None of which worked. Things to do such as cough a lot, especially after you-know-what, take a hot bath if your period is late, jump up and down, drink Castor oil, go horse-back riding, drink a whole bottle of aspirins with a glass of whis-key, pray a lot. The women, their tired eyes glued to Lucy's face, sat speechless, waiting for more. But Lucy only twirled her bra strap, determined not to tell the chicks everything she knew.

Yeah, Lucy thought, every chick knows that nuthin works. The thing is to watch out for yerself . . . 'cause no guy in hell is gonna. She stuck her hands out, inspected her nails and pretended to be bored with the whole thing. But the girls, especially Rosie, kept their eyes glued to Lucy's face, waiting for the most hep chick in Taconos to get on with it.

"Come on, esa, tell us," insisted Rosie. "Tell me at least."

"Yeah, I wanna know too," added Sally, leaning closer.

"Well, I heard them say there's some weeds."

"Yeah?"

"Who said?" asked the chorus of women, their eyes glued on Lucy. "Who?"

"Uhhhhh. My aunt Noni only had two kids. My Ma said she drank herbs to stop her period. Or something, I forgets." Aware of being the center of attention in the group, and determined to make them beg for more, Lucy suddenly shut up.

"Well, find out. Ask your Aunt Noni," suggested Rosie from the window, trying not to sound too anxious.

"I can't," answered Lucy, suddenly quiet.

"Why? Why not?"

" 'Cause she kicked the bucket."

"Shit!"

"What bad luck," lamented Sally, looking as if she would cry.

"What she die of," persisted Rosie, beginning to pout. "How?"

"From the weeds!" said Lucy, looking serious.

"Oh shoot," sighed Blanca, looking up at the ceiling. "How awful." Suddenly everyone in the room was still.

"Well," laughed Sally, "That's that. There goes Rosie with ten kids. Ha, ha."

"Here come the guys," announced Rosie from her perch.

"Here they come! Gosh, it's getting late!"

"It's about time," cried a relieved Blanca. The conversation had taken a wrong turn.

Like most girls her age, Blanca was curious about how to keep from having babies and still have fun. She knew that good Catholics should do nothing to keep from having kids. Now and then Father Ranger, curious to know who was doing what, preached a sermon against the evils of birth control. His steely eyes ablaze, he would make reference to couples, sinners, who knowingly practiced contraception and disobeyed the precepts of Holy Mother Church. Everyone knew they were going straight to hell!

"The Holy Mother Church forbids . . . "

In Taconos it was common knowledge that abortions were hard to get. Girls spoke of such things in whispers, aware that just to think of abortion was in itself a mortal sin. Blanca remembered well the time Tina, a friend of her sister Lola, went to confession and told the priest she had had an abortion. Immediately after her leaving the confessional, the priest had followed her out and then later told her parents who, shocked at what the holy man said Tina had done, locked their daughter in her room and made her break up with Birdy, her boyfriend. Weeks later Birdy, tired of waiting for Tina to come out, eloped with another chick. And, as pretty as Tina was, she never married. After all, what kind of man would wanna marry a chick who had abortions?

Abortions were hard to get and terribly expensive! But those desperate enough found ways to get them. In San Cristobal, a certain Epifenia used herbs and other methods to help señorita's abort. But it was said Doña Epifenia never washed her hands, and two women who had sought her help later got infections and almost died. Worse, her neighbors were quite nosy and were always looking over the fence. Just to be seen going into her house was a topic for speculation and gossip.

Unmarried women, especially las americanas, it was said, drove to Tijuana, where for seventy-five dollars cash they could get an abortion from a doctor who asked no questions and carefully washed his hands. Lucy had once told Blanca of driving to Tijuana with Aunt Tottie and her friend Fita for an abortion. "The doctor's office was the chets," Lucy said, with dirty towels on the floor and the instruments inside a bucket. Ya could smell alcohol all over the room. Then the doctor found out Fita was too far along, all of four months, so he said he would have to charge more. He wanted one hundred dollars cach. He said that or nuttin. So my poor Aunt Tottie had ta find a pawn chop to sell her new ring. Even her watch. The guy at the pawnchop wanted everything. He was really filthy and wanted to take Aunt Tottie into the back room.

Then on the way back from T.J. we gots lost and was in Rosarito before we could turn around. We took the wrong turn to the border, and when my aunt gave a U-turn in the middle of the street, three Mexican cops chased us all the way to the crossing. Sheeet, I'm tellin ya, man. Poor Fita, she was bleeding somethin awful, 'cause the quack scraped too much. She could barely walks when we gots to Taconos."

"Poor chick! What happened ta her?" "Shit, two months later she gots knocked up again! This time she went to Doña Epifenia . . . and made her wach her hands."

"And did it work?"

"Sure! After dat I told Fita she should gets her thing sewed up . . . or buy some rubbers. But she gots hitched instead, and now she has six kids!"

"Oh yeah?"

"Yeah, her Pa made her have a big church weddin. That way people ain't gonna talk, he said. Ha, ha, ha."

Blanca stretched and rubbed her wide feet. The day had been long. She was tired. She waited until the conversation died down, then yawned so that the bridesmaids took the hint to leave. "I'll see ya guys in an hour," Blanca said, as Lucy, Rosie and Sally trooped out the door, "when we take off to the dance." She waved at Cricket through the window and noticed Cricket was about to take off in Tudi's car. She pulled down the torn green shade, then closed the bedroom door.

Once alone in her small room, Blanca laid down on the bed strewn with tissue paper, clothes and bent bobby-pins. She felt hot, feverish, tired. I wish this was a work day, she sighed, so I could just lie down and go to sleep. And think of nothing, not even them turkeys.

At times Blanca was content with her life as a working girl, a single chick who could do as she pleased, especially on days when she trudged home from the bus stop to her mothers warm kitchen, then directly went to sleep. My Ma always knows when I'm tired, Blanca thought, wrestling with the pillow. She thought back to one day the previous week, when too tired to eat dinner, she went to bed, then later woke to hear her mother saying, "Blanquita, dinner is ready and . . . "

"I ain't hungry, Ma. I'm too tired to eat."

"Tomate un caldito . . . "

"I don't feel like soup, Ma. I wanna sleep."

"Have some, andale."

"Okay, but just a liddle bit."

Suddenly Blanca sat up, aware she should be getting ready. I ain't single no longer, she sighed. From now on I'm nuthin but an old married lady. Cricket's ball and chain. His ole lady. For better or for worse. Till death do us part. Ain't no longer gonna come home to this house, to the smell of my Ma's good food. Nor to my bed that sags in the middle, she lamented. Starting tonight I'm gonna be wiz my honey. My husband. Mrs. Sammy Lopez. Blanca Lopez.

She went into the bathroom, ran the hot water, then took off the chenille robe that had replaced the wrinkled bridal dress which her mother had earlier ironed. She rubbed Palmolive soap (guaranteed to give a new look in just six days!) on her full breasts and stocky legs, then began to furiously scrub her neck, shoulders and, last of all, her armpits. She dried herself, then took a can of April Showers talc and dusted it on her round body, making sure to get some on her back. Satisfied that once again she was as good as new, she took down her dress, still warm from the iron, slipped it over her head and called to Aunt Chonita for help. She began the battle with the fifty-two buttons on the colonial-style dress. Darn it, groaned Blanca, them buttons around the waist are gonna have ta just hang there till I go out the door. I ain't sure them safety pins are gonna last. She fumbled with the cumbersome dress and checked the bed for the large safety pins she recalled putting there. Trying to remember where she had laid her bra, she walked around the small room, trying to remember what else she should do.

When she finished putting on her wedding clothes with the

help of Tia Chonita, now an expert on safety pins, Blanca sat down to think of what else she had to do. Should I pack my stuff now? Did I wash out my slip? Did I sew the hole in my panties? Tired of the whole thing, she carefully laid down on the bed, straightened out her wedding dress, then punched the pillow and plunked it on her face.

Blanca had felt sick all day, first with a stomach ache and now with a slight fever. She yearned to take a nap . . . even in her newly-ironed wedding dress, but time was running out. And although it wasn't all that late, she knew she better be ready when Cricket came for her. Or else. But dammit, she sighed, tossing the pillow on the floor, even if I had time ta takes me a nap, ain't no room in this house that ain't full of people. Worse, I'm gettin hungry.

She had barely touched the breakfast of bread and chocolate, because she had been too angry with Cricket, Porky and Petey for what happened in the church. The smell of the damaged cushions was still in the air. And the two servings of mole had made her sick. I ate too much, Blanca admitted. I ate too damn much. And now I gotta pays for it. She rubbed her stomach and began to fiddle with the fifty-two satin-covered buttons of her Scarlett O'Hara dress.

Chapter Nine

The Dance

When she heard Tudi's car honk in front of her house, an excited Blanca dashed to the window, pulled aside the dark shade and with a wave of her wide hand signaled to Cricket, pretty soon! She moved back and forth across the small room, trying to concentrate on what she should be doing, but was distracted by the pain in her belly. The stomach ache that during the morning came and went was really bothering her. Dammit, I shoulda only had one serving of mole, Blanca sighed. Now my stomach is gonna get worser, and I still gots the dance. She picked her chenille robe off the rumpled bed and swept a dirty bra off the dresser. She sat down and looked for her shoes. Remembering she had stuck them back under the bed, she bent over, then pulled out the baby doll shoes and cleaned them with a damp rag. She ran a finger over the material, satisfied it was dry, and put them aside. Once she had wiped the bottoms of her swollen feet, she thrust them into the shoes. She reached across the bed for the freshly ironed veil that, despite the times she had pulled at it, still looked fresh. She adjusted the wax petals in the headpiece that had somehow retained their creamy freshness. I'm sure glad I bought this veil, she grinned, running her hands through the waxy flowers. Them orange bloosoms are so purdy! They cost a lot of money, but . . . I gotta looks good tonight. For the dance. Them chicks from San Cristobal are gonna crach the dance, just like they was invited. They want ta see what kinda dress I boughts. Huh! Wait till they see my Scarlett O'Hara dress . . . and my veil. I'll chow them!

Most of the time a wedding dance was for the chicks, a good place to meet new guys, on neutral ground, away from the prying eyes of relatives. Better yet, everyone looked good. Even messy guys like Tudi and Paulie, El Pan Tostado, looked good. In the dark hall, they shone like blackbirds decked out in rented tuxedos. They were handsome . . . happy . . . and a little drunk.

Blanca glanced around the room, trying to remember what else to do before leaving. Mostly she thought of Cricket and of how he was acting so far. Although me and Cricket are already hitched, Blanca sighed, he still flirts all he wants with other dames, even at our wedding dance. Ain't nuthin new, but I sure wish he was nicer ta me. Worse, ain't much I can do about it.

Weeks before, she had been to a wedding dance where, during the break, the groom was seen outside necking with the Maid-of-Honor. "It's my last fling," he had snarled at the bride, not at all upset with being found out. "I gotta have me a last fling." But for us chicks there ain't no last fling, Blanca grumbled, combing out her hair with a pink plastic comb. Once the wedding is over, that's it. To the kitchen!

She took a large grocery bag from the kitchen, yanked open drawers, then filled the bag with an assortment of clothes and makeup. With her free hand she yanked at her wedding dress. The creamy satin looked almost new. Gone were the wrinkles around the waist. The lovely sleeves had been ironed to perfection. Even the soiled hem was no longer as bad. The large safety pins were still pulling apart and digging into her warm flesh. Well, ain't nuthin else for me to do, Blanca concluded, but get going. She called out to her mother who was busy in the kitchen talking with Tia Chonita. "I'm leaving."

"Are you coming back?"

"I'm not sure." Blanca leaned back against the wall, her stomach heaving. The smell of mole had remained throughout the house and was making her sick. This is my farewell, she realized. This ain't gonna be my house no more. God, what am I supposed ta say? I won't be coming back no more. At least I don't think so. The dance is gonna end way after midnight. And maybe Cricket gots ideas, she thought gleefuly. Yeah, lots of ideas.

The week before, Blanca had cuddled up to Cricket to hint about a honeymoon.

"Honey, are we gonna have a honeymoon?"

"Whatcha talking about?"

"The honeymoon! You know, huh?"

"I ain't gots time ta worry 'bout a honeymoon. I gots ta get ready for the dance, man."

"But . . . "

"I gotta show them batos from Sancristofas and my cuzzins from Fresno I'm the Big Cheese."

"Just to Gorman, honey. There's a motel there and . . . "

"Yeah? And who's gonna pay for the gas? And the motel?"

Blanca shivered as she thought back to that night when Cricket, his large hands clenched at his sides, had glared down at her, at his wife-to-be and screeched, "No, I gotta take care of the dance first, get it?"

"Okay, honey." After that, Blanca dared not mention the honeymoon. Still, she was hoping for something.

She bolted out the front door, a happy grin on her round face. She took the porch steps three at a time, landed on her wide feet and dashed to the waiting car and to Cricket, her husband.

Once settled in the car, Blanca glanced shyly at Cricket. "It's almost over now, honey," she whispered as she moved across the seat to make room for her wedding train. "All we gotta do is make it to the dance."

"Yeah," grumbled Cricket, his eyes narrowing behind the dark glasses.

Blanca reached into her purse, took out a tiny bottle and began to dab Evening in Paris perfume on her perspiring neck and inside her wrists. She snuggled up to Cricket and put her arm through his. In the dim light she could barely make out the brooding face of the tipsy man who sat next to her. He was now her husband for life. Cricket, Her guy.

"Gee, honey, I sure hope the dance is good," she whispered as Tudi put the car in gear. "I wanna dance a lot." She hiked up her dress, leaned toward her partner, then jokingly put her leg over Cricket's. "We're gonna have fun, huh, honey?"

"Yeah," answered Cricket, adjusting his tuxedo jacket. Suddenly he spread his legs across the seat, pushing Blanca against the car door. "Watchet wiz my drapes," he hissed as he smoothed his pant leg. "Watch it, man, I don't wanna look like them dudes." Cricket inclined his greased head toward the front where the everfaithful Tudi sat in his rumpled tuxedo.

During the break before the dance, Tudi, usually content with how he looked, had not thought to have his pants pressed nor his shoes shined. I'm okay this way, he had felt. But not so Cricket. Once home from cruising the streets of Taconos and San Cristobal, Cricket took off for his pad to make sure his doting mother plugged in the iron, laid a wet cloth on his pants and ironed in a razor-sharp crease.

In the back seat, Blanca, momentarily stunned, huddled against the car door, her clear eyes suddenly bleak, her full mouth trembling. In the past weeks she had noticed a change in Cricket, a certain meanness she had not noticed before. She had told only Lucy about this.

"Gosh, Cricket is getting mean!"

"Getting? He was born mean."

"He used ta be so nice. Uhhh, so different when we was first goin out."

"Yeah? Well now he's got you where he wants you. He ain't gonna be nice no more."

"How come?"

"'Cause that's how guys are, stupid. They treat ya good at first, then throw ya to the dogs."

"Gosh! I thought if I was good to Cricket, he would change and . . ."

"Change? Only his underwear, esa! That guy ain't gonna change for nothing. He's just a mean son of a bitch."

"But I thought you liked him!"

"He's good for a cuppa coffee and a cigarette." Lucy giggled at this line used by real hep chicks to describe a guy who was cute, had a car, but was too square. "He's too mean for my taste," Lucy had said. "Too damn mean."

"Well, I'm gonna change him," challenged Blanca, hands on hips. "You'll see. Once we're hitched . . ."

"Yeah. Sure." Lucy stifled a yawn, then went inside, bored with the conversation.

I guess Lucy was right, sighed Blanca, as she opened the car window and took in the fresh air. I guess she was. Overhead a full moon lit up the sky so that from the back seat Blanca could almost count a hundred stars. Gosh, it sure is a purdy night, she sighed to herself, crossing her thick ankles. It sure is a nice night for a honeymoon.

In the front seat Tudi put the car into third gear, then sped swiftly down San Cristobal Road towards the Elks Hall in Burbank, where the most important Valley dances took place. Now and then he looked back to make sure they were not being followed by the Planchados. The near rumble earlier that day had unnerved him, as had Cricket's challenge to Skippy to settle the score. Tudi was fed up with Cricket and Los Tacones and the fights between them. Many of these guys worked together during the day and, if they weren't so macho, could be good friends. "Shit, man," he often told his co-workers, "I ain't gots nuttin against ya. We should learn to get along. I don't wanna gets knifed just fer nothing. This ain't the war." Just the same, he was careful to avoid starting something. Tudi glanced into the car mirror and met Cricket's scowl with a cheerful grin, his blunt hands relaxed on the steering wheel. He ran his hands through his duck-tail, then wiped them on his pants. So far, so good. Unlike that morning, this time there was no special formation. Everyone had been told to make it to the dance hall by eight o'clock . . . or else.

Tudi drove carefully, grateful to Lucy for the detailed instructions. He had been to many dances at the Burbank Elks, but in the dark, all the streets and buildings looked alike. By the time he swung the car into the street that led to the Elks Hall, traffic was thick. Ahead of him were the guys from Taconos, many of them his friends. Others were relatives of Blanca and Cricket, including the cousins from Fresno. By the time Tudi drove the bride's car into the parking-lot entrance, most of the ushers and bridesmaids who followed in assorted cars had fallen into a loose formation behind the festooned blue Chevy. Through the front mirror Tudi spotted the brown 44 Ford that belonged to Frankie, the low-slung maroon Mercury driven by el Topo and a snazzy red convertible he did not recognize. He smiled into the car mirror, trying to catch Cricket's eye. He was anticipating the festivities, the music and the dancing with Sally. "Honk, honk, honk," the cars bleated, announcing their timely arrival. "Honk, honk."

Once Tudi parked the car, Blanca quickly got out, brushed at imaginary dust on her dress, adjusted her veil, rewound the white ribbon on her bouquet and took a deep breath. The September night was cool, pleasant. The morning nausea had all but disappeared. Still, she felt warm, feverish, anxious for the dance to begin. Blanca smiled at Lucy and the other bridesmaids who flocked around her. She knew once the dance was over, she would no longer be the center of attention, the bride on whom the morning sun had so brilliantly shone. After this she would be just someone's old lady. She was determined to enjoy the night to it's fullest, which meant putting up with Cricket.

Cricket sat inside the dark car while the newly arrived bridesmaids and ushers hugged and kissed as if they had not been together all day. The girls pulled at each other's dresses, adjusted their partners' lapels, lit cigarettes and passed a flask around while they waited. "Shit," snarled Cricket, "them dudes actin like jerks."

The minute the cars in the bridal party had parked next to each other, Lucy had turned the car radio on full blast, and in the parking lot, with everyone watching, the partners began to dance to a Woody Herman tune. Lucy was quickly joined by Sally, who twirled around Paulie, his dark face gleaming in the soft light. Tudi grabbed Rosie while Sapo, not to be outdone, picked up Josie and turned her upside down. Man alive! groaned Cricket. What are people gonna say if they see Los Tacones actin stuped? I gots my pride ta think about. Goddamm Lucy!

"Come, on you guys," yelled Sally to the bride and groom, "let's warm up."

"Uhhhh, not yet," answered Blanca, smoothing her dress.

"She pisses me off," snarled Cricket, looking straight at Lucy. "Whatta beesh!" Blanca said nothing, merely smiled in the dark while tapping her swollen feet on the uneven blacktop.

When finally the wedding party trooped into the hall, Cricket turned to glare at Lucy. He gave her his meanest, darkest look, one that usually sent shivers up Tudi's back. But Lucy, equally fierce, looked him straight in the eye and snarled, "What's bothering you?" Not to be intimidated by a mere woman, Cricket adjusted his boppers, cracked his knuckles and glared once more at the Maid-of-Honor in her bright purple dress. Lucy turned nervously away.

Sometimes Lucy hated Cricket with a passion. "He thinks his shit don't stink," she often told Blanca. "You coulda done better."

"Better?"

"Yeah. That guy ain't gonna make it no how."

"Why?"

"'Cause he ain't got a pot to piss in, that's why."

"But I love him. He's my honey!"

"That's your tough luck! Shit, when I get hitched, I'm gonna gets me a guy who gots a steady job."

"Gosh, you're mean! You're supposed to be my best friend. How come ya hate Cricket so much?"

"I didn't say I hated him, it's just that . . . "

Sometimes, when she looked into Blanca's round, pleasant face, Lucy wanted to blurt out her real feelings, but kept quiet instead. She squeezed Blanca's waist and smiled through clenched teeth.

Inside the dance hall the waiting guests elbowed each other, impatient for the bride and groom to start to dance. The band was warming up; everyone waited.

"Hey," said a young woman standing to the side, "that chure sounds like 'Perdido!' "

"Who's lost?"

" 'Perdido,' 'Perdido,' ya dummy, ya know that new tune by that guy who plays jazz."

"What guy?"

"Here comes the bride!"

The younger couples, tired of standing around, began to jitterbug, then just as suddenly they quit. Near the front entrance, gaily dressed people moved away from the door as the bandleader, Gato Cortez, signaled the musicians to take their place. Gato, a tall, medium-sized man with premature grey hair, paced nervously across the bandstand. During the wedding reception Cricket had cornered him to hiss that for this wedding he was expected to play lots of "slow ones," and not the stuff he usually played, or else.

Gato took the threat seriously. More than once he had to corner a groom to collect money owed the band. Once he was forced to follow the newlyweds to the groom's house, where the embarrassed groom, still decked out in a shiny black tuxedo, woke his father, who lent him money to pay the band.

Gato's group, known as Gato Cortez and Band, had played in the San Cristobal Valley for more than ten years and was usually booked solid in summer. He was dependable, always gave a discount if booked three months in advance, and did not become angry when asked to play a special request.

When the wedding party was finally in position, Blanca turned to Rosie, who as the shortest bridesmaid led the march, and asked, "Now?"

"Neh. We need Sally," answered Rosie, tugging at her headpiece. "She went to the toledo."

"Shit," hissed Lucy, rearranging her wilted bouquet, irritated at this new delay.

"Man, that chick's always in the can," lamented El Pan Tostado to Tudi. "She's always gotta take a piss."

"Yeah," agreed Tudi, pulling at his bow tie. "That's how women are, always in the pisser."

"Here she comes," cried Blanca as she spotted Sally scooting through the doorway. "Let's begin, okay you guys?"

"It's about time," snickered Lucy as she moved to let Sally by.

"Oh, shut up," retorted Sally. Her full lips, resplendent with layers of Tangee Bright Red, moved up and down to display even white teeth.

"Make me, you big fat . . . " Lucy moved toward Sally, her fist at the ready. "Come on."

Just then Gato Cortez raised the baton; the "Wedding March" began. Slowly the tipsy ushers and sweaty bridesmaids moved forward, keeping time with the music. Arm in arm, right foot first, they advanced. With Rosie and her partner in the lead, they marched to the middle of the floor, then each couple split up, the ushers to the left, the bridesmaids to the right. Each person then moved to the end of the hall, keeping time with the music. Like a coiling serpent, they moved around the polished floor, the bridesmaids' dresses rustling to and fro, the ushers trying to look bored. When Rosie and her partner each reached the end of the hall,they turned, clasped hands, then formed a circle with the other couples. When all ten bridesmaids and ushers were in place, Blanca hooked her muscular arm through Cricket's lanky one, tucked in her stomach, smiled at everyone. Then Mr. and Mrs. Sammy-the-Cricket glided across the wooden dance floor. When they reached the middle of the dance floor they began to dance, arms entwined around each other as the crowd clapped hands and stomped feet. The wedding dance had officially begun.

Immediately following the wedding march, Gato Cortez played "Blue Moon," followed by another slow tune, favorites of Cricket and Los Tacones. Satisfied that this indeed was a dancing crowd, he raised the baton and began to play a mambo.

As though injected with a sudden spurt of energy, Paulie began to twist and bend his portly figure as Sally, her bright lips glowing, began to gyrate to the beat. To Paulie's left, Lucy, her small feet encased in three-inch heels, twitched to the rhythm of the huge conga drum. "Mambo, mambo, jambo," sang Gato, his eyes bright, "Mambo, que rico es."

Blanca stood next to Cricket, staring with envy at the dancing crowd. "I oughta be dancing too," she thought wistfully. "It's my wedding! I wanna dance but . . . " Just then Cricket turned to her and said, "Esa, ya wanna try et?" Unable to believe her ears, Blanca stared at Cricket, who behind the black boppers smiled down at her. Then, afraid he might change his mind, she slung her bouquet at Rosie, grinned up at her new husband and said, "Sure honey, I wanna dance."

Once they had shoved their way through the crowd, Cricket, his long legs bent at the knee, began to jerk to the left, then to the right. He twisted his thin frame back and forth, just as he had seen Paulie do, but try as he might, he couldn't get the beat. From behind the dark hoppers he spotted Paulie dancing away, his big stomach heaving to the call of the cowbell. To his right, Tudi was bent from the waist down, just like a puppet. Behind Cricket, near the bandstand, Rosie pouted at her partner, making sure he appreciated her toework and dimples.

Cricket hated the mambo. And the cowbell. And Perez Prado. "That mumbo shit ain't fer me," he often told Tudi. "All that jumpin and twistin is fer the birds. This ain't Africa." Cricket felt like a dammed fool dancing the mambo. But I gots ta try it, he grumbled, twitching to the left, trying to appear sophisticated, or the guys are gonna say I ain't hep. Next to him, Tudi swayed back and forth, trying not to step on Sally's dress. Just then Cricket spotted his cousins from Fresno, both of whom were dancing the mambo with ease. Determined not to appear like a small-town hick, Cricket bent his long neck and whispered to a radiant Blanca, "Let yerself go, man. We gotta chow them guys whose the Big Cheese."

Like a herd of cattle following a cowbell, the dancers stomped around the dance hall, jerking back and forth to the new Latin beat. On the bandstand, Gato Cortez, smiling to the beat of the band, banged away on a metal cowbell and in a loud falsetto sang, "Mambo, mambo jumbo."

As he sang, Gato Cortez glanced down at the crowd. He calculated the next set. He was as determined as Cricket that tonight he would outclass all wedding dances . . . and bands.

When Cricket staked him out to discuss tunes to be played at the wedding dance, Gato was not surprised. Few couples, he knew, agreed on anything, other than to getting married. Nothing new, he thought, the one paying is the one I gotta please. From past experience Gato knew he should first please the groom, or end up trying to collect. More than once he had made the mistake of playing too much boogie woogie and was told by an angry groom to slow down or collect the money owed him at the unemployment office.

From the first, Cricket and Blanca had disagreed on just about everything, except who should pay for Blanca's wedding dress. For weeks they argued over who should play at their dance.

"I ain't sayin Gato's no good," Blanca explained, trying not to look at Cricket, "but he plays too many slow ones."

"Yeah? Says who?"

"The Tequilas play better. They really go for the fast ones."

"Yeah? Whatcha wanna do, dance that jive shit? Ain't nobody beats Gato, esa, and ya better knows et."

From experience Gato knew brides liked slow, romantic tunes like "Stardust," "Fools Rush In," and everyone's favorite, "Blue Moon." Most grooms, he found, cared less what the band played, just so it sounded good. And, during the dance, arguments between the newlyweds got worse as the night progressed. The month before, at a wedding dance, the shy bride, loaded to the gills with champagne, had demanded the band play "Little Brown Jug" over and over. By the third set, the drunk groom, weaving from side to side, went up to the stage, knocked the mike down, then yanked the bride toward the door, and off they went on their honeymoon.

Gato sighed with relief when once the dance got going, Blanca let him be and did not insist he play a particular tune. Gato was unaware that Blanca had made other arrangements, as was Cricket, still fuming from having to dance the mambo.

When first dating Blanca, whom he thought of as just a simple chick, Cricket ignored her at dances, content with shooting the breeze with Los Tacones. Later he began to see that Blanca, while not a 'real hep chick,' was a cool dancer. He felt threatened by her popularity, especially when they began to go steady and Blanca danced every number while Cricket appeared to support the wall. It pissed him more when Los Tacones, trying not to look at him, asked her to dance. Time and time again he sulked near the sidelines, trying not to look towards where Blanca and her partner were cuttin' a rug.

"That chick tinks she's so hot," he grumbled to Tudi. "Just 'cause she gets ta dance all the time. Shit, ain't nuthin' I can't do."

"Yeah, Cricket. Ain't nuttin ya can't do . . . 'cept the mambo."

"Whatcha mean,? Ain't ya seen me wiz . . . "

"Get wiz et. This one's slow . . . "

Los Tacones prided themselves on being good dancers. Even Paulie, who weighed over 200 pounds, could dance with the best of them, providing there was enough room.

But Cricket knew he was not a good dancer. Not even as good as Paulie. His legs and arms were too thin and long. From afar he resembled a giraffe with weak knees. When dancing the boogie woogie, he could hardly balance his torso above the buckling of his skinny knees. Worse, it made him madder than hell to know Skippy, the leader of the Planchados, was a terrific dancer. Skippy not only did the mambo, but was even seen dancing a faster number. Gads! Now, sitting out a fast-paced tune, Cricket looked around, checking on the action, worried that people watching would not think him cool.

"I gotta look cool at the dance," he had told Tudi "and learn ta dance better than that mudder, Skippy. I gotta chow my chick I'm not only the best fighter in Taconos, but can swing wiz the best. She gotta know I'm the boss. I ain't about ta stand around like some asshole, while my chick twirls around like a top."

Weeks before the wedding, Cricket thought of asking Lucy to teach him some new "moves," aware that Lucy often went to the Zenda and knew the latest dances. But he sensed Lucy hated his guts, and he wasn't about to beg no chick fer nuttin. At parties he sometimes tried to dance fast ones, but his legs would go sideways; they appeared to cross each other like scissors. Tudi and the guys, Cricket knew, snickered behind his back, calling him el fly-boy, because of how he appeared to be taking off like a fly. But tonight, as he cased the joint from behind his dark glasses, Cricket was determined that Gato's band play enough slow ones for him to look tall, dark and handsome. The Big Cheese. He flexed his feet in anticipation, just as Gato reached for the baton to begin the last set.

Blanca loved to dance. Although not as tall as Josie or as lithe as Lucy, she was fast on her feet. Her sturdy body gave her an advantage in that when dancing, she rarely got tired, but could outdance most of Los Tacones. Just before she and Cricket began to go steady, Blanca lived only for Saturday night, when she, Lucy and whoever had a car, dressed up to the "nines" and drove to the Avadon and Zenda Ballrooms near Los Angeles. There, at the most spacious and popular dance halls, the chicks literally danced the night away. Later they lingered in the parking lot, trading names and addresses with guys from L.A. They knew in advance about other dances, other bands and new dance steps.

During those carefree days, they felt free to stay out late and dance with whom they pleased. There was safety in numbers and, although at times girls disappeared during the dance, they reappeared just before the last slow dance, disheveled but happy. They drove home along San Cristobal Road, softly humming, trading jokes, comparing the guys, looking forward to the dance the following week. The next morning, half-dead from lack of sleep, they trooped to ten o'clock mass, or slept in, dead to the world.

Although not as popular as Sally, Blanca was well-liked in the barrio and,like most of the chicks, rarely missed a wedding dance. She even went uninvited to some of them. Few of the chicks, or guys for that matter, cared whether or not they received a formal invitation to a wedding dance. Mostly they assumed they were welcome, so dressed to the nines. Once inside the door, they went up to the bride and groom, brazenly offered congratulations, then hung around, waiting to be asked to dance. Which is why wedding dances were such fun.

Blanca rarely tired of dancing. Before she got serious with Cricket, she and Lucy often got together during the week to practice different steps. They liked to warm up just before a dance and, music blaring, twirled around the room until exhausted. Soon Blanca got into the habit of spending Sunday afternoons at Lucy's, where, once they had pushed the bed out of the way and piled the odd pieces of furniture in a corner, the chicks listened to music played on Lucy's new record player. The record player, made of light oak, with thin legs and a black turntable, was Lucy's pride and joy, as was the collection of records daily dusted and placed in dust covers. Once they decided what turns they would practice, the two girls stacked a selection of 78s on the record player, then danced around the room until exhausted. Afterward they slumped down on the linoleum floor. Once rested, they began all over again until a step was perfect.

"Don't turn so fast, man."

"Put your arm higher, so I can turn under ya."

"Ouch, ya stepped on me!"

"Well, move yar feets."

"Whose leading? You or me?"

"You."

Three weeks before the wedding, Sadie, a woman at work had told Blanca about Gato Gortez's son, Cat Junior and his new group. They were experimenting with new sounds.

"Ya oughta check em out," she encouraged. "After all, it's your dance too. Ya wanna dance fast ones, then find yarself a group ta play em . . . "

"But . . . "

"Ya gotta do et, Blanche. Or do ya just wanna watch yer friends having fun at yur weddin?"

"No, I wanna have me a good time, but what if . . . "

Sadie went on to mention Neto, who played the vibes in Gato's band, and who was also trying to start a group with Cat Junior. One night Blanca sneaked over to listen to Cat and his group. She liked what she heard, and liked it even better when Cat mentioned a low fee. She sat down on a worn bench inside the garage, took a sip of the soda offered and began to calculate how much she would have to save for Cat and the Cool Cats. She remained a while, wanting to hear more cool sounds, until the musicians left. There, in the dim-lit garage she told Cat Junior exactly what she wanted.

Cat and the Cool Cats locked themselves inside the cluttered garage and practiced nightly during the two weeks before the wedding. They rehearsed, "Perdido," "Peanut Vendor," "Quiet Village" and, last of all, a combination of Latin Jazz with solos for Neto on the vibes. Towards dawn, when exhausted, they packed up their instruments and locked the garage. They vowed not to say a word about their secret musical arrangements to anyone.

Gato made his way to the bar, his dark tie flappping to and fro, relieved to be taking a break at last. The third set, usually the most demanding, had gone on and on, and he was now beat. He had made the mistake of playing an old boogie-woogie tune, one which the old-timers liked so much that when the music stopped, they kept dancing. There was nothing else for Gato to do but signal the guys to keep playing. Ten minutes later, and ten times more irritated, Gato finally swung the baton down, wiped his brow and stepped to the microphone. "That's it for now, folks," he smiled wearily. "We gotta break." He now made his way to the crowded bar and ordered a cold beer.

"Hey Gato, good sounds tonight, ese!"

"Yeah? Thanks."

"Why don't you play some Glenn Miller tunes?"

"Glenn Miller? Man, that stuff is old."

"So are we, man."

"Uhhh, good beer, eh?"

The musicians still on stage fiddled with their instruments. Neto rolled the vibraphone close to the piano and adjusted the shorter mike while Slick, the saxaphonist, looked around for the extra reed stored in his case. Foxy, still looking as handsome as ever, sipped warm water kept in a thermos and waited for the next set when he would get to "croon" to the dancing chicks. He slipped out the small mirror kept with the sheet music, checked to see if anyone was watching and smiled at his reflection. Foxy smoothed his moustache, polished his French cuffs on his jacket, then checked out the chicks and waltzed down the steps. On the steamy stage, the musicians finally put down their instruments, wiped their sweaty brows and left to mingle with the crowd. The minute Cat saw them leave, he grabbed a drumstick, then tapped it on the piano bench until he had Neto and Jimmy's attention.

At the piano Cat softly played the opening bars to "Perdido," his bright eyes on Neto and Jimmy. He waited till the guys had the sheet music in front of them, then said, "Ready?" Neto nodded. Jimmy smiled, then in a soft voice Cat said, "Let's go!" In a firm, clear voice Cat counted, one, two, one, two, one. On the third beat, Jimmy started drumming, followed by Neto, whose bony hands moved skillfully back and forth across the vibraphone. The stage filled with the sound of vibes, drums and piano. The crowd below began to clap. It was time for Stan Kenton's "Perdido."

"Perdido, Perdido, Perdido."

"I lost my heart in Perdido . . . "

When he first heard the introduction to "Perdido," Cricket almost choked on the cigarette dangling from his thin mouth. "Chet," he hissed, taking off his boppers, "I told them dudes ta play some slow ones. All they been playin is that mambo chet, and . . . " He glared at his bride of one day, took off the dark glasses to make sure she was getting the message, then, out the side of his thin mouth, he grumbled, "I ain't gonna dance this chet, esa, so don't be askin me ta . . . " But a tired Blanca, no longer caring what her new husband said, took one look at Cricket's red-veined eyes and moved away to stand close to Tudi. Blanca began to tap her foot.

"Gosh, I wanna dance to a fast one so bad!" she groaned, pushing back the orange blossoms. "I wanna . . . " Just then she felt someone tap her shoulder. It was Sonny, Cricket's cousin, his young, round face set in a wide smile.

"Wanna try et, Cuz, uhhhhh, Blanche?"

"Gosh, I dunno. Whatcha think, honey, chould I?"

"Aint nuttin ta me," snarled Cricket, dusting cigarette ash from his drapes. He hitched up his pants, threw back his bony shoulders and stomped off to where Topo and Los Tacones were holding down the fort.

In the short hallway that led to the men's bathroom, Gato, full of beer and good will, stood puffing at a Camel, his legs swaying back and forth.

"What's the matter with the toilet," asked Gato, trying not to sound too irritable. "I've been here five . . . "

"I been here all night, man. I tink somebody put in too much paper. It's clogged up . . . or so they sez."

"Who?"

"Them guys just came out. Man, they don't fix it soon, I'm gonna chet in my pants!"

Gato groaned, then moved closer to the hallway door and poked his greying head out. "I can't hear a damn thing," he sighed, blowing his nose. "I can't tell what the guys are playing."

"Sounds good ta me," offered the man in front, now moving toward the open stall. "Sounds like jazz."

Earlier Gato was surprised, a little angry even, to hear the start of "Perdido," an upbeat piece he didn't care for and which he knew Los Tacones hated because it was too fast. But he calmed down, sipped the cold beer and grinned. Cat's just feeling his oats, he smiled. The kid just wants to have fun. Nuthin I ain't done. I gotta give him a break. The beer had cooled him down; the faint beat of the vibes sounded agreeable, cool! Later, as he guzzeld peanuts and swapped jokes with the guys hanging out at the bar, he forgot all about Cat, and "Perdido." Suddenly the loud wail of a trumpet cut through the noise. Hector, the trumpeteer was now blowing to the tune of "The Peanut Vender." Gato almost choked on the beer. Damn it, now Hector's got in the act. Ain't no tellin what he's gonna want to play! I gotta get back to the guys or the band's gonna be in trouble. But first I gotta take a piss. He drained the tall glass, then ambled off towards the toledo, his dark jacket flapping to and fro.

Inside the crowded dance hall, Lucy, trying to imitate Hedy Lamarr, her favorite star, tossed back her dark hair, which began to bounce to the beat of the music. She yanked a curl across her eyes and wet it with spit, hoping it would stay down. Once more she adjusted the purple gloves that kept slipping off her thin arms, then glanced around the hall to see what new guys had come in. The dance was beginning to bore her, as were the gloves which itched. But, she grinned, I gotta look charp! And my arms are to damm skinny, so . . . I'll keep the mudders on! She smoothed her dress front to assure the falsies were in place, then leaned against the wall, puffing on a Kool cigarette, which tasted awful, but was the latest with the San Cristobal chicks. She swayed to the music, blowing smoke at random, then frowned as she saw that once more Blanca was dancing away, her orange blossoms swaying with each step.

Darn et, Lucy grumbled, stomping out the Kool, I ain't even dancing! Blanca and Sally ain't sat down the whole night, but . . . Ain't nobody here worth a chet. Nobody I seen, anyways. That Willy tinks his chet don't stink, just cause he dances the mambo so good and Cricket is his cuzzin! But his brother Sonny looks like he's gots the mumps. Or somethin. I sure ain't gonna go fer a guy that looks like a chimpmunk. Ain't that hard up! Her restless eyes roamed the dance hall, then zeroed in on Blanca, now dancing with Paulie, El Pan Tostado.

In the bathroom, a furious Gato struggled with his pant's zipper, now stuck halfway up his fly. Shit, he silently screeched, if this zipper don't open up, I'm gonna piss in my pants! He squatted down a little, trying to force the zipper up, then down, then, afraid to bust the metal zipper, decided to try it once more or give up and do something else. In the toilet stall next to him a guy was whistling "Perdido."

Lucy walked over to where Sally stood, smiled in a friendly way and accepted the piece of Spearmint gum Sally offered the chicks standing round. Lucy chewed away as she tapped her foot to the beat of the music. Man, Lucy sighed, that kid ain't played nuthin but "Perdido." All that Latin jazz is good ta hear, but I ain't chure how ta dance et. She puffed on another Kool cigarette, enjoying the taste of menthol, when suddenly Rosie poked her in the ribs and pointed to a bunch of guys coming in the door, none of whom she recognized. "Hey Lucy," cried Rosie, "lookit over there. Some guys just came in. They from the Valley?"

"It looks like Poncho. He's from Razgo . . . drives a truck for them turkeys. I tink Blanca invited him . . . "

"Yeah, I figured it ain't Cricket who asked dem."

"Poncho's okay, s'long as he don't drink . . . "

"Oh yeah?" asked Rosie, adjusting her dress. "What's he do dats new?"

"I ain't chure, but dey says he likes ta break windows."

"I think he's kinda cute. Maybe I'll dance wiz him," offered Lucy, pulling at the net gloves. "I tink I'll give 'im a break." She slipped a lipstick tube from her satin purse, dabbed it on her thin mouth, then looked toward Poncho, hoping to catch his eye.

Once more Blanca twirled around Paulie, her face wet with perspiration. She spotted Uncle Ernie talking with Gato, but when she looked again, Tio Ernie had disappeared. I'm sure in a dancin mood, gushed Blanca, smiling at the world. She grabbed at Paulie's thick waist, trying to stay on her feet, then, once she found her footing, twirled around once more, dancing to beat the band. Now and then she felt a pain in the pit of her stomach, a short, sharp jabbing that came and went each time she danced. Must be that damm mole, she grumbled, swinging underneath Paulie's thick arm. When the music stopped, she staggered to the bathroom. Clutching the gardenia bouquet in her sweating hands, she bunched up her colonial-style dress, and, unmindful of the parade of women waiting to get inside the toilet, she rushed in, bolted the stall door and sat on the toilet, beads of perspiration on her round, pale face.

Cat edged up to the bar, determined to act sophisticted, suave. He was about to order a soda when a glass of beer was plunked in front of him. "Drink up, kid," said a stranger. "Let me buy ya a drink."

"I'm under age," whined Cat, pushing the beer away.

"Ain't nobody lookin. Here, drink ta 'Perdido.' "

"Perdido?"

"Yeah, that's the kinda music I laks."

"Well, just this time," grinned Cat. He drained the tall glass, feeling more and more like a real man. Just then he saw Tina, a girl from Taconos that he liked, so he remained at the bar, hoping Gato would not find him.

"Hi, Cat! Gee, I didn't know ya drank!"

"Uhhhh, just now and then," smiled Cat as he signaled to the bartender for a refill. "Can I buy you a . . . "

"A Shirley Temple?"

"Uhhhhhhhh, I was thinking you could try a . . . "

"I'll try a Whiskey Sour, okay?"

"Okay." Cat slipped a fiver to the bartender, then smiled at Tina. He sipped the beer, munched on peanuts and hummed a few bars from "Perdido."

Inside the bathroom stall, Blanca spread out her Scarlett O'Hara dress, trying to keep it from getting dirty. The bathroom smelled, as did her armpits. She flopped onto the black toilet seat, breathing in and out, hoping the sharp pain that had forced her to stop dancing would go away. Just then she felt her stomach cramp, then a sticky wetness run down her thigh. Her round face froze in fear, her heart about to burst through her white bride's dress. She sat quietly, hoping someone familiar would walk inside the bathroom. She took a deep breath, then with one sweep of her hand, brought down the orange blossom crown, crushed it in her hand and slung it on the floor.

In the middle of the dance floor, where everyone could admire her tiny waist, Rosie, feeling no pain, danced with the round-cheeked Sonny. She had already guzzled three Singapore Slings and was now dancing better than ever. What Lucy says is true, she thought. A chick can dance better when she's high. She threw her head back, brown curls bouncing, pouted once more, and smiled at Sonny whom she had to admit, looked better after each drink. Can't be my eyes, Rosie giggled, so it must be da booze . . . cause that Sonny wiz the chipmunk cheeks is startin ta look good.

When he felt the coast was clear, Tudi eased his way out of the smelly toilet stall long vacated by Petey. He had twice flushed the toilet, then waited. Ain't nothin else ta do but get outa the can, he grumbled. He took off his tuxedo jacket, splashed water on his sweaty face, wiped it on a dry paper towel, and combed back his dark hair with his wet hands. He stared down at his shoes, then lifted a foot, smelled it and frowned. Shit! While hiding from what he thought was the Planchados, Tudi had squeezed next to Petey, who startled by the intrusion, missed the toilet seat . . . , and sprayed Tudi's shoes.

"Watchet kid," Tudi had yelled, forgetting momentarily he was in hiding from the Planchados.

"Ain't my fault," Petey had snarled, "ya didn't lets me finish pissin." The piss had dried and was now beginning to smell. Once free of Petey, Tudi swore to clean the shoes, then burn them. He now leaned down, wiped them off with his handkerchief, and prepared to leave the safety of the toledo to join Cricket and the guys.

Lucy lit a cigarette, took a few puffs, then surveyed the crowd. Willie and his chick were nowhere to be seen. Lucy saw that Blanca was back from the toilet and Rosie was flirting with Sonny, with whom she had earlier danced cheek-to-cheek. Man alive! grumbled Lucy, sliding her long nails along her arm. Ain't nuttin happenin.   She licked her lips and was about to walk to the bar for a drink when she spotted her Aunt Tottie's purse swinging through a bunch of people. She quickly stomped out her cigarette . . . and dashed to where the purse was flying in the air.

"What's goin on, man?" Lucy snarled, pushing her way towards her aunt.

"Same old chet," offered Topo, massaging his stony face. "Tottie and Chita are tradin punches."

"Oh yeah? Tottie and my sister Chita?"

"Ain't the first time them dames tangle. Watchet, here comes the purse!"

Lucy moved back just as Aunt Tottie, eyes blazing, chest heaving, smashed her purse against Chita's retreating back. "Ya fuckin bitch," she screeched. "You come near my man, I'll knock the chet outta ya." Tottie came to a screeching halt next to her favorite niece, who stared at her with alarm.

"Man, Tia, whatcha fightin wiz my sister fer?"

"Ain't fightin, Lucita, just teachin yar carnala a lesson. She don't keep away from . . . "

Wham! Unobserved by Lucy and Aunt Tottie, Chita snuck up close and pulled Aunt Tottie's peroxide hair.

"You whoreing mother . . . " hissed Aunt Tottie, trying to keep her balance. "Ay, ay, ay."

"Watchet wiz my Ma," Lucy warned her favorite aunt, or you're gonna gets et from me!"

"Not you, Lucy. That fuckin Chita is . . . "

Just then the band, with Foxy at the front, began to play the introduction to "Stardust." Aunt Tottie, purse swinging, yellowish hair bobbing, trotted off to the bar as Chita disappeared toward the back of the hall, accompanied by her old boyfriend Fish, now hoping for a reconciliation. I better find somebody ta dance this wiz, Lucy sighed, or I'll look like a a dummy. If I sit this dance out I'm gonna chet in my pants! She looked around for the bridesmaids, then headed in their direction.

Inside the baby-blue Chevie parked behind the dance hall, Tudi and Sally cuddled tight, waiting for the last set to begin. Sally took off her bridesmaids hat, slipped off the net gloves that had already split down the seams and kissed Tudi on the cheek. "Gee Tudi, if ya wanna go now, I can goes wiz ya. Ain't nobody gonna say nuthin."

"Neh. The guys will know . . . and Cricket's gonna say I'm chicken. Ya know, maybe I am."

"Huh! Just 'cause you don't wanna gets killed don't make ya chicken. Let's go ta my house till the dance is over . . . then ya can go home, okay?"

"Tanks, but I better gets back. Them Planchados said they'd be here, so . . . "

"But the dance is almost finished! They can't start something now."

"Ha, ha, ha," laughed Tudi softly, opening the car door. "Them guys start somethin anytime they wants " He took Sally's arm, guided her up the concrete steps and past folks leaving the dance. They were almost at the door when Tudi looked back and saw two cars, one of which was a low-slung navy-blue Ford slowly coming up the street. Instinctively he pushed Sally inside, squeezed past her and the crowd and ran up to Cricket. "Ese Cricket, I just saw Skippy's car comin down the street," croaked Tudi, his eyes bulging. "Deys comin dis way."

On stage, Cat smiled at the world. He, Neto and Jimmy, playing non-stop for almost a half hour, had already played "Peanut Vendor," "Manhattan" and "Perdido," all of two times each. He had even let Neto take over while he went to the toledo, then lingered to sip a beer, a thing forbidden by his father. He was feeling no pain, his dark head moving back and forth with the rhythmn. Now and then he looked around for Tina, the girl he had seen at the bar, but she was nowhere to be seen. And although the regular musicians later joined in (none of whom knew the arrangements) and almost ruined the night, Cat was happy. When finished playing his favorite "Perdido," he flipped through the music, yanked out "Quiet Village," a popular tune that few bands played well. He waved the sheets of music at Neto and Jimmy and tried to avoid looking at Hector, the saxaphonist, who awaited his cue. Just then Cat spotted his dad walking towards the stage. Gato was holding a magazine in front of his pants. Cat quickly counted the beat and began to pound on the piano, his eyes bright.

Lucy was feeling no pain. She had twice danced with Poncho, a seedy-looking guy who smelled of Three Flowers Hair Pomade. She thought he was kinda cute, even though he wasn't wearing a tailor-made suit. Twice, while trying out a new turn, she had stumbled on Poncho's big feet, but quickly recovered. He's gots a steady job, she admitted, baring her perfect white teeth at him and trying to look sophisticated. He's better than nuttin, Lucy told herself, but he chure dresses like a square. Worse, he can't dance worth a chet, but I ain't about ta stand around while Blanca and Sally dance. She edged away from Poncho, looking around for Willy, whom she saw was talking with a group of girls.

It was the group of girls said to be from "up north," chicks who were dressed to the nines and walked into the dance hall, acting as though they owned the place. They had sidled up to Willie and Sonny while the Taconos chicks, green with envy, watched. "Dey don't look like hicks," observed Rosie, "staring at the young women wearing shiny, stylish dresses.

"Yeah," added Sally, blowing smoke-rings at the ceiling, "I thought they was from L.A.! And look," she tapped Lucy on the shoulder, "that one is chure clinging ta Willie. Anybody tink she owned him or sumthin."

"Oh yeah? Ya think them chicks are so hot? Well, watch this." Lucy pulled back her shoulders, stuck in her stomach, then sashayed over to Willie, determined to dance the next set. With a nudge from her shapely hips, she eased her way between the girls bunched around Willie.

"Hey man, whatcha say!"

"Orale, Lucy."

"So, ya gonna dance wiz me or what?"

"Uhhhh, I gots ta dance wiz my chick first, man!"

"Oh yeah? She yer boss or what?"

Suddenly, one of the chicks, a round-faced girl with reddish hair who was wearing a magenta jersey dress with a sweetheart neckline, pushed her way to Lucy and snarled, "Ya want somethin, man?"

"Not from no dame!"

"Oh yeah? Well, I gots somethin fer ya. Here."

The girl stepped back, bunched her fingers, then brought her hand up and out and smacked Lucy on the face. "Here," she screeched, hand held high. She retreated, aimed her knee, then waited for the slap she was sure was coming.

"Take that yerself, ya god-damn hick." Wham! Lucy smacked the girl in the nose, yanked at her curls and the fight was on.

"Fight, fight." The noisy crowd picked up the word and passed it around. "Fight, fight! It's Lucy and some chick from up north . . . "

"Ha, ha, ha," screeched Cricket, his dark eyes crinkling behind the boppers. "Ha, ha. Lucy's gonna get what's comin ta her, the bitch. Let em knock the chet outta her. Ha, ha, ha."

"Give it to her," shouted Aunt Tottie, running to the rescue, her round arms flaying to and fro. Suddenly she was in the middle of the pack, slashing out with her purse at the startled chicks, one of which cried, "Watchet wiz that ole lady. She gots rocks in her bag or sumthin."

A winded Lucy, hair askew, stared at the blood running down Willie's nose and onto his white shirt. She was itching to smack the chick with the orange-brown hair who was now clinging to Willie, but Lucy held back, waiting to catch her breath. She saw Aunt Tottie swing her purse once more, then land it on the chick who had started the fight. "Owwwww," screeched Willie's girlfriend as she ran toward the bathroom, her hand over her head. Unwilling to let this chance go by, Lucy yanked off the net gloves, flicked her fingers back and forth, and took off behind Aunt Tottie, Willie right behind her. Just then the band began to play a corrido. Willie grabbed his chick, hustled her toward the music and away from Lucy.   Once safe next to Sonny, Willie and his partner slowly began to dance. "Da fights over," Willie whispered in the girl's ear. "Ain't no sense fightin wiz Lucy," he said, putting his arm around his girl and massaging her round cheek. Once more, Lucy had won! Once more Gato Cortez had played a corrido and stopped a fight. But Lucy, itching to dig her fingernails into someone, was still angry. She shook her fist at Willie, then strutted off, high heels clanging. Just then the noisy crowd quieted down to better hear the loud screech of car tires coming from the street. The startled dancers looked at each other, then toward the door and toward Los Tacones.

"It's the Planchados," yelled Paulie, running towards Cricket. "They'ze gonna crach the dance, ese!"

"Let em," snarled Cricket, trying to look bored. "Let them mudders come." He took a drag from the cigarette dangling from his mouth, cracked his knuckles and flexed his feet. "Let em come." He stayed close to the wall, his eyes on the door as Frankie moved next to him. In his right hand was a pair of shiny brass knuckles! Without being told, Paulie, El Pan Tostado, bolted out the back door to check the parking lot. Just in case.

Tudi stood inside the crowded bathroom, waiting patiently while Petey took a fast piss. His tuxedo was wrinkled and his tie had come undone. The commotion outside, now getting louder, had startled him, especially the loud shouts of the wedding guests. He opened the toilet door halfways, urged Petey to hurry up and pee, then adjusted his pant's buckle which felt suddenly tight. Just then the sound of running feet came closer. Tudi looked around to see who was watching, then squeezed inside the toledo as a round-eyed and surprised Petey stared.

Inside the dance hall, those not dancing waited to see what the fuss was all about. Was it really the Planchados? Dare they come inside? Los Tacones, huddled together in a corner of the Salon Parra, traded cigarettes and took sips from Frankie's flask, all the while trying to look cool. They waited for their rivals, the gang of Planchados, to barge in and start throwing blows that would bring Los Tacones charging. To the guys from Taconos, it was a matter of pride, honor even, to let the invaders hit first, or as Cricket often said, "Them mudders gotta make da first move, dat way ain't nobody gonna say we'ze chicken-chet." And so they waited, eyes alert, hands at the ready.

Across the hall, Lucy could hardly contain her excitement. Twice she ran to the hall door to check-out what was happening outside; twice she was disappointed to see nobody moving in the street. She ran into the bathroom, adjusted her bra straps, licked her lips, added more spit to her falling curl and checked her tits. Forgotten was the fight with Willie's chick, the slap across her face and Aunt Tottie's unexpected contribution with her swinging purse. *I chowed that chick whose really tough. Ain't no way she's gonna try and gets me.* As much as she hated to admit it, Lucy had a grudging respect for chicks who fought for a man. For their guy. The truth was, Lucy needed no excuse to throw a few punches. *I ain't about ta fight over no man,* Lucy often said, arching her eyebrows (just like Joan Crawford). *Ain't no man worth gettin my nose busted for.* Still she wished something would happen. *Let the Planchados bust in,* she prayed, pissed-off knowing that a stupid corrido had ended her early performance with Willie's girl. But, Lucy sighed, *the night is still young, and it looks like somethin just might be happenin.* Flanked by Rosie and Sally, Lucy waited to see what was next.

The nervous musicians played without enthusiasm. The set was almost over, they were tired and put out by the fight between the Maid-of-Honor and Willie's chick whom everyone could see was a very pretty girl. Gato was irritated at Cat for the fast numbers and at the pachucos for having to switch to a corrido, just when the dance was peaking. Even the mild-mannered Foxy was getting pissed. Twice he had dodged Aunt Tottie's purse as it flew across the room. The musicians knew that during fights they were perfect targets for flying beer bottles and purses, but they were also aware that Gato, their leader, was determined to keep playing, regardless of fights. Gato, his mouth set in a firm line, swung the baton back and forth, marking time. The band began the introduction to "Cottage For Sale," a romantic tune Foxy crooned to the chicks below who stared at him as if he were a god, their young, moist mouths salivating. Just then a bunch of well-dressed guys walked into the hall and headed straight for Cricket and Los Tacones.

When he first saw the five guys in tailor-made drapes walk through the door (none of whom he recognized), Cricket felt a shiver down his back. "Sonavaviche," he hissed to Frankie, "ets a deal! The Planchados gots a deal! Dem guys comin in iz gonna get us first, then them mother-fuckers are gonna finich the job. Chet, I shoulda known they wass gonna strike a deal." He took off his dark glasses, rammed them inside the tuxedo pocket, flexed his big feet, and waited.

"Ese, Cricket," began the taller of the five as he came close to the startled groom, "ya guys knows where the weddin dance fer Pinole is?"

"Pinole?"

"Yeah. Dey said ta take San Cristobal Road to the railroad tracks . . . buts we gots losted."

"Where ya from? L.A.?"

"Right from White Fence. We was told da weddin dance is supposed ta be near da Elks . . . ya wanna chow me and the guys how ta . . . "

"Chure, ese. Lemme look fer Tudi."

When he realized the newcomers weren't the Planchados nor looking for a fight, Cricket lit a cigarette, threw back his bony shoulders and passed Frankie's flask to them, acting as if the guys from White Fence were honored guests. From his place in the huddle, Frankie snickered to Sapo, "Lookit Cricket puttin on the dog! Man, that guy chure knows how ta deal wiz guys from L.A."

"Yeah, but they ain't the Planchados," retorted Sapo, touching up his moustache. "Diz guys don't count fer chet." As Sapo talked, Cricket put on his boppers, wiped his large hawklike nose, then took a drag from his cigarette and blew smoke into Frankie's face. Cricket knew people were watching. And wondering. I gotta look tough, he decided, or them guys from L.A. are gonna say Los Tacones are chicken-chet. "Tell ya what, he finally said, one of my vatos can chow ya where ta go." He looked around for Tudi, then decided to walk out with the dudes from White Fence, making sure everyone in the hall saw him. With a show of disdain and a cigarette dangling from his thin mouth (just like Humphrey Bogart), Cricket sauntered out to the street, followed by the guys from Los Angeles. He pointed to where they should turn, then once the guys roared off, stalked back inside the hall, the thick heels of his shoes striking the sidewalk with a vengeance. Once more Cricket had proven to Los Tacones and everyone else who watched that he had guts to be out in the dark and act cool with guys who carried switchblades, knives and guns. He returned to the Tacones just as the band began to play "Blue Moon."

Afterwards no one remembered exactly what happened at the dance. Who had started the fight. Who was hitting whom. Who called the coppers. When the first ambulance came. Whom they carried off. Everyone in town had a different version of how Blanca and Cricket's wedding dance ended.

It was late, past eleven, but the band still had another inter - mission to go. A car full of Planchados went by. Skippy was driving. Anyway, they had put out the car lights and were going real slow when Tudi, who was outside with Sally, saw them and ran inside to tell Cricket and Los Tacones.

By then Cricket was real drunk and acting tough, just 'cause he kicked out the guys from White Fence who wanted to break up the dance, or so everybody thought. Anyway, Los Tacones ran outside, right behind Cricket and Topo. They stood outside and waited for the Planchados to cruise by once more. But they waited and waited for nothing. As they were about to go inside again, they saw Skippy, dressed to the nines, walking toward them, smiling as though he was one of Los Tacones. The Planchados probably didn't know Burbank very well. That was because they only went there for dances. But what happened is the police station had been moved to a new building, one block away from the Elks. The Planchados had to park in the lot next to the police headquarters, not knowing the coppers were inside. Not all the Planchados got out, some stayed behind in their cars. Skippy, who was higher than a kite, took off with two other guys. He was laughing so loud, like he was drunk. She heard him all the way to the door. Anyway, when he got to where the guys were, Skippy went up to Cricket and said, "Conratulachens, ese." He took a flask from his jacket and drank from it, then said to Cricket, "here's ta ya and yer chick."

Cricket didn't know what to do. He just stared at his number-one enemy, then lit a cigarette and blew the smoke into Skippy's face and said, "Whatcha want, ese?"

"Pos, I came ta dance at yer weddin," answered Skippy, a sly grin on his face. "Don't tell me ya fergot ya invited me."

"Uhhhhhhh," Cricket mumbled something, then just stood there. From where he stood he looked at Skippy and his blonde hair· Cricket was still wearing the dark boppers. Just then Sapo pushed Cricket aside, went up to Skippy and growled, "Man, you Planchados chure tink yer chet don't stink. Ya wanna tangle asses . . . or what?"

"Yer de one wants ta fight. Me and the guyss just came ta dance. Nuttin wrong wiz dat, is et?"

"Dey ain't playin yer song, man, so ya better . . . "

"Ooooooo," grinned Skippy. "Oooooooo. Ya chure scare me, ese."

Just then Cricket grabbed Skippy by his pin-striped lapel, stuck his pock-marked face close to Skippy's startled mug and said, "Ya wanna dance? Okay. I'll let ya dance. Just ta chow ya. I gots class." Together the two guys walked into the dance hall as everyone stared at them.

The first person to scream was Blanca. Nobody knows why . . . but when she saw Skippy walking in with Cricket, she yelled real loud, then bent over, like she was sick. She almost passed out. Lucky for her Sally was nearby. Sally took her to the toledo. Cricket didn't even stop to see what Blanca was screamin about. He just kept walking with Skippy. People whispered that the guys were drunk and probably full of marijuana too. Anyway, when they got to where the band was, Cricket yelled up to Gato, "Hey Gato, let's hear dem danzon." Gato stared both at Cricket and Skippy, then he shrugged his shoulders, shuffled through the music to look for "Juarez." Everyone stood around, not knowing what to do. Then Cricket pushed Skippy towards the middle of the dance floor and said, "Well, gets wiz et, man! Ya gots the floor! Come on, chow us how ya . . . "

"Ya thin ₖI can't do et?" asked Skippy, laughing aloud. "Sheeet! I can dance ta anythin. Anythin." He took one look at the crowd, bowed, then puffed on a cigarette, and waited for the music to begin.

Gato looked really scared, but his son Cat was laughing really loud. Cat began to play something that sounded like "Perdido." Just then his father said something to Cat and he stopped playing. But he kept on laughing. Anyway, all that time Skippy was standing in the dance floor. When the music started he looked around for a partner, laughing like he was having fun. Then he saw Lucy standing with the bridesmaids, so he went up to her, grabbed her by the waist and said, "Hey Lucy, I hear ya always wanted ta dance wiz me! So come on, esa, here's yur chance." He put his face really close to Lucy's. It almost looked like they were kissing, except that Lucy had her eyes open. Anyway, he pulled Lucy by the arm to the middle of the dance floor, then turned her around and they started dancing!

Everybody was laughing, even Cricket who always looks like he hates you. The whole place laughed at Skippy, who was so drunk he kept stumbling. But mostly they laughed at Lucy in her high heels, trying to get loose from Skippy, who almost fell down when her shoes slipped. The whole thing was so funny! Skippy kept hugging Lucy closer and closer. She could hardly breathe. And suddenly a purse came at them.

While Skippy was forcing Lucy to dance, her Aunt Tottie kept wanting to get into the act and help Lucy get away from him. Maybe hit Skippy. But Blanca's Uncle Ernie, a big fat man who was roaring drunk, kept pulling at Tottie to stay put. But even he was no match for Tottie. When he let go of her, Aunt Tottie pushed her way to Skippy and Lucy and, with a swing of her purse, hit the leader of the Planchados on the head.

"Whammmmm. The purse hit Skippy right in the kisser. It totally surprised him, and for a minute he didn't know where he was. He just kept staring at the crowd then put his hand on his blonde head and checked for blood. He staggered to the side of the floor, and kept bumping into people.

Suddenly Chita, Lucy's older sister, who earlier had slapped her aunt, grabbed Aunt Tottie by the hair and smacked her across the mouth, cussing at her the whole time.

By then there were at least three fights going on. The Planchados and Los Tacones, Tottie and Chita, and Skippy and Lucy.

Chita was smacking Tottie and Tottie was ramming her purse into Skippy. All this time Lucy was trying to stay on her feet, as the band played away.

When finally Skippy let go of Lucy, she took off her purple shoes and began to hit him on the head. Skippy just kept laughing and laughing, as he dodged the ankle-straps. He grabbed Lucy again and tried to do a fancy step and he almost dropped Lucy on the floor. Lucy got really pissed-off.

When the two Planchados that were with Skippy saw Los Tacones making fun of their leader, they started to punch away. The first one to get it in the kisser was Tudi the Best Man. His face became a bloddy mess. Next, Frankie tried to hit a Planchado with his brass knuckles, but instead of hitting the guy, he hit Blanca's Tio Ernie, who hated Frankie's guts.That was a big mistake. Tio Ernie let Frankie have it with a left to the jaw, just like Joe Louis! By this time it was a free for all.

Just then the other Planchados who had stayed in the parking lot came running into the dancehall. They spotted Skippy, trading punches with Cricket, then each one took on a vato, and began to punch away. Paulie, El Pan Tostado ، pushed a Planchado with his big stomach. The poor guy turned purple, then slumped to the floor. But he got up again and went after Paulie.

Tudi played it smart staying in the restroom during most of the brawl. When Tudi had gotten hit, his new teeth fell out, and embarrassed at being seen toothless, he ran for cover.

Lucy started arguing with a real cute guy. Lucy scratched him in the face with her huge nails. The poor guy screeched, then grabbed Lucy by the arm and said something to her. His face was really close to hers, almost as if they were kissing! Next thing, Lucy and the guy walked out the door together. She took off so fast that she left behind her orchids. Porky grabbed the orchids and was not about to give them up. Just then Cricket and Skippy, caught in a clinch, fell right on top of her. Poor Porky, she pushed at Cricket probably thinking that Cricket was going to get her for what she had done to the cushions. But Cricket hardly saw her, he was too busy banging at Skippy. Just then Gloria yelled at her to stay where she was. Cricket let go with a right rook and hit Skippy so hard that Skippy's nose began to bleed. The blood was coming down fast. When Porky saw all that blood, she scrunched down as if she had a bad stomach ache and vomited all over the floor. Cricket and Skippy, who were still at it, skidded all over the vomit.

Cricket slipped and barely missed being punched by Skippy. By the time he got up, Skippy was fighting with Topo. Cricket started to clean his shoes with his hand, all the while looking around for Skippy. Just then Gloria went up to him, said something, and kicked him in the shin. Cricket was shocked. Nobody ever hit Cricket and lived! He called Gloria "beesch," then pushed her away and took off after Skippy. Finally Porky and mother were able to escape out the door.

The band was playing throughout the fight. The fight seemed like part of the dance! People in the back of the hall kept dancing making sure to keep away from where the Planchados and Los Tacones were beating each other up. Nobody was taking the fight seriously, not even the guys, except for Sapo and Topo. It seemed as if the pachucos were fighting in slow motion.

Something was wrong with Blanca. She stayed in the bathroom the whole time. Sally would go in and out of the bathroom without saying anything to anyone. Not even to Cricket. Later on, Lucy who had disappeared earlier, came back. She and Sally stayed with Blanca in the bathroom. They locked the door and would not let anybody in. Now and then they came out to get water. Said it would help her get over what was bothering her.

By that time people knew something was wrong, not only with the groom, but with the bride. Blanca, Lucy and Sally finally came out. Blanca looked really bad. Lucy pushed everyone out of the way. The trio made its way to the parking lot, to Tudi's car. Sally and Lucy held up Blanca, her colonial-style dress dragging over the cement. Her veil was hanging from her pompadour—what was left of it. Blanca got in the back seat then lied down. Sally told Tudi to go call an ambulance.

All during this time nobody had called the police! That was incredible, because the police station was right around the corner. It seems that someone had called the police to tell them that there was a rumble going on in San Cristobal between Los Tacones and the Planchados, and that they better get out there. Pronto! There were no cops left to go to the Elks. They had roared out to the Valley and even had called in back-up units from L.A.

The first ambulance pulled up just as Cricket was kicking Skippy brutally. The ambulance people did not know who to take first. Skippy, who had just about passed out, looked yellow. Cricket, who was bleeding from his mouth and nose, rocked back and forth in his shoes. He kept saying, "I gots him now. I gots him now." Then he keeled over. The ambulance attendants decided to take them both. They put Skippy in first and made room for Cricket. There lay the two toughest batos in the whole San Cristobal Valley. I could hardly believe my eyes. The ambulance backed up and was about to take off, when right around the corner came another ambulance with the siren at full blast. This one pulled up to Tudi's car.

The attendants rushed out and helped Blanca into the ambulance. Poor Blanca was a pitifull sight, crying loudly with her veil hanging from her head and her hand clutching the azares. Each time Lucy whispered into her ear, Blanca cried harder. And harder. Finally, Sally pushed Lucy   and got in the ambulance with Blanca.   The   medics closed the door so that they could take off. But right before they did, Lucy, madder than hell at Sally and crying almost as hard as Blanca, stuck her head inside the ambulance and shouted, "Now ya don't havta stay with him, Blanca. Now ya can . . . "

Blanca looked as if she were in pain. But when Lucy said that to her, she let out a loud scream and then pushed herself up from the cot and grabbed Lucy's hand and screamed, "But he's my honey! He's gonna change! You'll see!"

As the ambulance pulled away, Lucy screeched, "Ferget him!" She ran behind the white ambulance, her purple shoes scraping the pavement. "He ain't worth a chet, Blanca. Lissen ta me! He ain't ever gonna . . . "

The ambulance sped up and away, its siren going full blast. Lucy kept running after it, then tripped and fell. She lay there crying and banging a fist on the ground. Rosie helped Lucy up and to the bathroom. In a little while Lucy came back out, her face made up so that you could not tell she had been crying. Within a few minutes she was dancing with some guy, but she did not look at all happy. When the crowd saw Rosie and Lucy, everyone figured that the newlyweds had taken off for their honeymoon.

As the nurse was wheeling Blanca into the emergency room, Blanca turned to her and whispered, "Man, you shoulda seen my wedding. It was the best wedding in the barrio." The nurse thought Blanca was delerious until Sally told her that it was true, that Blanca was a brand-new bride. The nurse then smiled and said to Blanca, "I'll bet it was a beautiful wedding."

"Yeah," Blanca answered. "The best wedding, in all of Taconos." Then she passed out.